THIEVES BREAK IN

This Large Print Book carries the
Seal of Approval of N.A.V.H.

THIEVES BREAK IN

CRISTINA SUMNERS

Thorndike Press • Waterville, Maine

Copyright © 2004 by Cristina J. Sumners
A Divine Mystery

Published in 2005 by arrangement with Bantam Books, an
imprint of the Bantam Dell Publishing Group, a division of
Random House, Inc.

Thorndike Press® Large Print Core.

The tree indicium is a trademark of Thorndike Press.

The text of this Large Print edition is unabridged.
Other aspects of the book may vary from the original edition.

Set in 16 pt. Plantin by Minnie B. Raven.

Printed in the United States on permanent paper.

Library of Congress Cataloging-in-Publication Data

Sumners, Cristina.
    Thieves break in / by Cristina Sumners.
        p. cm. — (Thorndike Press large print core)
    ISBN 0-7862-7431-X (lg. print : hc : alk. paper)
    1. Women clergy — Fiction. 2. Tour guides (Persons) —
Fiction. 3. Americans — England — Fiction. 4. Oxford
(England) — Fiction. 5. Police chiefs — Fiction.
6. Castles — Fiction. I. Title. II. Thorndike Press large
print core series.
PS3619.U46T48 2005
813'.6—dc22   2004030708

Colin, this one's for you.
Hard to believe, but after eighteen years
it just keeps getting better.

National Association for Visually Handicapped
------------------------ serving the partially seeing

As the Founder/CEO of NAVH, the only national health agency solely devoted to those who, although not totally blind, have an eye disease which could lead to serious visual impairment, I am pleased to recognize Thorndike Press* as one of the leading publishers in the large print field.

Founded in 1954 in San Francisco to prepare large print textbooks for partially seeing children, NAVH became the pioneer and standard setting agency in the preparation of large type.

Today, those publishers who meet our standards carry the prestigious "Seal of Approval" indicating high quality large print. We are delighted that Thorndike Press is one of the publishers whose titles meet these standards. We are also pleased to recognize the significant contribution Thorndike Press is making in this important and growing field.

Lorraine H. Marchi, L.H.D.
Founder/CEO
NAVH

* Thorndike Press encompasses the following imprints: Thorndike, Wheeler, Walker and Large Pr int Press.

ACKNOWLEDGMENTS

Mostly I'd like to thank my splendid editor at Bantam Dell, Kate Miciak, for refraining from murdering me while I kept her waiting an extra year for the manuscript.

I suspect that thanks are also due to my equally splendid agent Linda Roghaar, who explained to Kate what was going on. ("They call it an accommodation problem, Kate; no, it has nothing to do with a shortage of hotel rooms; it means little thingys in her eyes can't accommodate fast enough and she can't see.")

Finally, although this story is not about Oxford nor set in it, Oxford permeates the novel. I could never have written this book had I not lived and studied there, and the plot would never have occurred to me if I had not the good fortune to spend a term under the tutelage of the never-to-be-forgotten Malcolm Parkes, professor of Paleography, now retired. To him many thanks.

In case you're wondering, gentle reader, I am feeling very much better now, thank you.

Do not lay up for yourselves treasures on earth, where moth and rust consume and where thieves break in and steal, but lay up for yourselves treasures in heaven, where neither moth nor rust consumes and where thieves do not break in and steal. For where your treasure is, there will your heart be also.

Matthew 6: 19–21

CHAPTER 1

LATE JULY 1997

Wednesday

Nobody knew where Rob Hillman was.

Curious. Very curious, Sir Gregory thought. With all the staff he had rattling about the place, one would have thought that somebody would have found him by now. After all, young Hillman was conspicuous for many reasons: his height, his clothing, his American accent, and his very novelty — he had only been among them a matter of mere weeks, whereas everybody else at Datchworth had been ensconced there anywhere between fourteen and eighty-two years.

Sir Gregory St. John Bebberidge-Thorpe was feeling his age, which was seventy-three, and also his health, which was intricate and tiresome and ensured that he got every penny he paid in taxes returned to him in the form of free medical care from Britain's National Health Service. Most people in Sir Gregory's tax bracket paid for private medical care, but the Bebberidge-Thorpes were famous for thrift. Not that they were miserly, it was simply that they didn't see any point in paying for something one could get for free. Sir Gregory had never been a snob, and he preferred to spend his money on things that were more enjoyable than going to the doctor.

But at Sir Gregory's age, the list of things one can enjoy decreased with every passing year, and when his time came, he did not plan to rage against the dying of the light. With one white finger he pressed a button on the right arm of his wheel-chair. Emitting a well-mannered hum, it rotated decorously until it faced the window, allowing him to gaze from his library out over the formal garden. What a pother that had been! — having it restored to its eighteenth-century perfection. But worth it. Definitely worth it.

He had done everything possible to pre-pare Derek, and he was confident the boy was ready. Which was just as well, for at the rate his own health was declining, it wouldn't be very long before Derek would get the baronetcy (which both of them re-ferred to as "the Sirdom") and everything that went with it. Well, almost everything. Possibly. That would depend on Rob Hillman.

Tom Holder was trying to pull the fangs out of the anxiety he was feeling by entertaining himself with it. "I would rather," he muttered to himself, "go unarmed against a homicidal maniac with a black belt, an Uzi and a sinus headache. I would rather eat a meat loaf made of earthworms. I would rather stand naked at the front of the church with the whole congregation watching while I sang the 'Hallelujah Chorus' to the tune of 'Rudolf the Red-Nosed Reindeer.' "

What he *least* wanted to do was have the conversation with his wife that he really had to have this evening, because any minute now he was going to have to start packing, and if Louise found out what he'd done before he'd talked to her, it was really going to hit the fan. Of course, it was going to hit the fan anyway, but at least if he told her now and tried to make it sound good, less of it would hit the fan than if he put it off another day. He had already left it until far too late.

You've always wanted to have Flora and the kids come and stay, he would begin. No, he wouldn't. Louise would never swallow that. He might mollify her, after telling her about what he was doing, by saying Flora and offspring could come stay in his absence, but Louise would never believe that was actually the reason he was going. *Good news, I'm going to relieve you of my presence for a while, you'll like that.* No, no, no. Too close to the bone. How about something more direct? *Louise, I just couldn't pass up this opportunity. It may never come around again.* That, at least, had the advantage of being true. When you're trying to pull the wool over someone's eyes, it's always comforting to know you're doing it by telling the truth.

James Crumper was trying to decide whether to go over the same ground again in his search for Mr. Hillman, or to try to think of somewhere nobody had looked yet. The cook, Mrs. Drundle, had advised him to give it a rest, have a cup of tea, and wait for the American lad to turn up of his own accord. That suggestion did not recommend itself to Sir Gregory's butler.

Jim Crumper belonged, according to his wife, in another century. Crumper took that as a compliment. He had grown up reading the Regency romances of Georgette Heyer, pressed upon him by his father Albert ("Old Crumper") with the admonition, "Forget all the romance rubbish, that's for women; pay attention to the servants. That's how you're supposed to behave in a house like this." Old Crumper, now in semi-retirement in the south wing, had reason to be proud of his training methods. His son had taken to Heyer's Regency world like the proverbial duck to water.

But the son, cleverer than his dad, had seen the tongue in Heyer's cheek; he knew that when he assumed the mantle of butler at Datchworth, he'd be playing a character in a long-running pageant, part historical re-creation, part comedy of manners. Now, at forty-five, after eight years in the role, he played it very well indeed, and he loved it.

Part of the character of The Good Servant was extreme dedication to The Master. For that reason, Crumper was disinclined to give up searching for Mr. Hillman, because that would mean failing to perform a perfectly simple task that his master had laid upon him. Or at least, it ought to have been simple.

Mr. Robert Hillman was a creature of habit (which had endeared the young American to the staff, since routine was awfully helpful in running a household as vast as Datchworth). Every weekday he took his breakfast with Sir Gregory and Miss Daventry (and Mr. Banner when he was in Oxfordshire); he went to the muniment room at nine a.m. promptly and set to work. He took elevenses at his desk, being careful, of course, to move the manuscripts out of range of his coffee, not that there was much danger of Mr. Hillman spilling anything, as he was always tidy and careful, especially where the manuscripts were concerned.

He invariably came down for lunch within two minutes of being called, and returned to the muniment room precisely one hour later. There his tea was brought to him at four-fifteen; he would eat the thin sandwiches he preferred while drinking his first cup. He would then pour a second cup, and mount the spiral staircase to the parapet, where he would walk along the rooftop and admire the view over the west lawn and the woods. This he did, come shine or showers. When asked why he subjected himself to the worst of England's summer weather, he replied, "Oh, I like rain. We don't get enough of it where I come from."

After tea came the only variable part of

Mr. Hillman's schedule. He would either stop work for the day, as Sir Gregory always urged him to do, or, if something had piqued his curiosity among the manuscripts, he might return to the muniment room for another hour before going upstairs to change for dinner.

Since it was just before five o'clock that Sir Gregory had asked Crumper to find Mr. Hillman, the task was slightly more complicated than it would have been earlier in the day. Even so, there were a limited number of places where the young man could reasonably be expected to be. He could be still on the parapet with his cuppa. Or he could be back in the muniment room working again. Or he could have gone back to his room, either to read or to send and receive emails on the laptop he had brought to Datchworth with him. He had told Crumper he liked to keep in touch with his friends.

The butler had silently given the American credit for not adding, "while I'm out here in the middle of nowhere." Crumper suspected that's how the young man felt, because every Friday at four-fifteen he left the muniment room, forsaking his tea (these Americans!), throwing an overnight bag in his little car, and motoring out past

15

the gatehouse no later than four thirty-five, on his way to Oxford for the weekend.

Crumper had not found Mr. Hillman in the muniment room. The tea tray was there, but Mr. Hillman's cup and saucer were not on it. So Crumper had confidently mounted the stairs to the roof and gone out onto the parapet; the young man, however, was not to be seen. Crumper had then sought him in his room, but he wasn't there, either. Of course, Mr. Hillman could have gone for a walk in the grounds, but he usually did that after dinner, taking advantage of the seemingly everlasting daylight of the English summer evening.

Crumper went so far as to go out onto the veranda and gaze across the garden (which appeared to be an American-free zone), but searching the grounds was out of the question. It would take an army. He went though the public rooms of the house, which were sufficiently impressive to move people to pay twelve pounds to see them on open days. Mr. Hillman was particularly fond of the fan vaulting that the third baronet had seen fit to install in the State Dining Room, but he was not to be found admiring it this afternoon. Nor was he in any other of the public rooms. No one on the staff admitted to seeing him since Jenny had taken his tea to the muniment room. It was at this point that Crumper had informed Sir Gregory, with regret, that the young gentleman could not be located. Sir Gregory had kindly told Crumper to let it be, he would see Mr. Hillman at dinner; Crumper had murmured assent, but the butler had no sooner left the library than he recommenced the hunt.

"You what?"

Kathryn sighed. Her mother was, as usual, failing to understand her. Feeling it would be rude to say, "You heard me," she merely shifted the receiver to her other ear and waited.

Mrs. Koerney continued. "With all the money your father left us, I can't imagine what you're doing, taking up a summer job."

"It's not a job, Mom, I volunteered. They aren't paying me anything."

"Then why on earth are you doing it?"

As several people at the church had already asked her that question, Kathryn had a ready answer. "Because I love Oxford. I want to show it to people, show them how to look behind the horrible commercial bits and find the quiet little islands of the Middle Ages and the eighteenth century."

"But Kathryn, people can hire a tour guide to do that. Surely they can afford it, if they can afford the airfare. Why do they have to make you do it?"

Kathryn sighed again. "Mom, they're not making me do it. I want to do it. I'll enjoy it."

It was her mother's turn to sigh, but Mrs. Koerney's exasperation was followed immediately by a short laugh. "Well, you always were a weird child."

Kathryn smiled. "Thank you, Mother dear."

"You're welcome. So tell me about it. Anybody going that I know?"

"Well, you remember the Rector?"

"Beautiful profile."

"Exactly. He and his wife are coming."

"How about Tracy?"

"Insufficient funds. If I could figure out how to buy her a ticket and leave her insufferable husband behind, I would do it, but I can't, so I won't. Ben and Celia Smith are coming, which is good, and so are the Folgers, which is not so good."

"Folgers. Have I met them?"

"Probably not, since I wouldn't waste your time bringing them to your notice."

"That bad, huh?"

"That bad. Oh, but back on the good side, my friend Tom Holder is going, and without his awful wife, thank God; I told you about him, the Police Chief."

There was the briefest pause. "Yes, you've told me about him, but you didn't introduce me to him."

"That's because the last time you were in Harton, he was just an acquaintance. It was only last November that we got to be friends, when all that missing-person stuff happened. The next time you're here, I'll introduce you. He's delightful."

"Uh, Kathryn, has your mother ever given you lecture number forty-seven, 'Being Friends with Married Men'?"

Kathryn emitted a laugh of genuine surprise. "Not to worry! Mom, if you could see him; somebody told me he's forty-eight, but he looks fifty-eight, his belly hangs down over his belt, he's going bald —"

"Hey! Who are you trying to fool? This is your mother, remember? Since when have you cared what a man looked like? That Phil what's-his-name was the ugliest —"

"Mother!" Kathryn exclaimed in the vexed tones of a heavily parented teenager.

"I grant your point. It doesn't matter what he looks like. But still, Tom's just, he's just not . . ."

"Does he not recognize quotations from Hamlet?"

On second thought, maybe her mother did understand her. "Ouch," Kathryn admitted. "Got it in one."

"My daughter, the intellectual snob."

"But you love me anyway."

"Of course I do. But answer me this: if you're showing all these people around all the time, how are you going to have time to see Rob?"

"Clever planning, that's how. I've told the church group in no uncertain terms that they are utterly on their own on weekends, and Rob has weekends free. He's making all sorts of plans, he informs me; he's reserved a punt for our first Saturday, and we're going to do Oxford's Greatest Hits. You know: Addison's Walk, the Ashmolean, all that stuff. And — get ready to turn chartreuse with envy — Rob has a summer job somewhere in rural Oxfordshire in a *castle* for heaven's sake which is really a fortified manor house but who cares, sorting out some manuscripts for a baronet, I am not making this up, with the most marvelous name: Sir Something St.

John Beverage hyphen Something Else. And I am invited for Dinner, capital D, so I can check out the castle. Not to mention the baronet."

The Baronet was dozing lightly in his chair, exercising a talent younger people rarely have, that of sleeping while sitting upright. His eight-year-old self was playing with his brother Richard in the woods; they were hunting dragons. Great fun, that had been. But something was wrong. Something had happened to Dicky. A shadow of unease fell across the Baronet's dream; somewhere in the distance a woman screamed. Voices. Shouting. People never shouted at Datchworth. Running footsteps.

The library door was flung open, something else that never happened at Datchworth. Sir Gregory awoke with a start. His imperturbable butler stood in the doorway, perturbed beyond measure. One could actually hear the man breathing. In his shaking hands he held some fragments of a china teacup.

Crumper said, with something approaching anguish, "I beg your pardon, Sir Gregory. I'm afraid we've found Mr. Hillman."

CHAPTER 2

JANUARY 1997

Almost Seven Months Before Rob Hillman's Death

What ultimately would culminate in tragedy began as a minor domestic inconvenience — or a domestic inconvenience that would have been minor in a more modest household than Datchworth Castle. One of the lesser staff members, changing a light bulb in a narrow passageway on the ground floor, noticed a crack in the wall.

Unfortunately, the wall in question dated from the twelfth century. When in 1403 the Knight Sir Edward Thorpe had commenced building upon the land granted to him by King Richard for services rendered in the west of Ireland, he had thought it good to incorporate into his new home the sprawling Norman ruins of Datchworth Castle. Family legend differed on the reasons for this decision; either Sir Edward believed the ruins occupied the best building site on the estate, or he thought every knight should have a castle, or he figured he could save a bundle on building costs by using the old walls, where they were still standing, and the old foundations. Sir Edward left to his descendants the nightmare of taking care of them.

The current owner, having maneuvered his wheelchair down the passageway in the wake of Ralph Carlyle, his estate manager, to view both the crack and the evidence that it was slowly widening, did not have the luxury of summoning one of his numerous maintenance staff to simply patch the thing up. Datchworth was a Grade I Listed Building.

"Damn and blast," sighed Sir Gregory wearily. "Notify English Heritage."

English Heritage duly arrived in the form of a single official whose placid manner, upon inspecting the offending crack, gave way to a concern bordering on alarm. His report clearly telegraphed the urgency of the situation up the line of command, for a more senior inspector of masonry arrived at Datchworth instantly — that is, two weeks later. In the blink of an eye — that is, by the first of February, the place was crawling with English Heritage.

They took photographs. They drew diagrams. They took (Sir Gregory swore to his neighbors) X rays. They scraped minute bits of mortar from between stones, and even more minute bits from the stones themselves, with tools they had obviously stolen from dentists. They sealed the resultant sacred milligrams of dust in tiny plastic envelopes, and dispatched them to undisclosed destinations.

At some location remote from Datchworth there were meetings. Arguments. Reports. Recommendations. Finally, on a disagreeably overcast morning shortly before Valentine's Day, Sir Gregory received a polite letter with the verdict. At least two-point-three-six-five square meters of the wall would have to be Disassembled and Rebuilt.

Sir Gregory informed his nephew Derek that the upshot was that the masonry work would be a doddle, but the state-of-the-art scaffolding required to keep the rest of the wall supported while they delicately punched a bloody great hole in it, that was going to set them back a packet. Because of course the Family was going to have to pay for it. English Heritage only told you what you had to do, they didn't foot the bill.

And the bill was not going to be a trifle, because for one thing they had no idea what was behind the crack. When the original inspector had asked to see "the other side of this wall, please," consternation had ensued. No one, it seemed, had the remotest idea where the other side of the wall was. That part of the house was an architectural hodgepodge, Sir Edward having been particularly assiduous in utilizing castle fragments in that area. The passageway, which Sir Gregory had taken to calling "the Scene of the Crack," led from the old castle stillroom (now the site of a desperately uninteresting display entitled "Datchworth through the Ages," which, even on public days, attracted no more interest than it deserved) to a modern hallway leading past the visitors' rest rooms into the original wing of Sir Edward's manor house.

A forty-seven-minute search by the English Heritage official, Mr. Hitch, accompanied by no less a personage than Crumper himself, through a miscellany of centuries, architectural styles, and rooms used and unused that together made rabbit warrens look as if they were laid out in right-angle grids, had produced no joy. Recourse was had to the muniment room.

There the architect's drawings for the modern hallway were unearthed, paper-clipped (English Heritage was shocked) to a four-centuries-old floor plan. Alas, when Mssrs. Crumper and Hitch had returned to the place which should have been the other side of the wall from the Scene of the Crack, they had discovered that neither drawing, old or new, entirely coincided with the layout of rooms and hallways in which they found themselves. They came dispiritedly to the conclusion that the architects hadn't been able to find the other side of the wall, either, and had faked it.

"Which means," said the Baronet to his nephew, "that we've no idea whether the Crack is in the face of a hundred cubic feet of solid stone and is merely a cosmetic problem, and we might just as well stuff it with common or garden concrete, or whether it runs clear through a strategic supporting wall, which means that whole damn wing could fall down on top of us any minute if we don't repair the thing correctly. And soon."

Derek made a face and a noise, both eloquent of understanding, and drained the last of the tea from his plain blue mug. He rose and picked up the teapot from the table between them, refilling first Sir Gregory's china cup and then his own mug, saying, "Not something to take chances with, then."

"Alas, no. Ah, thank you, Lovely Boy."

Derek's Mediterranean features softened into the smile he'd inherited from his Italian grandmother. For as long as he could remember, his uncle had called him that, and he liked it. Nice to be somebody's Lovely Boy. He had certainly never been his mother's. Nor Julie-the-Crumpet's, either, though she had once used the term on him. He had rather bitten her nose off for it, which, as they'd been in bed at the time, was a bit ungentlemanly of him. Derek had tried to explain to her why she mustn't use his uncle's term of endearment for him, but found that the word "presumptuous" was tickling his tongue, and obviously he couldn't say it. She'd have told him off for being a snob. She'd have been right.

Derek shook thoughts of the Crumpet from his mind and resumed his seat. "So, Uncle, break it to me gently. How deep do we have to dig to finance this project?"

"Impossible to say before we know what the wretched wall is holding up."

"Worst-case scenario?"

"At this point it would only be a guess."

"Guess, then."

"I'm bracing myself for seventy thousand."

"Jesus," said Derek, quietly.

Sir Gregory, in deference (still) to his late wife, habitually refrained from taking the Lord's name in vain, but he tolerated the practice in his heir, just as he tolerated the abominable mug that Derek fancied over a proper teacup. Besides, it was a reasonable reaction. Seventy thousand pounds out of the estate was seventy thousand less for Derek to inherit, and only an indecently wealthy saint could fail to care about such a sum. Derek would of course be indecently wealthy when his father died, but he would never, thank God, be a saint. Sir Gregory found saints tedious.

"So sorry, Lovely Boy."

Derek summoned a laugh for his uncle's sake and waved a lavish hand. "What the hell! We can sell the plantation in Cuba."

That had been a family joke since the time of George III. (There were, presumably, lots of plantations in Cuba, but none of them had ever been owned by the Bebberidge-Thorpes.)

The old man's face crinkled into a smile, and he raised his teacup in a toast. "The plantation in Cuba it is, then! Meanwhile, I shall write to this Mrs. . . . ." He set the cup down on the marquetry table next to his chair, picked up the letter from English Heritage, and peered at it through his steel-rimmed spectacles. "Mrs. Roghaar. I shall tell her to storm the Castle and do her worst."

Miranda Roghaar, in fact, had been careful in her letter to prepare Sir Gregory for the worst, but she was very much hoping it wouldn't come to that. Not just because she took no pleasure in inflicting huge expenses on those who owned and cared for the ancient buildings that were her passion, but because a wall whose other side could not be located might possibly have a function immensely more interesting than merely holding up half the castle. Reluctant, however, to create expectations which might never be fulfilled, she did not confide her hopes to Sir Gregory when she arrived at Datchworth. Instead, she proceeded to set up her invasion of his home in the most tactful and least intrusive manner possible.

In this respect Mrs. Roghaar found the Scene of the Crack close to ideal. In a passageway rarely used in winter, right around a corner from the rest rooms that had been constructed for summer tourists, she and her team were well out of the family's way. She hated jobs when they had to work in the owner's bedroom or the family's favorite sitting room or — worst of all — the kitchen. Here, the closest they came to the kitchen was a message from the cook informing them that if it suited their convenience, their elevenses (coffee and pastries) would be laid out for them in the Visitors Café (past the rest rooms, across the small courtyard), which was being opened for their exclusive use during their stay at the Castle. Lunch would be served in the same place, and were there any vegetarians or other dietary requirements to cater for?

I'm in Heaven, thought Miranda Roghaar, and set her team to work. A drill scarcely thicker than a needle was carefully positioned, and a tiny tunnel began to creep through the wall at a rate of slightly less than one inch per minute.

Some time later Crumper was in the library reporting to his master and to the young gentleman, a frequent and welcome guest at Datchworth, who was facing Sir Gregory across a Victorian games table. "Mrs. Roghaar now confirms her earlier estimate, Sir Gregory. The wall is no more than six inches thick, and she believes it is not — her exact words were, 'structurally significant.' "

"Well, thank God fasting. Better yet, thank God drinking. What do you say, Kit?" asked the Baronet, turning to his visitor.

Kit Mallowan grinned first back at his host and then, man to man, at the butler.

"I say the good sherry at least. What do you say, Crumper?"

The butler allowed himself a small smile and murmured in his best courtly manner, "Very good, my lord."

"Yes, and Crumper," added Sir Gregory, relief shining in his tired eyes, "when you've poured for us, get Mr. Banner on the telephone. We should put him out of his misery."

So Derek, who was entertaining a lady friend in his Victorian house in north Oxford, was informed that the amount he was not going to inherit was probably going to be rather less than seventy thousand pounds. He and his uncle exchanged heartfelt congratulations.

"Kit and I are having a sherry on it and I suggest, Lovely Boy, that you do the same."

"Good idea, only I think I'll make it a G

and T. Ring me again the minute they guarantee it'll be less than ten thousand, and I'll switch to champagne."

By teatime the champagne was on ice, not at Derek's house, which he had departed in jubilant haste, but at Datchworth, whither he was bound. The repairs, after all, were going to be comparatively modest, but the repair bill was now the last thing on anybody's mind.

Not Crumper, but Miranda Roghaar herself, had brought the next report to the library; Crumper merely ushered her into the room. It was immediately evident both to Sir Gregory and to the young man, whom the former was still ruthlessly drinking under the backgammon table, that Mrs. Roghaar had large news. Her demeanor was cool and competent, but the excitement crackled from her like static electricity.

After the team had drilled several of their slender holes through the wall and determined its thickness, she reported, they had inserted fine rods with conspicuously colored tips through the holes, pushing them far enough to extend several inches out the other side. They had then recommenced the search for the other side of the wall. Floor plans, architects' drawings, a compass, much persistence, and even the advice of Mrs. Draper, the retired housekeeper who had actually been born (unexpectedly) in the cloakroom off the entrance hall eighty years before and who knew every inch of the Castle, had not availed to locate the other side of the wall, even when it should have been obvious to a nearsighted hedgehog because it had funny little pointy things sticking out of it. "In short, Sir Gregory," Mrs. Roghaar explained, "those rods are protruding into space about six inches, but they are *not* extending from any wall in any room that might conceivably be on the opposite side of the wall with the crack in it."

It took about two seconds for the light to dawn, and it struck the young visitor first.

"Pull the other one!" Kit cried in high delight. "You don't mean it!"

But by that time Sir Gregory had caught up. He eyed the woman whom he had heretofore regarded as a polite nuisance and a necessary evil, and whispered incredulously, "A secret room?"

CHAPTER 3

SUMMER 1933

Sixty-four Years Before Rob Hillman's Death

With intense pride of ownership, he surveyed his domain. It was without doubt the best room in the Castle. And it was his. Of course, everything was going to be his one day. Pater had told him so.

Some people (naming no names!) didn't like that. Well, that was just jolly rotten luck for them. After all, it wasn't his fault he was the Heir.

As the Heir, he would have to learn to take care of Datchworth, Pater had told him. Not just the Castle and the servants and all — the farms, the tenants, the whole estate. It would mean more lessons, and he wasn't frightfully keen on lessons, but that was a long way off. Years and years. Probably not before he was seventeen. Right now there was just him and the room.

He called it the Round Room. That wasn't its proper name, but he fancied the sound: Rrrrouound Rrrrooom. And be-sides, that's what made it special. Anybody could have a square room, or a rectangular room. And the windows, they were special, too. They were huge, bigger than any others in the old part of the Castle, and looking out of them you could imagine stepping down into a boat and sailing across the wide, wide place in the moat to all sorts of adventures. He'd asked Mater and Pater for a boat, just a little rowboat was all. He could tie it under one of the windows, and go straight onto the water from his room. All the chaps at school would be so jealous! But M & P had said that until he could swim better they didn't want him "playing on the moat." Playing! He wasn't going to play, he was going to explore. But one could never get one's par-ents to understand things like that.

In fact, they'd even told him not to get up onto the windowsills when the windows were open. But he did it almost every day in the summer. It was too spiffing, really, to pass up, he thought, as he clambered up onto the one he liked best. One could look out over the moat when one was standing down in the room, but up here one could look down into it, down into the murky green water. Terrific fun to think what might be under it. Lost treasure from old Sir Edward he bet.

Couldn't stand up there for very long, of course. Mater might come by any time, and if she caught him, they wouldn't let him keep the room. He didn't want to have to move back to his old digs by the nursery. That was for little people.

He turned his head to check the door. Crikey! It was opening. Jumping down from the windowsill, he grabbed the closest thing he saw: one of the woods from his set of golf clubs. Whistling casually, he strolled to the middle of the room, the big empty space, where he sometimes practiced his swing. He was carefully not even looking at the door, but when after a few moments he heard nothing, he turned to stare at it.

What a gudgeon he was! It hadn't been opening at all. It was just a teeny bit ajar. He must have forgotten to shut it properly when he came in. That was bad. A chap had to have his privacy. He crossed the stone floor to the door, opened it, and looked down the corridor. Nobody there. Good show. He closed the door with a strong push and heard the satisfying *choonk* of wood and the clack of the iron bar dropping into place.

What he did not hear was the slow, careful breaths of the person who now crouched low behind the faded red leather trunk in the corner. Getting in without being spotted had been the first victory. The second victory would be to prolong the invasion, stretch it out for minutes and minutes until some great triumph came crashing . . .

Meanwhile, back in the open space, the Master of the Round Room discovered he still had the golf club in his hand, and decided that practicing a few swings might be a good idea after all. He didn't want Fletcher to laugh at him at his next lesson.

So he swung the wood for a bit, but it was a lot more fun with a ball, so he tossed the wood onto the bed and got out the putter, the three balls, and the tin that Cook had given him.

The figure hiding behind the red leather trunk, finding it easier to breathe quietly now that the initial thrill of invasion was over, spent several minutes trying to figure out what was happening. The noises sounded somehow familiar, but what were they exactly? A little click, then a louder noise that sounded like metal and something. Then after what seemed like a long time, a proud voice shouted that it was the champion golfer. Oh, he was knocking golf balls into a tin. Stupid, really. No kind of fun. But the noises stopped. Now what was he doing?

The Master of the Room had looked under the big chair to find a ball that had missed the tin, and found his slingshot instead. Oh, that's where it had been hiding! Jolly good! Now, where had he put the pebbles he'd collected for it last month? He'd wrapped them in a handkerchief, and he'd put the handkerchief . . . in the bottom drawer of the dresser, he thought. Yes, there it was! He grabbed the grimy white bundle that scrunched in his hand, scooped up the slingshot from the chair where he'd dropped it, and trotted back to his favorite windowsill.

Having scrambled up onto the sill, he stood facing the moat while he struggled to untie the knot in the handkerchief. His supplanter, bored with sitting silent and undiscovered, peered from behind the red leather trunk.

Up on the windowsill the handkerchief had yielded up its store of small stones. Fingering them thoughtfully, he looked out over the moat. He hadn't a hope of hitting the far bank, of course. But he could see how far out into the water he could get a pebble. Carefully he chose his first missile: smooth, brown, the largest of the lot. Could he get it halfway across? He drew back the sling as far as he could and let go. There was a small *ploop* and a widening ring of ripples out on the water. Rats! Not nearly halfway. He wondered if a smaller stone might go farther. He pawed through the pebbles, looking for a likely candidate. But he never got to make his second shot.

Both literally and figuratively, he never knew what hit him.

CHAPTER 4

WEDNESDAY, THE DAY OF ROB HILLMAN'S DEATH

Close to Midnight

Detective Sergeant Meera Patel was feeling unusually useless. Unusually, because normally at this point in an investigation she was feeling like one of the best-oiled cogs in the machine. The machine itself might be plowing full steam ahead, or it might be floundering in the ditch, but Meera's part in the investigation was, nearly always, operating at peak efficiency. Meera Patel was awfully good at her job. She knew it, and her sights were fixed unwaveringly on the advancement that was nothing less than her due. So when she felt useless, she also felt frustrated and therefore impatient. These emotions had to be kept under control, because they got in the way of her work.

Her job was Family Liaison, which meant that in a homicide investigation she was the officer in charge of dealing directly

40

with the victim's family. She was the sympathetic face of the police force. While other faces, solemn and dispassionate, asked endless boring, pointless, or painful questions, probed and pondered, made notes, and went away again, Meera Patel actually *answered* questions. The grieving widow, the bewildered child, the parent stunned into incoherency found in Meera an invaluable ally. Here was somebody who understood how they felt, and moreover, understood what was going on in the abruptly alien space that had been, until hours or days ago, their normal lives. They trusted her. Frequently they poured out their hearts to her.

Their willingness to do so was created not only by the Detective Sergeant's compassionate attitude but by her appearance. Central Casting, asked to provide a convincing policewoman, would never have sent over anybody remotely resembling Meera Patel. She stood a reasonable five feet five inches in her stocking feet, but her slender figure and delicate head made her look petite, even fragile. The raven hair, worn in a neat, chin-length crop, framed a perfect Asian face: huge dark eyes, olive skin, sensuous mouth. She looked as sturdy as porcelain and as dangerous as a bunny rabbit, and the last two-hundred-and-twenty-pound villain who had taken her at face value had spent three days in the hospital on his way to prison. In the department she was referred to — cautiously, behind her back — as the Bengal Tidbit.

Meera, whose self-awareness was matched by her appreciation of irony, relished the contrast between her appearance and her abilities. Besides, a disarming front was much more useful to a Family Liaison officer than a formidable presence would have been. Many a distraught relative, after stammering broken, useless answers to the official questioners, turned voluble when Meera was the only police officer in the room. This was useful for two reasons: the families got to dump some of their intolerable emotional burden, and Meera picked up a fair amount of information that no formal interview could ever have elicited.

Meera was scrupulous never to abuse this trust. The ethics of Family Liaison were stern, and Meera clove to them, letter and spirit. She always reminded the family, carefully and specifically, that she was a police officer, and that although they could get as comfortable with her as they wanted to — Call her Meera? Certainly! — they must never forget that anything they told her that might assist the investigation would be passed on to her fellow officers. This rarely stopped the flow of confidences, however, because normally the family was every bit as anxious to find the perpetrator as the police were.

But this time it was different. For one thing, there wasn't a family — or at least, it wasn't the victim's family. The victim was American, and his parents, apparently too traumatized to essay a transatlantic flight, had deputed the victim's cousin, who was bound for England that week anyway, to come to Datchworth Castle, or at least to the nearby village of Wallwood, as proxy for her bereaved aunt and uncle. This woman — an Anglican priest, Meera had noted with interest — had yet to arrive, although she was expected on Saturday.

Meanwhile, what Meera had on her hands was the *Family*. She had been at Datchworth Castle only a couple of hours when she noticed that she had begun, in her mind, to assign a capital "F" to the word: her acute ear had picked it up from the staff and servants. Servants, for heaven's sake! She felt as though she had stepped into a costume drama, only without the costumes. There was even a butler, who probably rated a capital letter, too: the Butler.

He had been standing on the front stoop as their cars had crunched across the gravel of the drive onto the paved area by the front door. The door was a massive affair of wood and iron, living up to the crenellated tower that rose above it to the height of five stories. The honey-colored stone, perforated here and there with arrow-slit windows, was smooth and unpocked by the weapons of long-dead enemies, and the tower exhibited that storybook perfection which tells the initiated eye that the building in question does not possess that medievality to which it pretends. Most of the police personnel climbing out of their cars, having spent years in and around that open-air museum of architecture which is the city of Oxford, pegged the entrance tower at a glance as Victorian.

But the man at the foot of it was the Real Thing. He was perhaps in his late forties, stocky but not flabby, of average height with a face containing no remarkable features and wearing a gray suit of utterly forgettable blandness. The moment he spoke, however, the mild stir of arrival stilled: every cop there instinctively recognized a voice that was accustomed to being listened to.

He said impassively, "Good afternoon. Sir Gregory is in the library; I will take you to him" — here the man's eyes turned unerringly to Chief Inspector Lamp, the senior investigating officer — "as soon as his physician feels it is safe for him to see you. I am Crumper, Sir Gregory's butler. The body is in the side drive" — Crumper made a small efficient gesture to his left — "where it is being watched by our local constable. Prior to the constable's arrival I stationed three members of the staff around the area so that it would not be disturbed. The young man who discovered the body is in the front hall, waiting to answer your questions. A room on the ground floor has been set aside for your use."

No doubt about it, the butler was impressive. But he was one of the principle reasons Meera was feeling useless. Or perhaps it was merely that the uselessness came into sharper focus when she spoke to Crumper. Not that the butler wasn't cooperating; Crumper was the soul of cooperation. Not that he wasn't pleasant; he smiled at her in an avuncular fashion whenever he brought her tea, and having discovered her preference in that matter, made certain that the kitchen supplied her with Darjeeling rather than the Earl Grey which was brought to Chief Inspector Lamp.

But there was a wall there. It was invisible, like those force fields you saw in sci-fi series on the telly, but it was an impassable barrier. Meera and all her colleagues were on one side, and Crumper, polite and untouchable, stood on the other. No, Meera decided, that wasn't quite accurate. Crumper himself was the wall, standing between her and the Family, between her and the entire household. He was Datchworth Castle's defending army, entire in the body of one man.

At first they had thought Crumper was going to be their ally. When he had telephoned 999 he had said, "There's been a death, a sudden death. It may not have been an accident." Since it often was tricky, to say the least, to break the news to a shocked household that what they were assuming was an accidental death was in fact a homicide, it was a small but welcome relief to find that here this bridge had already been crossed.

"First of all, Mr. Crumper," Chief Inspector Lamp began with a faint, official smile, "I want to say that you've handled this situation quite well."

Crumper nodded as though Lamp had done nothing more than state the obvious, and murmured an uneffusive "Thank you, sir."

They were sitting in the parlor favored by Sir Gregory's late wife. Crumper had caused a library table and chairs to be installed in the area where the light was best, and for good measure had arranged for the presence of a miscellany of cords and cables, ready to receive the plugs of telephones, computers, or whatever other machinery might be deemed essential to the modern crime fighter. All this had occurred before they arrived.

"Can you tell me," Lamp continued smoothly, "why the broken cup was removed from the scene, and yet afterward you went to a great deal of trouble to see that nothing else was disturbed?"

"Certainly, sir. As you have spoken with young Donovan already, I assume he told you that it was he who picked up the pieces of the cup. He told me that he did it without thinking. I presume it was a result of his shock at finding Mr. Hillman dead. When Donovan came to me, he was stammering, unable to speak clearly. He held out the pieces of the cup to me and I took them. I saw that the cup was one of the set that was used for Mr. Hillman's tea, and we had been looking for Mr. Hillman for an hour without success. I assumed at that point that there had been an accident, a serious one, to judge from the lad's behavior. But when he led me around to the west side of the house and I saw, ah, what had happened, I thought it might not be an accident. So I made arrangements for the area to be watched by three different members of the staff whilst I rang for help."

Lamp tapped gently on the table with the well-sharpened tip of a yellow pencil. "So, you think Robert Hillman was, what? A likely candidate for suicide? Or homicide?"

Crumper's eyebrows rose half an inch, in an expression equally compounded of surprise and disapproval. "Neither, sir."

"Then why were you so quick to assume that he didn't just fall off the, um, that walkway along the edge of the roof?"

"Mr. Hillman was lying facedown. He was wearing shorts. On the back of his right calf there was a dark stain that I took to be blood. Resting against it was a large stone from the crenellations on the parapet

48

above. The stone had a similar stain."

There was a brief silence. These observations had, of course, been made by everyone from the village P.C. to Lamp himself. The Chief Inspector pursed and unpursed his lips. "But doesn't that suggest an accidental fall? He leans on one of the stones, looking out at the view, stone comes loose, bloke loses his balance, they both fall, man and rock. Stone lands on his leg." Lamp knew it wasn't right, but he wanted to see what the butler was made of.

He found out. Crumper said calmly, "If that were the way of it, sir, the man would fall on the rock, not the rock on the man. Besides, the stain was relatively small. That suggests that Mr. Hillman's blood had already stopped flowing when the stone struck his leg."

Lamp smiled. "Ever thought of joining the C.I.D., Mr. Crumper?"

"No, sir," Crumper replied without returning so much as a hint of a smile.

Lamp perceived that the butler was impervious to flattery. Well, that was all right. They wouldn't need to cajole the facts out of him; it was clear that the man was going to be forthright with them.

Twenty minutes later, Lamp was less confident of Crumper's cooperation.

Crumper had no idea who had killed Mr. Hillman, and no idea who might have wanted to kill him. Mr. Hillman had no enemies that Crumper knew of. Certainly no one in the household had the slightest reason to want him dead. Everyone there liked him; Mr. Hillman had been, in fact, a very likable young man. No one in the household had known him longer than the few weeks he had spent at Datchworth, first during the Easter holidays, then the past two weeks. Except, of course, Miss Daventry; Mr. Hillman had been her tutor at Oxford.

"Were Miss Daventry and Mr. Hillman, ah, close?"

"No, sir."

Lamp wondered how the butler, with no discernable alternation in expression, managed to cram into those two words half the disdain in the civilized world. Crumper might just as well have said, "If you expect me to encourage nasty insinuations about the Family I serve, you are as stupid as you are crass."

The pattern continued. Crumper returned unhelpful but perfectly polite replies to all Lamp's questions, until Lamp asked one that might remotely imply any untoward behavior, much less a motive for murder, among the residents of the household. Then the "No, sir" or the "I couldn't say, sir" was tinged with implacable frost. The ice in the reply was so subtly conveyed, however, that it was impossible to accuse the butler of being either rude or unhelpful. Chief Inspector Lamp, not an arrogant man, knew that he had met his match. He decided he would let Meera Patel have a go at Crumper later, but he didn't expect miracles, and he told her so.

Meera, meanwhile, had been attempting to make headway with the Family. Sir Gregory's physician, whom Crumper had called immediately after summoning the police, had turned over his late afternoon appointments to his colleagues and made haste to Datchworth (there are some circumstances under which even the NHS makes house calls). Having arrived a scant two minutes before Chief Inspector Lamp and Company, he had temporarily denied access to Sir Gregory while he took the old man's pulse and blood pressure and satisfied himself that his patient was somewhere this side of shock.

That left Meera talking to Meg Daventry. Meg was a pretty girl, eighteen or nineteen, Meera guessed, and Meg, not to put too fine a point on it, was in shreds.

"Oh God, oh God," she wailed. "It's my fault, it's all my fault."

This was a promising beginning; Meera could make herself well and truly useful to the bereaved and at the same time garner immediate information about what might have happened to Robert Hillman. But it emerged that all Meg Daventry meant in assuming the blame was that it was she who was responsible for getting the young American to the Castle in the first place.

The three and a half minutes Meera was allowed with Sir Gregory produced even less satisfaction. What she got was punctilious civility delivered in a shocked and shaken voice. She assured the Baronet that she would be there should he need to talk to someone about what was happening; he assured her that he would let her know should such a need arise. Recognizing her cue, she departed, resisting the fleeting urge to bow herself out. The doctor had been sitting ten feet away from Sir Gregory's wheelchair throughout the brief conversation.

Shortly after eleven thirty p.m., Lamp convened a meeting in the parlor Crumper had allotted them. There the entire team compared notes, and it wasn't happy hearing. The postmortem was not complete, but preliminary indications were, first, the deceased had died when he hit the ground, which nobody had doubted; second, the stone had landed on top of him very shortly after he died, which again nobody had doubted; and third, when examined at six thirty-five p.m., the body had been dead somewhere between one and two hours, which everybody knew already.

"I don't think we can expect anything more from that department, frankly," said Lamp. "So either Hillman jumped and somebody pushed the stone after him to make it look accidental, which doesn't seem probable because why should anybody here cover it up if he committed suicide? And besides, everybody from the Baronet to the maid who took him his tea says he was in good spirits, no sign of trouble or depression, and again, why should everybody here lie about that? So I think we file 'jumped.'" There were nods.

The Chief Inspector continued. "Next, did he fall? Anybody have a reasonable explanation for why somebody would push a stone after him?" Everybody shook their heads. "Which leaves us with the obvious. He was pushed, and the stone was pushed over afterward to give the idea that he fell because the stone gave way. Has anyone got anything at all that challenges that?" Again, heads shook unanimously.

"All right. Motive. Anybody got anything to offer, anything at all?"

Detective Inspector Griffin suggested, "The girl? Meg Daventry?" There were a few murmurs of assent.

"What about her?"

"Well, she's the only one who's really upset, and she's more than upset, she's hysterical. She keeps saying she's the only reason Hillman was here. And she's expressing remorse. Lover's quarrel, maybe?"

Lamp looked at Meera. "What do you think?"

Meera had seen this question coming even before the meeting had started. "I think it's the only possibility we've dug up so far."

Lamp looked at her, waiting for more, but when all he got was a steady gaze from the big, dark eyes, he shrugged and turned back to Griffin. "All right, then. We'll have a team — Duncan, Morrisey, you take the girl. Anybody else smell a motive? Anywhere?"

Silence.

"Well, let's hope she's it, because I don't see anything else promising. We've got at least eight people so far who could have followed Hillman up the tower stairs and shoved him off that roof, and the only people we can eliminate positively are first, the old man, who's been in that chair for ten years and couldn't push a teddy bear off a table, if we believe the doctor, and second and third, the cook and the butler's wife, who were together the entire time from the brewing of the tea to the finding of the corpse. So if nobody has any other suggestions, I think we call it a night."

Meera wondered what it would do to Sir Gregory if they pinned a murder on his niece. She also wondered where the nephew was, and whether it was significant that they couldn't find him. And finally, she wondered if she had accomplished anything remotely useful that day. She decided she probably hadn't. The only bereaved person who'd found her any use or comfort was Meg Daventry, and it somehow didn't count if you comforted the perpetrator. As for helping the investigation, Lamp would have set an inquiry team onto Meg even without Meera's report; the girl had had her hysterics openly, uninhibited by the presence of the law, heedless of the suspicions she drew upon herself.

She probably did it, said Meera's harder side to her softer, which didn't want to believe Meg guilty. *And either Duncan and Morrisey and a little more digging among the staff will wrap it up, or we won't find anything that's not circumstantial and it'll go unsolved, and in either case, what was I doing here?*

So it was that as the police vacated the Castle for the night, Detective Sergeant Patel was feeling frustrated. Not one to allow herself to wallow in negative emotions, however, she found herself looking forward to Saturday. If they hadn't wrapped it up before then, or even if they had, maybe she could be of some use with the cousin from America. She wondered what a woman priest would be like.

CHAPTER 5

FEBRUARY 1997

Five Months Before Rob Hillman's Death

Miranda Roghaar eyed Sir Gregory and his young guest with a touch of dismay. They were so eager, so excited.

"Please don't get your hopes up," she said. "We don't know that what's behind the wall is a secret room. It may just be a hollow space, quite small. There may be nothing in it. There may just be some rubble. That's frequently the case."

But both her listeners had seen the suppressed excitement on her own face, so it was too late to tell them not to expect much. Sir Gregory tried unsuccessfully to arrange his features into a semblance of indifference and inquired, "When will you know? How do you find out?"

"First we have to put supports in place to hold up the stones over the area where we're going to make the hole; that's under way as we speak. We need to drill several more holes at the top of the area, then erect a counterweighted scaffolding. Since the wall, as I told your man earlier, does not appear to be structurally significant, we might finish the scaffolding by early afternoon. Then we'll start removing stones. One at a time. Very carefully."

Sir Gregory smiled. "I should jolly well hope so. Is there anything we can do to help?"

Miranda hesitated. "Well . . . if it wouldn't be too much trouble, could we take our elevenses there in the passageway? Nobody really wants to leave the site." She smiled ruefully at him, knowing she'd just given the game away. If her team, the professionals, were that keen, then there was little point trying to pretend to the owner that nothing particularly interesting was about to happen.

Sir Gregory's smile widened. "Of course, dear lady. Simply tell Crumper on your way out; he'll be standing the other side of the door there."

So Miranda Roghaar returned to supervise the assembly of scaffolding and the disassembly of the wall; Sir Gregory asked his guest if he'd care to say; Kit assured Sir Gregory he wouldn't miss this for the world and phoned home to say he was lunching, tea-ing, and quite possibly dining at the Castle.

After luncheon Sir Gregory announced he would take his daily nap, leaving Kit on his own in the library: "Dear Sir Greg! Two hours of uninterrupted dalliance with your books? Heaven, I assure you! Besides, I can make a few phone calls home and get a bit of the business done that I really ought to be home doing, but wild horses couldn't drag me out of here at this point. You run along and have a good kip."

Kit was an easy guest in anybody's house, but especially at Datchworth Castle, which had been his second home for most of his life; he and Sir Gregory, despite their age difference, were firm and comfortable friends. So the ailing Baronet wheeled away for the rest he needed, and returned shortly after three.

At that point the scaffolding was safely established and the removal of stones had begun. With the first stone out, Miranda Roghaar had shone a small but powerful flashlight into the dimness beyond the hole, and Crumper had reported back to the library that the hidden space appeared to be an irregular triangle, about two feet at its deepest. Shortly thereafter, with a second stone removed and Mrs. Roghaar employing a flashlight and a small mirror set at an angle on the end of an eighteen-inch rod, the news sent to Sir Gregory was that there was a respectable pile of objects in the enclosed space.

"They are irregular in size and shape," Crumper reported, "and of course they are covered with dust, but Mrs. Roghaar says that she does not believe that they are rubble. More than that she does not wish to say at this time. However . . ."

As Crumper was not given to significant pauses, both his listeners pricked up their ears.

"She did ask me," Crumper continued, "if I knew if the Family had hidden any silver from Cromwell in the Civil War, and if so, had it ever been found?"

Kit let out a whoop of celebration and his host suddenly seemed ten years younger. "Crumper," said Sir Gregory, "chill half a dozen of our best bubbly, ring Mr. Banner and Miss Daventry, and tell them" — here the old man assumed an air of mock grandeur — "to make haste to their ancestral halls."

"With pleasure, Sir Gregory," the butler replied, allowing a small smile to adorn his face as he withdrew from the room.

"They found a small batch of our

silver," Kit remarked, "in eighteen sixty-something, but my folks always held that there was a lot more under the lawn next to the knot garden. I asked why they didn't just dig it up — I think I was ten at the time — and they said in shocked tones, 'You can't dig up the grass!' as though I'd suggested dynamiting the dower house."

Sir Gregory chuckled, and began to regale his young friend with some of the lesser-known (and less illustrious) exploits of the Bebberidge-Thorpes in the Civil War, and how they (in company with most of the major landowners in Oxfordshire) had pledged their arms and their wealth to the King while burying the very best of the household silver, ostensibly to hide it from Cromwell, but simultaneously making sure that the King didn't stumble across it, either. Kit had some stories of his own to offer, of course, and the exchange of family legends was creeping toward the apocryphal when the next guest arrived: Will Tandulkar, cordially summoned from his labors at the Morgan Mallowan home farm by a phone call from Kit. ("Oh, of course, dear boy, ring him by all means; the more the merrier!")

Will had known that Kit had gone to Datchworth that morning to see Sir

Gregory through the invasion of his domain, and was delighted to learn that what earlier was deemed a damn nuisance now looked like it was turning into a cause for rejoicing. Sir Gregory explained that congratulations might be somewhat premature, but that he himself was passing from cautious to incautious optimism as the afternoon wore on.

Tea was served, and Will was just offering to pour Sir Gregory a second cup when the door opened and Crumper pronounced, "Miss Daventry; Mr. Banner." Meg and Derek, having made record time from Oxford, swarmed into the room demanding to know if the Old Silver had really been found.

"Patience, children!" beamed Sir Gregory, receiving a kiss on each cheek from his niece and a warm handclasp from his nephew. "We shall know presently. Meanwhile, do have some tea."

"Uncle Greg," said Meg, having greeted Kit and Will and accepted a cup of tea from the latter, "I'm confused. How can it be the silver? The wall with the crack is twelfth century, didn't you say? — and the silver would have been hidden about, what? Sixteen-thirty?"

"My clever girl! I asked Mrs. Roghaar —

she's the English Heritage woman — that very same question. She says they have no way of knowing at this point how old the *other* wall is, the wall at the back of the enclosed space. They can't get to it until the hole in the twelfth-century wall is considerably bigger than it is now."

And so they all discussed ancient walls and the complications involved in partially dismantling and repairing same, but everybody knew they were just killing time. When a slight click signaled that the door was being opened, conversation died instantly as everyone in the room turned toward the sound with a collective intake of breath.

It was Miranda Roghaar herself who opened the door. She said nothing, but smiled conspiratorially at Sir Gregory, and stepped aside to make way for Crumper. The butler bore a large, serviceable tray (borrowed from Mrs. Drundle in the kitchen) on which were laid a number of nondescript and unidentifiable objects. Most appeared to be roughly cylindrical in shape, about eight inches long and four inches in diameter.

Crumper had claimed the right to bear the precious burden to Sir Gregory, but had selected a battered old kitchen tray for the task. Sir Gregory, who knew his butler's face as well as he knew his own, noted with amusement that there was a faint quiver of distaste visible in the man's left nostril. Crumper wouldn't sully the tea tray with these dusty lumps; their odor offended his fastidious nose. The butler laid the tray on his master's desk and was in the process of making a punctilious withdrawal when he was kindly bidden by Sir Gregory to stay.

Miranda Roghaar had pulled on a pair of snug latex gloves. Delicately she peeled away the leather husk of one of the cylinders, then unwound cobweb-frail wisps of fabric which bound, mummy-like, the object within. A rousing cheer met the emergence of a metal goblet, gray with tarnish. This trophy Miranda placed on the desktop and invited her audience to "Look, but don't touch."

Most of them hadn't waited for this invitation, but had already drawn close to inspect the treasures as they were disclosed. To cries of ever increasing appreciation and excitement, the collection on the desk grew to seventeen more goblets (slightly mismatched) and, as other members of the English Heritage team came bearing more bundles, a generous collection of miscellaneous trays and plates together with three bowls, one of them footed.

On the fourth goblet, Sir Gregory had dispatched Crumper for the champagne, adding kindly, "And Crumper: bring a glass for yourself."

"Thank you, Sir Gregory."

"Oh, and tell Mrs. Drundle to locate a very large fatted calf."

"Yes, sir." Then as everyone else's attention was clearly fixed elsewhere, Crumper murmured quietly to his employer, "I believe I saw one tied to the kitchen door this morning."

When Crumper returned, this time with the Charles II oval tray (1662, Special Occasions only) laden with chilled bottles and the Regency glasses (Very Special Occasions only), it was to a scene of near delirium. A new pile of dusty lumps, delivered in his absence, had contained an especially irregular package that had turned out to be the lid to the footed bowl. Instead of a knob on the top, the lid featured a five-inch, narrow, pointed spike.

"My God!" Meg had exclaimed. "It's a steeple cup!"

Miranda Roghaar eyed her with respectful surprise and started to say something complimentary about a rare knowledge of old silver, but Meg disclaimed, "They have one at our college, bigger than this."

Kit chimed in, "College legend has it that it's so far beyond priceless that Lloyd's won't insure it."

Derek was imploring one of the English Heritage team to loan Sir Gregory a pair of gloves so the Baronet could handle his own treasures; Mrs. Roghaar was telling Sir Gregory about a silver expert she wanted to telephone right away; Will Tandulkar had hopped up to assist Crumper in the disbursal of champagne to all and sundry; Crumper was informing Sir Gregory, as he handed him his glass, that Mrs. Drundle had the fatted calf, plus accessories, well in hand.

The application of alcoholic bubbles did nothing to dispel the excitement, so perhaps it was a good thing, considering the Baronet's age and health, that the last package fetched to the library from the Scene of the Crack constituted something of an anticlimax. It was a flat box, lined with tin and with waterproof seals, and it proved to contain nothing but a few nondescript books and a stack of quite unremarkable-looking manuscripts.

CHAPTER 6

JUNE 1944

Shortly After D-Day
Fifty-three Years Before Rob Hillman's Death

It's a fairyland. A bloomin' fairyland, he thought, unaware of the pun he'd made. What had stopped him at the church door, making his jaw go slack in amazement and his eyes go round as buckets, were the flowers. They were everywhere. They were tied in bunches at the ends of the pews. They were hanging like vines on the rood screen. They were like a wall in front of the altar. And a bunch of them were shooting up in front of the pulpit. *Like they was growin' out of the floor!* he exclaimed to himself in silent wonder, unable to see, from where he stood, the tall vase that held them. *Crumbs,* thought Bertie. *You can't hardly see through the rude screen!*

And they were all *white*. Bertie had never seen so many white flowers in his whole life. Of course he'd seen some white roses in the formal gardens at the Castle (you could sneak in early on summer mornings, before the Family woke up), and of course every Easter they had them lilies that smelled so sweet, they smelled up the whole church. But never anything like this. Did all swell weddings have white flowers? he wondered. There hadn't been anything like this in Wallwood for a generation, so he had no way of knowing.

He would have liked to ask somebody whether this was what all posh weddings looked like, but everybody was too busy. And besides, if they even knew Bertie was here, they'd probably tell him to leave, so he was careful not to stand where anybody'd see him.

The Vicar was talking to the organist, Mr. Pockets. Both looked excited and maybe a little worried, but anybody could tell they agreed about something because they kept nodding at each other the whole time. Mrs. Pockets was hopping around the church like a fat brown rabbit, fussing with the flowers, moving a little one here and there, like she was worried they wasn't perfect yet, which anybody could see they was.

"Bertie Crumper!"

The voice wasn't angry, more like surprised, but it made Bertie jump.

"Beg pardon, Mrs. Collins, I was just looking at the flowers."

"They are pretty, aren't they?" said the Vicar's kindly wife. "If you've had a good look at them now, though, I think you'd better toddle off. See, Mr. Pockets is going up to the organ now, so the music should be starting soon. And then the guests will be arriving."

He didn't need to be told that if he was still there when the guests started to come, he'd be sure to catch a couple of mean licks from his Pa later for bein' in the wrong place. Bad thing, bein' in the wrong place. Gettin' in the family's way. Bertie took a final look at fairyland and slipped out of the church.

Mrs. Collins watched him go, wondering what the boy had made of all this extravagance. Wartime shortages being what they were, the Bebberidge-Thorpes were rumored to have ransacked every florist from Southampton to Birmingham to produce this show. The cost of the roses alone would have supported Bertie's entire family from Petertide to Advent. Had that thought even crossed the boy's mind? She doubted it.

Mary Collins had spent five years in the

slums of the East End while her husband labored to better the physical and spiritual lot of London's poor. The futility of the task, implacable and inescapable as the bombs raining down on them, together with (his wife suspected) his guilt at not being across the channel with the troops, had wearied him to the point of collapse. In the winter of 1943, his bishop became belatedly aware that if something wasn't done quickly, young Collins was going to wind up in hospital. His Grace sent a note to his old school chum, the Bishop of Oxford, and asked if the latter had a nice restful little living in the country somewhere. Thus the Rev. Winston Collins found himself Vicar of St. Swithin's, Wallwood, Oxfordshire. There his most arduous duty was trying to reconcile his conscience to writing sermons which neither offended Lady Bebberidge-Thorpe by their political content nor bored Lady Wallwood to tears.

His wife had been grateful to see him saved from irretrievable damage to his health; she admitted to herself that Wallwood was in almost every way a blessed relief from the East End. But something about this pastoral paradise disturbed her. She had finally decided it had something to do with the apparent contentment of the rural working class. The urban poor had seemed to sense the injustice of their lot, even as they ignored it in the patriotic fervor of surviving the German bombs. They were aware, however deeply buried that awareness was and however inarticulate it might be, that the rich were using, abusing, and ignoring them.

But these country people! As far as she could tell, they didn't seem to mind that much. They were like little moons, content to shine only by reflecting the light cast upon them by their "betters." Mary Collins was several furlongs short of the outright socialism of the British Labour Party, but she had (rarely, for 1944) allowed enough of the Gospel to penetrate her English sensibilities that she was vaguely disquieted, not so much by the class system itself as by the failure of those at the bottom of it to resent it.

Her reflections on Bertie Crumper and his ilk, perceptive though they might be, extended only to the sociopolitical. It was her husband whose sight penetrated to the spiritual. The Vicar, turning from his conversation with the organist, caught fleeting sight of the Crumper lad scampering out of the church. Of course. The boy was bound to make an appearance. Bertie would be drawn to this celebration of wealth and privilege like a moth to a flame.

The Vicar knew all of the village urchins as well as all of the children whose families worked on the two great local estates, Morgan Mallowan and Datchworth Castle. He had seen them line the road, wide-eyed, when the Earl and Countess had swept through Wallwood in their silver Rolls-Royce, swathed to the ears in ermine, bound for the opening of Parliament. The Vicar had seen the children close-huddled by the gates of the Castle on a summer evening, watching in vicarious delight as huge cars rumbled past bearing white-tied gents and bejeweled ladies to the parties which, even at a subdued war-time level, presented heights of spine-tingling glamour to those for whom serious luxury would have been a new pair of shoes. But in the eyes of young Bertie Crumper the Vicar had discerned a crucial difference from the excited wonder of his peers. Something in the wideness of the gaze; something in the open, unsmiling mouth. The boy was one of those who worshiped.

The Vicar had made this diagnosis the previous summer. As he knew very well that people's lives are shaped by what they worship, he had hoped for the boy's sake that when Bertie's soul elected its object of veneration, that object would prove worthy, and would lead the child in the paths of righteousness. Or at least, out of serious trouble. But today his mind was altogether too busy to ponder Bertie Crumper.

He was as ready as he could be, and so was the church. The florists (there seemed to be about two dozen of them) had arrived at dawn and transformed his humble village church into the anteroom to paradise. Sir Harold, father of the bride, had descended upon the church shortly after the florists had finished, beamed his approval, tipped them all generously, and — to the Vicar's intense relief — shooed them off the premises.

"Everything under control, Vicar?" he had boomed from the doorway, having rid the church of aliens.

"I believe so, Sir Harold." Then, as a kindness to the Baronet, who was unfailingly pleasant and unendingly generous to the church, Mr. Collins added, "It looks quite wonderful."

Sir Harold emitted a bark of laughter. "Well, the girl wanted flowers, and flowers

73

she got." He rolled a rueful eye toward the Vicar. "She also got everything else she wanted."

Collins smiled. "Well, a girl is only a bride once," he said excusingly, although privately he agreed with his wife that this level of extravagance was probably inexcusable.

"Thank God for that!" the Baronet replied, drawing a genuine laugh from the Vicar. "Well, I'd better get back to the house. Clarissa's screaming for a report on the flowers, and Lady Bebb will kill me if I'm not there when the Banners arrive. Mrs. Banner, that's the groom's mum, is pretty frail, you know. Lady Bebb's in a pother about it."

He departed with a wave, and the Vicar returned to his own preparations, hoping for Sir Harold's sake that the bride's "screaming" was only hyperbole. Winston Collins's opinion of Clarissa was not high. A stunning beauty, of course. Huge, glittering smile. But the smile was a stretching of beautiful lips over perfect white teeth. It did not extend to her eyes. Evidently John Banner had not noticed. Or perhaps Banner, rich beyond the dreams of avarice and utterly middle class, cared more about allying himself to the old blood of the

Bebberidge-Thorpes than having an amiable wife.

Who knows, Collins reflected, *they might be made for each other.* This thought made it possible for him to contemplate his duty for that day with a shade less guilt. It was hard enough, even with the most pleasant of bridal couples, to read the Prayer Book wedding service without a tinge of unease. All those pious promises about leading a specifically Christian life sailed right over the heads of most twentieth-century souls, who didn't understand the language of half of the vows they were making and wouldn't mean to follow them if they did.

Between his scrupulous conscience and his desire that the wedding should proceed without the slightest hitch — for the sake not of the bride but of her far more likable father — the Vicar's mind had no more time for the village children, who with intuitive good timing were beginning to gather about the church.

They were careful to stay out of the way; they knew their boundaries well, the older ones officiously restraining the younger ones. Most of them stood in the churchyard, between the graves but not on them. From this vantage point they had an excellent view of all the arriving cars and also of the elegant occupants as they emerged from their vehicles (assisted by their chauffeurs) and trod gingerly up the gravel path to the church door. The children giggled surreptitiously over the dowagers' hats, oohed with admiration at the young swells and young ladies, and generally enjoyed themselves so much that not one of them noticed that Bertie Crumper was not among them.

Bertie had discovered a small open window in the storage room behind the vestry. Wriggling cautiously through it, he had discovered with joy that the door from the little room to the vestry had been left open. This attempt on the Vicar's part to alleviate the growing warmth of the summer morning was seen by Bertie as nothing less than a divine invitation. Waiting in cautious silence behind a stack of boxes, he heard the Vicar's prayer with the servers, and the soft rustle of their robes as they filed out of the vestry into the church. He peered from his hiding place, ascertained the coast was clear, and crept over to the faded purple curtain that covered an old opening in the wall on the church side of the vestry. With the stealth of a stalking cat he pushed the curtain slowly to one side, inch by inch, until he could see the middle of the church, with all the gentry in the pews. If he moved a bit to his left and looked right, he could see the Vicar standing up by the altar. The posh bloke next to Mr. Collins looked too old to be the groom, but Bertie couldn't figure out who else he could be. Suddenly the music changed, and Bertie heard the wedding march. He moved to the right and peered leftward down the aisle to the church door. Almost in silhouette, framed against the bright sunlight, stood a tall couple, who as Bertie watched began to walk down the aisle in a measured pace. As they moved away from the light in the doorway, Bertie was able to recognize Sir Harold but he spared him a mere half a glance.

Bertie had seen Clarissa Bebberidge-Thorpe before, of course. He knew she was beautiful. But he'd never seen her this close. And he'd never seen her clothed from head to foot in sparkling white, white roses in her hair and lace all around her like a cloud. As she moved gracefully toward the altar, her brilliant smile lighting up the onlookers like a second sun, Bertie recognized dimly that here was the rightful queen of this fairyland. She was coming into it, claiming it. A tiny rustle of awe accompanied her as she walked, telling Bertie that she was also claiming the fairyland's inhabitants. They were her subjects. With every step she took, he could feel her power growing stronger.

As she reached the altar, she turned her perfect face upon the man she was about to marry and allowed the smile to rest on him, a regal gift. But the heart she enslaved in that moment was not that of her bridegroom.

CHAPTER 7

THURSDAY, THE DAY AFTER
ROB HILLMAN'S DEATH

About Seven in the Evening

Paddington Station was an old, familiar friend. It was she herself who had changed. On the positive side, she knew where she was going. She was much more self-assured. And there was no denying that it was pleasant to have money. As an ordinary graduate student she had lugged her own bags, hoisted them up into a second-class carriage, and struggled down the aisle with them to find a seat. This time she had paid a porter to carry them and hand them over to the guard in the luggage car.

No; luggage *van,* she reminded herself. She was vain about her ability to speak British, a language that differed in slight but significant ways from American, but she was out of practice. *What I need,* she decided, *is an Oxford accent to talk to. That'll bring it back in a trice.*

But the moment the thought occurred to her, she realized that she didn't want to talk to anybody, least of all a stranger, regardless of accent. There was a leaden weight the size of a fist somewhere between her heart and her stomach; it had been there since she had picked up the phone to hear her uncle's voice, dull with shock, and in the background her aunt's sobbing.

Rob. Dead.

Impossible.

Everything else had been blotted out. The insiders' tour of Oxford she had promised the people from St. Margaret's. The lunches and teas she'd arranged with old college friends who were still living there. Even the pleasures that hadn't yet happened — the punting, the Ashmolean — with Rob. Instead, her first appointment in Oxford would be at the police station with an Inspector — no, a Chief Inspector — by the name of Lamp. Lamp. A lamp unto my feet. My eyes? Let thy word be a lamp unto my — what was the damn verse. She couldn't remember.

Rob. Dead. Like her father.

When her father had died, it had been Rob who met her at JFK and held her while she cried all the way back to Texas.

There had been nobody to hold her on the flight to London. Her mother, of course, had gone to be with her aunt and uncle. Kathryn felt alone now in a way she had never been before.

She mounted the steps into the first-class carriage and moved slowly down the narrow corridor that ran the length of it, looking into the compartments as she passed them. She was assessing the desirability of the occupants as traveling companions in case she was unable to find a compartment that was empty. In the first one, three gray-suited businessmen were chatting in a desultory manner. *City gents*, she thought, and was faintly pleased at the readiness with which the British term resurfaced in her mind. The next compartment contained a young woman with two children — rare in first class — though a subtle quality in their seemingly casual clothes signaled to the experienced eye that here was a family who could well afford luxury. The occupants of the third compartment were more conventional; two fifty-somethings in skirts of well-worn summer tweed, twin sets, and yes, Kathryn verified with a discreet glance, there were the requisite pearls. *County ladies*, she noted. *I'm traveling with the great clichés of the English class system.*

Suddenly her steps halted. She had come abreast of the fourth compartment. There a reddish-blond man in his mid-thirties was talking animatedly to someone Kathryn didn't bother to notice. She caught her breath. It couldn't be. On second thought, maybe it could. A first-class carriage from Paddington was an entirely plausible place to happen upon a prominent British actor. Just then he laughed at something said by his companion, and he looked so beautiful, Kathryn felt a pang in her heart despite the lead weight. It had to be him. The finely chiseled (Fiennely chiseled?) profile, the pointed nose a fraction too long, the chin a couple of microns too small, the freckles — *freckles?*

As if he sensed her presence, the red-headed man turned his head and looked directly at her, the laughter still lingering on his face. There was no disguising the fact she had been staring at him. Kathryn felt her cheeks go hot.

"I — I — beg your pardon," she stammered, realizing her mistake. It wasn't her second-favorite actor, after all. She plunged hastily down the narrow corridor, no longer looking for an empty compartment, seeking merely to distance herself from her embarrassment.

A *teddibly, teddibly* upper-class accent called after her. "I say, don't run off like that!"

She turned. It wasn't the gorgeous redhead; it was the other person from that compartment, who turned out to be another wonderful-looking man approximately Kathryn's age. Over six feet tall, broad-shouldered but athletically trim, he had smoky brown skin that accentuated the brightness of his teeth, and that rare beauty that Kathryn had noticed before in her Eurasian friends at Oxford. He wore the right clothes for a gentleman (in the old sense of the word) coming into the city for the day, but he wore them haphazardly; his shirttail was untidy if not quite untucked, and his jacket, although the correct size, hung on him as though it hadn't made up its mind whether it planned to stay there or to move to some more stable location.

No normal woman would have given a damn. He was as handsome as he was big, and his smile would have melted a misanthropic lesbian.

Kathryn still had the stammers. "I — I — I'm so sorry, I know I was staring quite rudely, but I thought, I thought your, uh, friend was —"

"He's used to it," he assured her, waving away her apology with a dismissive hand. His smile, impossibly, got warmer. "What he's not used to is the person doing the rude staring being a stunning brunette. What would I have to say to get you to join us?"

Kathryn's cheeks were warming again, but this time the sensation was considerably more pleasant. She hesitated only two seconds.

"I think you just said it," she admitted, and retraced her steps.

The man with the red hair sat very tall in his seat, and there radiated from him a palpable energy, an intensity which at that moment focused on Kathryn with a rueful twinkle in his eye.

"Happens all the time," he told her. His accent was as posh as his friend's. "They pause, they stare, they think, 'My God, it's the Oscar Bafta Golden Globe–winning —' " He shook his head mournfully. "And then they notice the damned polka-dots."

They were hard not to notice, actually; his fair skin was liberally dusted with freckles, from the roots of his red-gold hair to the open neck of his blue shirt. But the blue was the next thing that caught Kathryn's attention, for his eyes were a shade somewhere between the pigeon's egg of his shirt and the royal of his blazer.

The freckles, the thin face, the elegant drape of the blue clothes and the self-deprecating humor, the red hair and the energy that hummed from him like an electric current, combined to create the most vividly attractive man Kathryn had ever beheld. She knew that by any sane standards his friend was better-looking, and furthermore, Eurasian good looks had always gotten to her in a very serious way. But it didn't matter. The truth was irresistibly drawn from her as she sank, a trifle weak-kneed, into the seat opposite him.

"I *like* the damned polka dots."

It was his turn to blush, a tinge of crimson creeping up under the orange freckles, but he pretended not to believe her.

"You *like* the polka dots?" he asked incredulously. "Does insanity run in your family?"

"Do polka dots run in yours?" she countered.

"Only since m'father went to Ireland to find a wife."

"The ones in England were all hiding?"

"I think he just fancied a bride from over the water."

"Does *that* run in your family?"

"Hasn't so far, but I think I hear it trotting down the track to the starting gates."

Minutes earlier, Kathryn would not have believed that she could laugh, but she did, and it felt surprisingly good. Both men laughed with her. Then the freckled one leaned forward and extended a hand as thin and elegant as the rest of him.

"Christopher Mallowan, please call me Kit. And this is Will Tandulkar."

Will had been standing in the doorway of the compartment ever since he had waved Kathryn into it, as though reluctant to break the line of vision between his friend and the American beauty. But as his name was pronounced, he stepped between them to return to his seat, dropped into it, and held out a hand.

Kathryn took it, saying, "Hello, Will. Run your last name past me again?"

"Tan-dul-kar. It's Indian."

"That much," she nodded sagely, "I had sort of guessed." She turned back to Kit and asked him, also, to repeat his last name.

"It's a bit unusual," he acknowledged,

"but basically one just says 'Allen' with an 'M' in front of it."

Will asked Kathryn what she was doing "in our green and pleasant land."

She studied him a moment, wondering whether the snippet of Blake was meant to impress or test her, or if the man naturally and spontaneously sprinkled his speech with scraps of poetry.

Taking no chances, she replied, "That's a brave phrase for someone sitting on a train that's shortly going to be chugging past the dark satanic mills of Didcot." This speech efficiently conveyed to both her listeners two facts: she was familiar with William Blake's "Jerusalem," and she knew that the Paddington to Oxford train went past Didcot and its nuclear power station.

"Touché!" cried Kit, applauding.

Will clapped one hand to his chest as if in pain, raised the other in a fencer's gesture, and acknowledged, "A hit! A very palpable hit!"

Kathryn knew instantly that a hit was precisely what she had made, and was grateful. She liked Will both for his quotations and for his clowning, but nothing and no one could divert her interest from his redheaded friend. It took willpower to ignore Kit and keep her gaze on the beautiful Mr. Tandulkar, but she didn't want to be humiliatingly obvious.

"To answer your question," she said as she forcibly closed a solid door in her mind against her grief, "I am brought to this green and pleasant land by the Dreaming Spires. My church in New Jersey is sending over a herd of Anglophiles and I volunteered to show them around Oxford, since so often American tourists get dumped in the middle of Cornmarket and are told to get on with it, then they wander cluelessly around in the noise and traffic wondering why anybody would bother to come to such a place."

"That's right!" Kit leaned forward again to eye her with fervent approval. "Oxford *hides.*"

"Yes! And you have to know where to find it," she responded. "Those little islands of the Middle Ages, tucked away down cobbled alleyways. Oxford is like a scattering of emeralds, set in —" She hesitated, hunting for a sufficiently distasteful word.

"Plastic," Kit supplied.

"Yes! Amid great, grinding noise."

"Exactly."

They regarded each other with immense satisfaction.

It was not that Kathryn had forgotten her cousin's death at the first sight of an attractive man. On the contrary, it was precisely because of that unbearable ache that her response to the redheaded stranger was so powerful. The ghost, the grief, the pain suffocated her; her emotions were crying out for relief, desperate for more pleasant sensations. Even as she rushed into this blessed relief, a fraction of her brain was remembering with cold-blooded clarity a little-known fact she had been taught in her seminary's pastoral counseling course: one of the most common reactions to bereavement is increased sexual drive.

Knowing very well why this man attracted her so devastatingly didn't lessen the effect.

So she further established herself as one of the Oxford cognoscenti (and therefore worthy of his full attention) by asking simply, "What college?"

"I'm from a long line of Nosemen," Kit informed her solemnly.

If he thought he might stump her with this bit of insider vocabulary, he was very much mistaken. "And I," Kathryn answered with equal solemnity, "I am one of the very first Nose*women*."

Thus they had informed each other that

they had both been students at Brasenose College, universally acknowledged as having the silliest name among all the Oxford colleges.

Kit was regarding Kathryn with nothing less than delight, but suddenly he seemed to remember Will, whom he had effectively ousted from the conversation. He waved a hand at his friend. "Will was at B.N.C. too. We were there together."

Kathryn took her eyes away from the object of her growing desire and turned again to his companion. "Really? When was that?"

It emerged that they had just managed to miss each other, Kathryn having been in the H.C.R. (Hulme Common Room; i.e., she had been a graduate student) two years after the men had left the J.C.R. (Junior Common Room; i.e., they had been undergraduates).

They swapped anecdotes about the more colorful members of the Senior Common Room (the faculty), the martinet in the Porter's Lodge (their college having been widely reputed to have the rudest Head Porter in Oxford), and the terminally grumpy groundskeeper who rejoiced in the incredibly Dickensian name of Doggerel.

Other college stories inevitably followed.

Will had Kathryn in stitches with the lurid tale of his and Kit's twenty-first birthday party (their birthdays being only eleven days apart, they had celebrated them together since they were schoolboys); the two of them, accompanied by several other drunken "Nose" friends, had spectacularly failed to duplicate a legendary Brasenose College stunt involving the theft of a deer from Magdalen College deer park.

Kit hardly let him finish before he said, "That reminds me. What we were doing in London today, actually, was having a late-ish birthday party for ourselves. Will was inconsiderately in New York last April so we couldn't do the thing at the proper time, so we figured we could do it this month and call it our long-play vinyl birthday."

Kathryn looked at Kit's mischievous little smile and informed him that he was a rat and that she hated riddles.

"You're right," he admitted, "not very gentlemanly, is it, testing people like that? I do beg your pardon. I mean that we are —"

"Thirty-three and a third," she said.

Will chuckled and pronounced judiciously, "Alpha plus."

Kit protested, "I thought you said you hated riddles."

"Doesn't mean I can't solve them, does it?"

Will asked Kit if he needed a towel to staunch the bleeding, but Kit just laughed and moaned, "I grovel, I grovel!"

Kathryn was wondering if Kit would be at all bothered if he knew she was thirty-five; she decided she would keep that information to herself for a while unless directly asked for it. As a card-carrying feminist she was ashamed of this decision, and felt the need for a change of subject.

"What keeps you fellows busy," she asked, "when you're not celebrating birthdays?"

Will started to say something but Kit interrupted him to say, "We're farmers."

"Pull the other one," said Kathryn, using the British version of "You're pulling my leg."

"No, really," Kit assured her, "although we are flattered by your skepticism. One would hate to think one *looked* like a farmer." The last part of this speech was directed, with an assumed shudder, at Will.

There was a private joke there, Kathryn realized, as Will grinned and riposted, "Better a farmer than a —"

"Shut up!" Kit commanded, as Will simultaneously said, "Mockie!" Or at least, that's what it sounded like to Kathryn. She started to ask what a Mockie was, but Kit was speaking to her again.

"Truth is, I was going to be a secret agent or a stunt pilot or perhaps a professional gambler, but fate intervened by summoning my uncle to his eternal reward and leaving my entirely useless aunt —"

"*Almost* entirely useless aunt," Will interrupted in a spirit of fairness.

"*Almost* entirely useless aunt," Kit agreed with a gracious nod in Will's direction, "squawking hysterically about having nobody to turn to and what oh what oh my deary me *what* was she going to do about the" — there was a tiny hesitation — "all the things she had to take care of, the house and the farm and all, and the long and short of it is, she twisted my arm into abandoning my plans for a life of adventure and going back to Hole-in-the-Wallwood to take care of the house and the farm."

"He's lying through his teeth," Will told Kathryn. "He loves it, and he would have made a terrible professional gambler anyway, a ten-year-old could beat him at cards —"

"I *beg* your pardon! Precisely what ten-year-old do you fancy in that role?"

"It's true and you know it! If you get a good hand, everyone in the room can read it right off your freckled face as if it were —"

But Kathryn ignored the jesting squabble and interjected pointedly, "Wallwood?"

They looked at her in surprise.

"Don't tell me you've heard of it," said Kit.

The sparkle of the conversation died for Kathryn, as she felt the cloud come back over her spirits, felt the lead weight again.

"Yes, I'm going there on Saturday. My cous—" She stopped, swallowed the last syllable of the word, got control of her voice, and continued, "My cousin was working there. He just, ah, died in an accident. Wait; if you live in Wallwood, do you know Sir Gregory St. John Hyphen-Something?"

Both men stared at her for two seconds, then simultaneously burst into questions ("You're Rob Hillman's cousin? You're Rob's Cousin Katy?") and exclamations ("How extraordinary! We're invited to the Castle to meet you!"), while Kathryn endeavored not to cringe — or cry — at being referred to as "Katy," which no one had called her since she was seventeen except for Rob, who had done it mostly to annoy her.

They consoled her on her loss in such a frightfully English manner that she found herself hard put not to smile. Rob had been "a capital fellow," "a jolly decent chap," everyone had been "shocked, stunned really." It appeared that their admiration for Rob had been genuine, and their grief, if moderate, was sincere; thus, although the conversation turned somber, the easy harmony that had charmed the miles from London remained intact. In fact, Kathryn's heretofore joyless errand to Datchworth Castle became the vehicle for the formation of definite plans for the three of them to meet again. In the midst of this comforting process, Will glanced out the train window.

"Good God, we're there already."

"Dreaming Spires ahead?" Kit asked.

"Hard upon us," Will replied regretfully.

Kit once more leaned toward Kathryn with an extended hand. "Shortest run from Paddington to Oxford in living memory," he pronounced.

"I was just thinking the same thing," Kathryn replied, placing her hand in his and finding his grip firmer than it had been before, and more reluctant to let go. She allowed herself to be held in that electric blue gaze for perhaps a second longer than was wise before turning to Will. "It was a pleasure to meet you," she assured him, shaking his less significant hand.

"Ring me," Kit ordered, "the instant you get to the Castle." He was holding out a card, which Kathryn took. "You must come for a meal. Oh!" there was touch of embarrassment, a hint of afterthought. "I mean to say, Will's house is just down the road from mine; we, um, could meet there." Then he made a quick recovery: "But the grub's better at my place!"

"He's right," Will admitted. "Let's meet at Kit's."

"It's a date," Kathryn promised, mustering a smile and sharing it equally (she hoped) between them as she rose and left the compartment. She made hastily for the door at the end of the carriage, descended to the platform, and received her bags from the sullen man in the guard's van in exchange for a tip so exuberantly generous that he almost looked grateful.

Back in the compartment, Kit was imploring his oldest and best friend to tell him the truth.

"I *am* telling you the truth. I might as

well have been your grandmother, for all the interest she showed in me."

"I didn't imagine it, then? She really did —" Kit faltered.

"Prefer you to me?" his sapient companion supplied.

Kit, long acquainted with Will's ability to read his thoughts as if they were indeed printed on his freckled face, was not discomfited. "Yes. Did she prefer me to you?"

"I'm trying to tell you, she didn't even *see* me. I've never been so humiliatingly ignored. I've half a mind to throw you off the train in a jealous rage."

"She really liked me." Kit closed his eyes and savored the unexpected blessing. "Liked *me*."

"Liked you? I'm surprised she didn't *jump* you. Never saw a woman so besotted, so fast, in my life."

Because they were men, not women, and English, not American, they did not say, Will to Kit, "I'm so thrilled for you," and Kit to Will, "Bless you for being so generous." But they both understood exactly what the emotional score was.

It was Kit who, as the train once more lurched into motion, expressed the other thing they were both thinking, and both gleeful about: "And she doesn't know about *either* of the Beasts!"

Christopher Mallowan, Seventh Marquis of Wallwood, regarded himself as afflicted by two beastly handicaps when it came to finding that elusive dream, True Love. "The Greater Beast" (greater only in the sense of being physically larger) was a combined package of wealth, title, and ancestral mansion so powerfully attractive to the opposite sex that he spent half his time trying to get rid of women who found him, plain Kit, only moderately attractive but who were nevertheless quite determined to marry the other him, Lord Wallwood.

"The Lesser Beast" (again, the measure being purely of physical size) in and of itself was a minor problem. Initially devastating, over the years it had become something Kit simply coped with. But when it came to women and their feelings about him, it was a demon from Hell.

CHAPTER 8

FEBRUARY 1997

Five Months Before Rob Hillman's Death

Meg Daventry had never liked having to wake up on winter mornings before it was light. But in February it wasn't light until after eight, and since it was a good forty-five minutes' drive from Datchworth back to Oxford, and she had a nine o'clock lecture at the St. Cross Building, she had resolutely set her alarm for an hour that would force her to fumble for it in the dark. She was dressed, if still yawning, when a soft tap at the door announced the arrival of her breakfast. Meg had discovered years ago that it was actually less trouble for the servants to bring a tray to her room than to serve a meal for one in the dining room at dawn. Still, it felt like an almost indecent luxury.

"Oh, Jenny, that's lovely. You are a sweetheart. Yes, this is all I'll need; you go back to the kitchen and tell Mrs. Drundle she's a sweetheart, too."

Jenny retired, giggling: in the opinion of the junior staff, Mrs. Drundle was far too fierce a figure to be anybody's sweetheart.

Meg hastened through her porridge, toast, and tea, donned her coat against the chill of the castle corridors, and set off on the two-minute walk from her bedroom to the front door. She carried nothing but her handbag, as there was never any need to bring luggage for an overnight stay at home; everything from pajamas to toothbrush to suitable dresses for dinner were all there waiting for her. It meant that popping home to see Uncle Greg was a doddle, which in turn meant she did it frequently, which suited both of them. She found Crumper in the entrance hall, holding her long woolen scarf and driving gloves.

"You spoil me, you know," she admonished him.

"I do, don't I?" he responded amiably, handing over her scarf and gloves one item at a time as she put them on. "Your car has been brought 'round. The motor's been running, and the heater of course, for five minutes. I hope you will find it warm enough."

"Crumper, whatever would I do without you?"

"I imagine, Miss Meg, that you would live in the squalor of student lodgings and entirely forget what civilized life is like."

One of the compensating factors in these early departures was that Crumper, alone with a single member of the Family and sure none of the other staff could overhear him, was likely to make quite unbutlerish remarks.

Meg left the house with a smile and a wave, got into her car, and glanced at the dashboard clock as she drove out of the gates. She was in good time; she would make the lecture. The car was warm, the roads were dry, and the gas gauge, as always after a night at Datchworth, showed full. (Amazing staff Uncle Greg had, right out of Edwardian times.) But the reason Meg felt as though her cup was most agreeably running over was none of these comforts. It was what had happened the previous night at dinner.

Dinner had been served early, of course, as it always was at the Castle, on account of Sir Gregory's health. He talked jokingly of "country hours," but the truth was that he had to be in bed by nine-thirty. So they had sat down in the State Dining Room, all ten of them, at seven. The original plan had been for delicious but informal fare to be served in the summer lunchroom for the three of the English Heritage team who preferred to eat before driving off into the night, plus a light invalid's supper for Sir Gregory in the Family Dining Room. The kitchen staff had known by early afternoon that there might be one guest joining the Baronet. But dinner for ten?

Mrs. Drundle had surpassed herself. How she had done it, God only knew. The table glittered with the postrestoration silver the Family had been accumulating ever since 1660, but that was to be expected; it was ready to hand, after all. Onto this elegant board, however, there appeared in all the proper stages a formal dinner from soup to nuts, and it tasted as good at it looked.

All five of the English Heritage team had elected to stay; such an invitation, even for people in their line of work, was a rare opportunity and not to be passed by. Sir Gregory had persuaded both Kit and Will to dine with them as well, and with Meg and Derek, that had made a fuller table than Meg had seen at Datchworth in years.

She was at the opposite end of the table from her uncle, being (for lack of any other) the Lady of the House on these occasions. Trained in courtesy from her cradle, she had concentrated on setting at their ease the two English Heritage employees who had been allotted places on either side of her. Both were nice enough chaps; one of them was lively and funny, and the other one was cute and smart if slightly ponderous in conversation, and neither was too terribly old for her. But Meg had felt no desire to stir the conversation in such a way as to give rise to sparks. Her eighteen-year-old fancy was elsewhere occupied.

Still, she had enjoyed the party; it was lovely to see Uncle Greg in such good spirits, Derek wasn't teasing her for a change, and Kit and Will were always great fun. And she had gotten to run the uncle joke, which she enjoyed. It was wonderful to watch people's faces as they tried to decide whether or not she was pulling their legs.

"So," said Davey, on her right, "you live with your uncle when you're not at Oxford."

"With one of my uncles. I have three uncles, and two and a half of them are sitting at this table."

Davey laughed and Bert looked dubious. Davey immediately threw himself into the puzzle.

"Right, then, one of them is obviously Sir Gregory, since you were introduced as his niece."

Meg smiled mischievously. "That was the easy bit."

"Too right. Who else have we got? Hang on, that Derek bloke, they said he was Sir Gregory's nephew?"

"Mm-hmm."

"So Derek could be your cousin, of course, but he could also be your uncle, couldn't he?"

Meg rewarded him with a grin. "Two down and one half to go."

But Davey couldn't figure it out, and Bert didn't seem to want to play. In the end Meg explained: "Sir Gregory is my great-grandmother's brother. Derek is my grandmother's brother. That's two uncles. And Will Tandulkar" — she gestured toward the dark, handsome man who was making Miranda Roghaar laugh very loudly — "is my mother's half brother, which makes him my half uncle, or so he tells me, and his twin brother is my other half uncle and between them they make a whole uncle. Total number of uncles, three."

Davey loved it, but Bert said pedantically that he didn't think there was such a thing as a half uncle. Meg sighed. *What a wet blanket!* she thought.

Oddly enough, however, it was Bert who had made the dinner party a source of lasting joy to Meg. He did it unwittingly, of course. He merely asked if her uncle Sir Gregory planned to hire anybody to catalog the manuscripts they'd found behind the wall. Not nearly so important as the silver, he admitted. But it should probably be done anyway. Might turn out to have some really interesting papers about the family and the Civil War. After all, somebody had gone to a great deal of trouble to hide them from Cromwell.

There was a brief silence after these remarks while both men waited for Meg to respond. She was looking at Bert as if she were in a trance, but after two seconds she seemed to recover. She told him his suggestion was excellent, and she would see to it that Uncle Greg followed his advice.

At the point in the evening when, in days gone by, the ladies would have left the table for the drawing room while the men remained to smoke and drink port, the custom at Datchworth was for everyone to rise and change places. Meg excused herself to Davey and Bert, maneuvered quickly around Kit and Derek, and plumped herself down next to her senior uncle. She put a hand on Sir Gregory's shoulder and leaned close, excitedly putting forward her suggestion.

He beamed, patted her young hand with a frail old one, and said, "What a capital idea! Do you think he'll be willing to spend his holidays here?"

"If you pay him enough. I think he's a bit strapped for cash, unlike most of the Americans one sees in Oxford."

"Ah! He's American?"

"Yes, dear Uncle, but quite housebroken, I assure you."

"If he dines on high table at B.N.C., I imagine he can sustain dinner at Datchworth."

It was this exchange, not the party, not the discovery of the lost family silver, that sent Meg driving through the gray, wintry countryside in a mood more appropriate to spring. She had a tutorial with Mr. Hillman at two-thirty that afternoon. All she had to do was get through six and a half hours without bursting like a big bubble of pleasure.

CHAPTER 9

MAY 1945

Two Weeks After VE Day
Fifty-two Years Before Rob Hillman's Death

Lady Bebberidge-Thorpe had expected the worst. It was for that reason that she had forbidden her amiable husband from accompanying her to Banner House. It was not going to be a pretty sight, Clarissa's lying-in. John Banner had sounded desperately weary when he had rung Datchworth to beg his mother-in-law to come a week early. "Dear Marjorie," he had said, "perhaps you can do something with her."

Clarissa had been willful from her childhood; Sir Harold always said, "Ah, she knows her own mind!" In his wife's estimation, that description fell far short of the reality, which was that their only daughter was selfish to the bone. Marjorie Bebberidge-Thorpe would not have objected to a *little* selfishness. Sometimes she suspected that she was a little selfish herself. Certainly the times that her husband did things her way seemed to outnumber the times she did things his way. On the other hand, Marjorie normally felt she had earned his cooperation; after all, she put up with all the bad habits he refused to break. He was much too familiar with the servants, for instance. Imagine, helping her into the car and then telling the chauffeur to "Take care of Lady Bebb for me!" Fortunately, Baker never encroached; he had merely replied, "Certainly, Sir Harold."

For all Harold's faults, however, Marjorie was sincerely fond of him, and was loath to expose him to Clarissa at her worst. And Clarissa had been at her worst ever since she had been married. No sooner had the newlyweds returned from their honeymoon in Scotland than Clarissa had bolted back to Datchworth for a visit, very much without her husband. Marjorie had known the moment her daughter stepped out of her cream-colored Bentley that they were in for it; judging from Clarissa's stony face, in fact, Marjorie guessed that it was *she*, Mother, who was in for it, not Father.

So it proved. Clarissa swept up to her childhood room with her mother in tow, dismissed the maid who was starting to unpack her suitcases, flung herself into the wing chair by the window, and cried with smoldering resentment, "Why in hell didn't you warn me?"

The genuine shudder that accompanied this accusation made it unnecessary for Lady Bebberidge-Thorpe to ask, "About what?" Instead she took a deep breath, got a stranglehold on her own anger at being thus addressed, sat down on the bed, and replied, "I was under the impression that I *had* warned you."

As a bride, Marjorie had received no more premarital advice from her own mother than the admonition to put a towel under her pillow. Came the night, Marjorie discovered what the towel was for, but she thanked God she had married a kind and patient man. She had resolved not to send any daughter of hers off to her wedding bed in a comparative state of ignorance. When Clarissa had elected from her numerous suitors a man nearly twice her age, Marjorie's first act — after persuading her own husband that John Banner's maturity and wealth probably made him a better spouse for their daughter than any younger, poorer man — was to take Clarissa aside and introduce her to the facts of life.

Birds and bees had not figured in that discussion. Marjorie was no coward; not for her the timid euphemisms of her day. It was unusual for the 1940s, but her daughter received a straightforward, biologically specific description of marital relations. And when this lesson was received with a distaste bordering on horror, Marjorie was not taken aback. She had expected as much, and had the second half of her speech as well prepared as the first.

"Yes, dear, I know it sounds repulsive. However, with time one becomes accustomed. One even grows to enjoy it, although I can tell from your face that you find that impossible to believe. My best advice to you is this: make sure you have something you like to drink, and I do not mean cocoa, in the bedroom. Encourage John to have no more than one glass, but you should drink two or even three. If he questions you about it, tell him you are nervous. I believe he will understand. If you are tipsy it will be easier for you. Of course I know that I do not need to warn you against drinking so much that you behave in a way that will disgust your husband. The trick is to do this unladylike thing in the most ladylike manner that you can. Oh — and put a towel under your pillow."

Many a girl in Clarissa's generation would have given her trousseau for so useful a talk prior to her wedding day. Clarissa, however, showed no sign of gratitude.

"You call that a warning?" she now shouted angrily. "You said it was unladylike. *Unladylike!* God, it was like *animals!* Like slimy, horrid —" There followed a noise so eloquent of revulsion that Marjorie wondered for a moment if her daughter was actually vomiting.

Lady Bebb was patient. She rang the bell and ordered tea for the two of them to be served there in Clarissa's room. She listened. She commiserated. She talked. She reassured. Nothing did a particle of good. Eventually she announced that it was time to change for dinner.

"Oh, Lord, Mother, I couldn't possibly! Just tell them to bring a tray up to me here."

"No, Clarissa. You will change your dress and powder your nose and come down to dinner and smile at your father and your brother, who have been looking forward very much to seeing you. They will ask polite questions. You will give them polite answers. And you will say *nothing* to distress your father, do you understand?"

Clarissa's eyes narrowed. "I think you're forgetting, Mother dear. I'm married now. I don't have to do what you tell me to do any more."

Lady Bebberidge-Thorpe again throttled the rage that rose up in her, and after a few seconds of icy silence replied in an even voice, "Then ring for your maid and order your car and leave. I believe The White Hart serves a tolerable supper."

Clarissa's narrow-eyed frown slackened to a look of high indignation. She started to say, "You wouldn't dare —" but a closer study of her mother's expression changed her mind, and she shut her mouth.

"Shall we see you in half an hour, then?" asked Marjorie. Her voice betrayed no trace of smug triumph, which in itself was so smug a triumph that her daughter all but ground her teeth.

"Yes, Mother."

Marjorie had won that battle, but before the week was over it was clear who was winning the war. Strictly obedient, Clarissa had said nothing to distress her father that first night at dinner. She had not been forbidden to distress her sixteen-year-old brother, however, and she spent most of the meal needling "Greggers" to within an inch of his life. As the Bebberidge-Thorpes had long followed the policy that siblings must learn how to get along without interference from their parents, they would say nothing to deter Clarissa. Marjorie's only satisfaction was that Gregory gave as good as he got. He always had, she reflected, even when he was quite young. Naturally he had never laid a finger on his sister; that would have been ungentlemanly. But he had always returned taunt for taunt, insult for insult. Sometimes brother and sister had managed to be civil to each other, but their mother knew there was little love lost between them. Since she had never had much time for her own siblings, she believed that this was normal behavior and nothing to be concerned about.

Clarissa seemed unusually hostile that first evening, and she remained particularly aggressive toward Gregory as the week wore on. Nobody was surprised when he announced five days after his sister's arrival that he'd had a letter from one of his Harrow chums, and if his parents had no objection he proposed to go visit Charlie immediately. His parents had no objection.

As Sir Harold was much occupied in the

summer with the farms, that left mother and daughter alone together most of the time. Marjorie took advantage of their privacy to try to persuade her daughter to return to her spouse. Nothing availed, and Clarissa simply alternated between shouting and sulking. On the twelfth day of her visit, however, that soul of patience, Sir Harold, put his foot down.

"Come now, darling, you can't just run away from your husband the minute you get back from the honeymoon. If he's not mistreating you, and you say he isn't, then you belong at home. Your *new* home. I'll order your car for tomorrow morning, there's a good girl." So Clarissa was dispatched, muttering furiously all the time, back to Banner House.

As Lady Bebberidge-Thorpe's car rolled through the stone gates to that lavish dwelling, she was trying to remember how many times in the last eleven months the bride had abandoned home and husband and fled back to her parents. Altogether too often, that was certain. There was gossip, of course, but Clarissa hadn't cared about that. Sometimes her mother wondered if Clarissa cared about anything but Clarissa.

Now, almost a year after the wedding, the reluctant wife was about to present her long-suffering husband with a child, possibly an heir. ("Please, God, let it be a boy," Marjorie had prayed for many weeks.) She had no reason to believe that Clarissa was happier, now, with John. True, the husbandless visits to Datchworth had grown fewer after Clarissa had discovered she was pregnant, but she had informed her mother it wasn't so bad at Banner House now that she could tell her husband not to touch her. The new Mrs. Banner had even insisted on separate bedrooms, which her mother informed her was a bit old-fashioned. Clarissa had merely retorted that it showed women used to have better sense.

It was a dreary day for May. Later, in midsummer, the flowers would show the benefit from all this rain, but in the meantime, thought Lady Bebberidge-Thorpe, it was rather depressing. If the sun had been shining, she might have dragged Clarissa out for a walk. No hope of that now. At least the dull weather obscured the raw newness of John's enormous redbrick residence. In bright sunlight Marjorie could hardly look at it without wanting to close her eyes.

As her car pulled up to the front entrance, one of the servants emerged with an enormous umbrella. No, not a servant. As the man descended the shallow steps, Marjorie discerned the limp that had kept John Banner out of active service in the war. How kind of him to come out to greet her himself. Unless, Marjorie thought with a flicker of mordant humor, it was only a sign of how desperate he was to have someone in the house who might, just might, be able to control his wife.

Her son-in-law got to the car door even before her driver did, opening it with a welcoming smile. "Marjorie!" he cried. "You are a gift from Heaven."

She emerged into the shelter of the umbrella and they kissed on both cheeks, continental fashion. It was a habit he had picked up in Paris before the war, and his mother-in-law had decided she liked it.

She returned his smile, but adjured him not to spread flannel over her until she'd earned it. "My presence is no guarantee she'll behave, I'm afraid."

"Well, you couldn't possibly do any worse with her than I have. The mere sight of me seems to infuriate her."

The unmistakable sadness in this admission moved Marjorie to real pity. She and her son-in-law had become friends; he was a gentle soul, only five years younger than herself, and she had hoped, once upon a time, that marriage to him would improve Clarissa. It was dishearteningly clear to her now, however, that she and Sir Harold, in bestowing their young and beautiful daughter upon John, had not done him any kindness.

Marjorie's low expectations of her daughter preserved her through the days that followed. In one sense it wasn't quite as bad as she had feared. Clarissa's greeting when her mother came into the bedroom was slightly sullen, but not actively hostile. It was as though the heavily pregnant girl had figured out that the suffering she had so far endured was going to get worse before it got better, and she was in need of an ally. As there were no available female Banners, and certainly none of the servants was suitable, that left Mother.

Mother obliged. She listened to Clarissa's complaints about the horrors of pregnancy and agreed with them. When Clarissa asked how on earth her mother had managed to go through it three times, Marjorie carefully drained the frost from her voice before she replied, "I was fond of my husband. I wanted children both for him and for myself." And she managed not to add, "And I knew my duty," although the words were marching through her mind like the Queen's Regiment.

There was silence for a minute while Clarissa brooded on what her mother had said. Then she said plaintively, "I *am* fond of John, really I am. It's lovely being married to him, all except for — oh, God, Mummy, how can you *stand* it?"

Lady Bebberidge-Thorpe's withers were slightly wrung, if only because her daughter so rarely called her "Mummy."

"Clarissa, darling, is he, ah, doesn't he make any effort to, ah . . ." but she found that it was more difficult to discuss the facts of life with a daughter who had already experienced them than with a prenuptial virgin. But she didn't need to finish the question.

"Y*es,* Mother, he *does* make the effort, I can see him trying to — to — be kind about it, he even apologizes, but oh I just *can't stand it!*" This speech ended on something approaching a shriek: Clarissa, to her mother's horror, burst into hysterical sobs.

Marjorie comforted her as best she could. She sat on the bed and held her weeping child and patted her and murmured into her ear such comforts as she could think of: "There, there, darling, you'll get used to it in time, and besides, when you see your baby you'll know it was all worth it, worth every bit of it. When I held —" Marjorie swallowed an unaccustomed lump in her throat and resolutely put away from her mind the child who had drowned — "when I held each of my three babies in my arms, I knew it was worth it. You'll feel the same way, you wait and see."

Marjorie Bebberidge-Thorpe had her share of faults, but dishonesty was not one of them. She believed every word she was saying, even though she knew that Clarissa didn't. Not yet, anyway. But when the baby was born, then Clarissa would understand.

Lady Bebb clung doggedly to this conviction through the difficult days that followed. Clarissa, as if determined to compensate for her display of weakness in front of her mother on that first day, returned to her usual petulant manner. Nothing the servants did was good enough, nothing her mother said or did was acceptable, and as for her husband, she couldn't bear the sight of him. When her mother insisted John be admitted to the bedroom in which Clarissa had confined herself, and even accompanied him to make sure her daughter was not rude to him, Clarissa would give him only fleeting glances between long sullen stares out the window.

As the time drew near, however, even the much-abused husband began to feel his spirits rising. Come the day, John was positively cheerful.

"I've sent for the doctor," he announced with ill-suppressed excitement. He had just joined his mother-in-law in the morning room.

"Poor fellow," replied Marjorie, referring to the doctor. "I imagine Clarissa must have been one of his least pleasant cases."

John Banner had not yet grown accustomed to Lady Bebb's extraordinary frankness regarding her daughter. He was sure she would not speak thus of Clarissa in general, and had concluded that she did it to comfort him. And it was indeed a comfort. He rather suspected he might have gone right 'round the bend if she hadn't been there for the last few weeks.

"Marjorie," he began awkwardly. "I really can't thank you enough for all —"

"John!" she interrupted in the voice of a schoolteacher who had run out of patience with a slow pupil. "You have thanked me far too much already. She is my daughter.

It was my duty." She looked at her emotionally exhausted son-in-law and relented slightly. "And my pleasure," she added graciously, nodding to him. "And I must go now to Clarissa." She put down her teacup, rose from her chair, and walked briskly to the door, which John held for her while muttering yet another sheepish thank-you in spite of himself.

She did not acknowledge it; it was doubtful if she heard it. She had set her face toward her daughter's bedroom.

It would be difficult to say who suffered most through the next five hours. Medically it was an easy birth; mother and baby were strong and healthy; labor and delivery were accomplished without any of the difficulties and disasters that might have attended them. But the servants and the grandmother-to-be had been well nigh deafened by the screams of the laboring mother before the doctor arrived; when he did arrive, and dared to touch Clarissa, he was sworn at for his pains, and was grateful for the expectant grandmother, who surged out of the dressing room to which she had retired upon his arrival, grasped her daughter's flailing wrist, and ordered her in implacable tones to remember she was a lady.

But the baby emerged, responding to a smack on the bottom with a good, healthy cry. Lady Bebberidge-Thorpe looked down at the product of her daughter's efforts and beamed, but cautioned the doctor to wipe off the infant before offering the mother a look. The cord was cut, the baby was cleaned and wrapped, and the nurse, defying tradition, handed the tiny bundle first to the grandmother. Lady Bebb, no fool, knew she was being rewarded for her beneficial influence over the termagant who now lay quiet, limp and sweating, in the bed.

"Here you are, Clarissa, here is your beautiful little daughter."

Clarissa's eyes had been shut. They flew open.

"It's a *girl?*" The word "girl" was uttered in a tone that might have led an onlooker to suppose it was a synonym for "slug."

"Now, Clarissa. I know you are disappointed not to have given John an heir. But you are young and healthy and you have plenty of time to produce a boy. Meanwhile, you have a very lovely baby girl." Again Marjorie held out the infant.

Clarissa did not move. Instead she stared at her baby as if it were something infected. Then she raised her eyes to her mother's face and whispered despairingly, "I have to do this *again?*"

CHAPTER 10

SATURDAY MORNING

Three Days After Rob Hillman's Death

Tom Holder couldn't remember when he'd been happier. He could scarcely believe it, after the unpromising start to his vacation.

The pleasure he'd anticipated in the trip to England had nose-dived when he'd heard, the night before Kathryn's departure, that she'd had a cousin over there who'd had an accident — a fall, they said — and died. She would have to spend a lot of time doing all those dreary but necessary things that survivors have to do. He was sorry both for Kathryn and for himself; obviously it would put a serious crimp in her vacation, and it would substantially reduce the amount of time she would spend with the church group, which would put a serious crimp in his.

Canceling, however, wasn't an option. It would be all too embarrassingly clear — to God, Louise, and everybody — that the presence of the Reverend Dr. Koerney was, in Tom's book, the chief charm of the Oxford trip. Besides, clearing up her cousin's affairs couldn't possibly take every minute of the two weeks; she'd still be spending as much time as she could with the gang from St. Margaret's.

Of that he was certain because he'd learned over the last year that Kathryn had an exaggerated sense of her obligations. She lashed herself with guilt whenever she thought she'd failed to meet expectations— her own or anybody else's.

As they disembarked at London's Heathrow Airport and threaded their way through lengthy corridors and tedious lines at customs and immigration, Tom was picturing how Kathryn would look — a bit harassed, but putting a brave face on it, and act — full of smiles and apologies in equal measure. She would bustle about them like a hen gathering her chicks, assuring them that she'd see to it that they were well taken care of whenever she had to be absent, and that she would be absent as little as she could possibly manage.

So when he saw her he was shocked. It was as if someone had pulled a plug and drained the life out of her. The color in her cheeks had faded almost to gray; the light in her eyes had gone out. Others in the group passed by him, greeting Kathryn with concerned noises, but Tom stood stock-still, swearing at himself under his breath, "You stupid dickhead. Just because *you* never had a cousin who meant more than another Christmas card every December!" He had blithely assumed that her cousin's death would mean little to Kathryn beyond inconvenience; now, he was ashamed of himself, both because the assumption seemed inconsiderate toward Kathryn, and because as a policeman he wasn't supposed to make unfounded assumptions. He watched as the women who knew her best abandoned the luggage carts they'd been pushing and went to Kathryn to embrace her and express their sympathy. More than sympathy: concern. Because Kathryn was behaving oddly, almost like an automaton, exercising a steely control not only over her face but over her body. Her legs and arms moved stiffly, as if she had been starched. Tom couldn't decide whether he should approach her or hold back.

The decision was taken out of his hands, however. Kathryn swept the little crowd with a jerky glance, raised an arm, and gestured for them to follow her. They rolled their luggage carts through the crowds after her, a haphazard caravan, out of the noisy arrivals hall into a soft English twilight marred by exhaust fumes. She led them toward a curb where half a dozen small buses were lined up nose to tail emitting noise and carbon monoxide. One of these, clearly, was to ferry them to their hotel on the outskirts of the airport. Kathryn stopped at a green and white one, turned, held up both hands, and asked for their attention. They gave it to her.

"You will have heard," she began with her customary volume and strength but completely without her normal animation, "that my cousin in Oxford died suddenly last Wednesday and that I therefore was going to have to absent myself from this tour for part of the time. I'm afraid it's worse that that. I am now informed by the police that my cousin was murdered. I am therefore," she continued without pausing for the gasps and cries to subside, "going to the village where this happened, some miles from Oxford, and I shall be there at least until the perpetrator is discovered and possibly longer." She explained that she had arranged for an old friend from her Oxford days to act as their tour guide in her stead; he would meet them at the station in Oxford when their train arrived the next day. She was extremely sorry, but it was unlikely that they would see her at all.

Tom was appalled, not because his happy expectations had been dashed, but because it was clear that Kathryn was not only in pain but in shock, and he couldn't do a damn thing about it. He wasn't a close enough friend to offer a shoulder to cry on, and he would not be able to assist her professionally because he was an ocean away from his own turf. Adding to his feelings of uselessness was the conviction that when her glance had swept over the group, she hadn't even noted his presence.

She had motioned for them to get on the bus, and they were beginning to do so. She pulled the Rector aside and murmured quietly to him. Tom watched a bit wistfully as Father Mark took one of Kathryn's hands and patted it, nodding repeatedly at whatever she was saying. Suddenly their brief conference ended; Kathryn turned and began to walk down the line of people and luggage carts in Tom's direction. His brief, urgent prayer that she at least acknowledge his existence was answered with a divine generosity that left him breathless.

She walked straight up to him and spoke

so quietly that only he could hear. "Tom," she whispered, "I know this is an outrageous request, and I have no right on God's green earth to make it, but would you come with me? Out to this place where Rob died? I've spoken on the phone to the owner of the house, and he told me very kindly that I could bring a friend if I liked, he said there was plenty of space for guests."

Tom was stunned beyond speech, and Kathryn misinterpreted the amazed look on his face. "Oh, forget it! It was selfish of me to ask, you came here to see Oxford, not to traipse around a country house in the middle of a murder —"

She was waving her hands in a "cancel that" motion. Tom reached out and caught one of them and held it in both of his. Forcing himself to speak calmly, he asked simply, "What do you want me to do for you?"

She caught her breath and blinked back tears. "Oh, Tom, you are such a dear. It's just that this was bad enough when I thought it was just a horrible accident. But now — now — I seem to be so rattled — I don't know, the fact that somebody actually killed him, I can't — and the last time I was around a murder I was a complete idiot and practically got —"

"You were *not*," he said sternly. "You were very smart and I — *we* — would never have cracked it if it hadn't been for you. We have had this argument before and I am not going to listen to it again. Now pull yourself together and tell me how I can help you."

It transpired that Kathryn felt that what she needed in her current state of mind was the steady presence of an experienced policeman who also happened to be a friend. Tom promptly pledged all the time and attention she needed, and added that he'd rather help her catch her cousin's killer than see the sights of Oxford anyway. He figured it was safe to say this because she wouldn't believe him. Sure enough, Kathryn gave him a wan smile, squeezed his hand, and told him he was a wonderful liar.

"Are you tired?" she asked. "Do you need to crash for the night with the others, or are you up to going straight to Oxford with me?"

He assured her (truthfully) that he was wide awake, and she led him off to the taxi rank.

So it was that Tom found himself the following morning being driven out of Oxford in the car Kathryn had rented. His duty was to navigate them through the rolling countryside to Datchworth Castle. Between the unfamiliarity of the British map (it showed *pubs,* for heaven's sake!) and the sure and certain knowledge that they would die any minute because Kathryn insisted on driving on the left side of the road (he knew it was correct but it felt idiotically dangerous), it was a wonder he didn't feel more anxious. But there was simply no room inside him for negative feelings.

England was as beautiful as everybody said it was, the sun was shining but it wasn't too hot, and the Reverend Kathryn Koerney, the incredible Kathryn, was his for the next several days. Well, "his" might be putting it too strongly, but she had solicited his companionship in a manner that had made it obvious that they were going to be spending a lot of time together. Tom wouldn't have been able to enjoy it if she had continued in the state of obvious distress he had witnessed at the airport. But on the ninety-minute ride to Oxford, as he had watched the taxi meter ascend by regular clicks into the fiscal stratosphere and wondered what it would be like to be rich, Kathryn had fallen asleep in her corner of the backseat and the nap seemed to do her good. At the hotel in Oxford she seemed to be suffering from no more than fatigue as she thanked him for the sixth time and bade him goodnight.

In the morning she was downright cheerful over breakfast, explaining to him that the English actually liked their toast cold and their bacon half-cooked and their sausages stuffed to blandness with bread crumbs.

"I assure you, the Randolph serves the best breakfast in town," she chuckled at him as he held up a piece of bacon as limp as overcooked spaghetti and stared at it incredulously.

Had he suspected that she was putting on a brave face for his benefit, he would have told her instantly to drop the act. But it was a very good act, and it fooled him completely. Kathryn had decided that since Tom had so kindly agreed to sacrifice several days of his vacation, the least she could do in return was refrain from acting the way she felt, and endeavor to make those days as pleasant for Tom as she could manage.

So on the drive she chatted lightly about the house they were going to; not really a castle, she said, but a fortified manor house built on the ruins of an older castle. Apparently every century from the twelfth to the twentieth was represented somewhere in its fabric. She added a few bits of information she had picked up from her cousin's gossipy emails about the family who lived there. The owner was a baronet, the lowest form of title, but his family was as old as the castle, which was actually more important in the circles where people cared about that sort of thing. And one of his middle names was St. John, but you pronounced it "sinjin."

"You're kidding."

"No, rhymes with 'engine.'"

Tom laughed, half from amusement and half from pure joy, as he realized that the tune that had been running at the back of his mind for the last half hour was, "Heaven, I'm in heaven. . . ."

They lost a few minutes to a wrong turn ("Sorry, that was stupid of me." "Nonsense, Tom, you're doing brilliantly.") but eventually they found the entrance to Datchworth. Around it were encamped a number of bored-looking people whose profession was obvious. Kathryn drove slowly through their midst, ignoring the questions that were called out to her and Tom, and guessing that the questions would have been more insistent if they'd known who she was. Tom was making her chuckle by smiling at the reporters on his side of the car and saying, "Hi, nice to see you, thanks for coming, I know how busy you've been." The car crept forward to the bobby standing guard, Kathryn showed him her passport, and they turned into the gates of Datchworth. The press fell back, and Tom and Kathryn gazed at the castle before them.

Kathryn, eyeing the entrance tower, remarked that she could see why they had resurrected the term "castle." She glanced at Tom and was surprised to see him frowning. "What's wrong?" she asked.

"I know I'm supposed to be impressed, but why does it remind me of Disneyland?"

Kathryn whooped with appreciation. "Because it's a fake, my clever friend! It's Victorian. The bit we're looking at here, at any rate, which is obviously hiding the older bits. This is no more than a hundred years old. Good grief, it's got arrow slits. I think that counts as pretentious."

By this time they had pulled up by the massive front door. As they got out of the car the big door opened, and the serene presence of Crumper emerged to greet them.

Twenty minutes later Kathryn knocked at Tom's door and was told to enter. She did so, looked around the spacious, well-lit room with its mellow antiques and picture-postcard view of the park, and shook her head in amazement. "If this is how they house strangers, I wonder what they do for honored guests."

"Your room this good, too?"

"Every bit. Oh, Tom! How 'bout that butler?"

"I figure he's an actor this Gregory Sinjin guy hires to impress the guests."

"Works, doesn't it?"

"Oh, yeah. Ready to go talk to the fuzz?"

"As I'll ever be."

They set off down the corridor, Tom muttering as it branched into three, "I *knew* I should have left a trail of bread crumbs."

But he led her without hesitation or error to where they were supposed to be, which was back in the wide entrance hall. There they were met by an officer who introduced herself as Detective Inspector Meera Patel, who looked so little like a policewoman that both Tom and Kathryn blinked in surprise. Meera gave Kathryn a firm handshake, a warm smile, and a short explanation of what a Family Liaison Officer was. Kathryn responded with her customary good manners, and introduced Meera to "my friend, Tom Holder." She did not mention Tom's profession. They had decided, for the time being at least, to keep that information to themselves, lest the local police think she had brought Tom along to horn in on their business.

D.I. Patel was leading them down a broad passageway toward the parlor that Crumper had allotted to the investigators, when a door opened on their left and Derek Banner all but walked into them.

"Oh, I, ah, beg your pardon, ah, Detective Inspector!" he uttered in short jerks, attempting a polite smile and making a poor job of it. Then he saw Kathryn.

Kathryn Koerney's physical appeal was directly proportional to her emotional state. In high spirits, she was exceptionally beautiful, lit from within. In a more somber mood, she was merely very, *very* good-looking. It was enough for Derek, whose dismal attempt at a smile gave way first to surprise, then pleasure, then with some deliberate magnification on Derek's part into a rapt expression that if made verbal would have been, "Where have you been all my life?" He did this while effectively blocking their path, forcing Meera to respond.

"Hello, Mr. Banner. This is —"

But he didn't need her. He reached Kathryn in two long paces, held out his hand, and asked breathlessly, "Are you Rob's cousin? Welcome to Datchworth! I'm Derek Banner. I'm sorry that my uncle — that's Sir Gregory — isn't available until lunchtime."

Kathryn introduced Tom, whose hand Derek wrung warmly before turning back to Kathryn a fraction of a second too soon. Kathryn began, "About your uncle, Mr. Banner —"

"Derek! You must call me Derek!"

"Derek," she nodded with a smile. "I'm aware that Sir Gregory's health is frail; Rob mentioned it to me. It's exceedingly kind of your uncle to invite us to stay, and I wouldn't dream of asking him to wear himself out talking to strangers."

Derek informed her earnestly that she was *most* considerate, rather implying that he didn't meet with such wonderful persons very often, and upon ascertaining that she and Tom were bound for their first session with the police, began to escort them down the corridor in that direction, leaving D.I. Patel to bring up the rear.

Derek inquired, as they walked, if Kathryn and her friend had found their rooms satisfactory ("Palatial," Kathryn assured him.), if they were tired or jet-lagged ("A bit."), if they needed anything ("Just a long nap after lunch, I think; you, Tom?" "Same here.").

When they reached their destination, Derek opened the door for them with a tasteful version of a flourish, saying, "I'm only sorry that you're here on such a sad occasion, but nevertheless" — he gave Tom a nod and a smile — "I am pleased to meet you and on behalf of my uncle" — he turned to take Kathryn's hand, which he bowed over rather than shook — "I present you with the keys to the castle. Figuratively, you know."

Kathryn could not help but smile, but her thanks were perfunctory, as her attention was promptly claimed by the policeman who had been waiting for her in the parlor.

Said policeman, George ("Gee Gee") Griffin, took one look at the victim's cousin from America and was instantly glad he was wearing his Harrods suit and his Sulka tie. D.I. Griffin was justly proud of his appearance, which lay approximately halfway between that of a smart, competent cop and that of a male model; he spent a goodly part of his salary making sure that his clothes tended more toward the latter. Probably nothing much could be stirred up with the lady minister, given the professional distance the situation called for, but one never knew. He hadn't been nicknamed "Gorgeous George" for nothing.

Kathryn shook hands with him and gestured toward Tom, introducing him as "my friend, Tom Holder; he's come along for moral support."

D.I. Griffin gave Tom a handshake and all the attention he merited, which amounted to waving vaguely in the direction of a chair off to the side, and courteously offered Kathryn a seat opposite himself at the table. Meera Patel sat down unobtrusively in a corner and prepared to be unimpressed. She and her best friend on the force had decided long ago that the double G actually stood for "God's Gift" (to women), because that was what the man so obviously thought he was.

Having condoled with Kathryn on her loss, Gee Gee put on his most charming smile to thank her warmly for coming to Datchworth and to make solicitous enquiries about her trip.

Kathryn replied civilly, thinking that English cops were certainly friendly. Pity this one was wearing a charcoal pin-striped suit and a brown paisley tie which, though each was ever so excellent on its own, together clashed so ferociously that Kathryn could scarcely bear to look in the man's direction.

He was running smoothly through the customary courtesies, commenting appreciatively on the cooperation she had shown in Oxford when she had met with Chief Inspector Lamp the previous day, stressing to her the importance the Thames Valley Police placed upon this case; explaining that Lamp had been called to a triple homicide in Reading or he would be at Datchworth even as they spoke, and finally apologizing for asking her to go through another interview and possibly repeat a lot of things she'd already told the Chief Inspector.

"You don't need to apologize," she assured him. "I'm ready to do anything at all that will be useful. Nobody wants to see this — this *villain* caught more than I do." It was clear that "villain" was an anemic substitution for what she really wanted to say.

The flash of anger was a mild surprise to everyone there, including Kathryn herself.

Until she'd needed to refer to the person who had deprived her — and her aunt and uncle, and the world — of Rob Hillman, she hadn't realized how furious she was. *I must be getting over the shock,* she thought.

Griffin nodded sympathetically and said, "Of course, of course. Now, I understand from Chief Inspector Lamp that you and your cousin were, ah, fairly close?"

"Not fairly. Very. We've been friends since we were children. We lived a six-minute bicycle ride from each other." She paused to swallow. "Rob is — was — a year younger than I, a year behind me in school. Once we were out of high school, that didn't matter, of course. We were always —" She broke off, memories welling up like tears. She struggled to address the policeman in businesslike tones. "Look, you don't need a biography. What you really want to know is, did Rob tell me any of the personal details of his life. The answer is yes, he did. He — we — tended to confide in each other all those things we would never dream of telling our parents."

Griffin leaned toward Kathryn with earnest sympathy nicely blended with a slightly conspiratorial air and asked her if she might divulge some of those confidences.

Kathryn was almost back in control of her emotions. "I thought you would be asking something like that, and since I have my laptop with me I made this for you." She extracted a floppy disk from her handbag and handed it across the table to him. "After I talked to Chief Inspector Lamp yesterday it occurred to me that this might be useful. Rob and I communicated mostly by email. There are two files there; the one named "Complete" contains every email Rob has sent me since he took up his post at Oxford two years ago. To save you time, the other file, "Datchworth," contains only the messages that mentioned his job here, or were actually sent from here, either back in April during the Easter holiday, or earlier this month. I thought you might like to look at those first."

Gee Gee Griffin gazed with undisguised amazement and delight first at Kathryn, then at the disk, then at Kathryn again. "Oh, I say! Reverend Koerney, this is brilliant!"

Meera Patel, over in her corner, was equally, if silently, impressed. Tom, unsurprised because Kathryn had told him about the disk on their drive to the Castle, was enjoying the sight of the overfriendly policeman shooting himself in the foot by addressing Kathryn as "Reverend."

The rest of the interview was uninformative — for the police, at least. Kathryn hadn't seen her cousin for over a year, as they were seldom "home" (in Texas) at the same time. She had no letters from him: "Rob gave up writing when email came along." She had no idea who might want him dead. She imagined the only people who profited financially from his death were his parents, who would presumably inherit his modest belongings. Kathryn knew of no quarrels Rob had had with anyone, no jilted lovers, no angry students who'd gotten bad reports from Rob, no enemies of any kind.

"I'm sorry to give you such a run of negatives," she said, shaking her head, "but I can't think of anything that you might call, oh, turbulent. Troubled. He was happy; he enjoyed his job in Oxford, he loved working here . . ." Kathryn spread her hands in a helpless gesture and fell silent.

"Did he have any, ah, romantic interest? Anybody special in his life right now?" The second question was delivered with a tiny smile equally compounded of warmth and wistfulness, the Detective Inspector meanwhile making direct eye contact.

She shook her head firmly. "No." Seeing

the next question coming, she continued, "Yes, I'm sure, and yes, I would know. We specialized in minute descriptions of our love lives, or lack of same. As I said, all the things we wouldn't tell our parents."

"When was the last time he was seriously involved, do you remember?"

For a moment or two Kathryn gazed past Griffin at the oak paneling on the wall. Then she nodded. "Yes, it's in there"; she gestured at the disk still in Griffin's hand. "Soon after he went to B.N.C. Brasenose. One of the dons there, Chris Something. But it's also in there that they dallied with sexual attraction for a while but then decided, amicably, that friendship would be a better option. Different kinds of friends, was the problem. Chris was a bit of a party animal, and Rob is a pipe —" She broke off abruptly, then took a deep breath and continued, "Rob was a pipe-and-slippers-by-the-fire type."

Griffin looked at the tight-shut mouth and gave her a moment before asking gently, "And that's all you can tell us?"

"I just can't think of anything useful," Kathryn replied, shaking her head sadly. "I'm sorry."

Griffin assured her earnestly that there was no need to apologize. He held up the

144

disk between well-manicured fingers and asked, "And everything you've heard from him in the past two years is in here?"

"Every word. And if you can find anything suggestive in it" — Kathryn mustered a stronger tone of voice — "you're a better man than I am."

Tom, unfamiliar with the quotation known to every English schoolchild, raised his eyebrows at Kathryn's referring to herself in such unfeminist terms.

But the cop, to Tom's dismay, promptly responded with mock pomposity: "Gunga Din!"

Kathryn smiled, or tried to.

Gee Gee smiled back.

Tom ground his teeth.

Meera Patel glanced back and forth between Kathryn and Tom, her mind busy behind her beautiful, expressionless face.

Kathryn gathered her inner resources and addressed D.I. Griffin. "May I ask some questions now?"

"Of course! I'd be happy to tell you everything I can."

"Starting with the big one. Why are you so sure this wasn't an accident? Chief Inspector Lamp said something about a rock, but I'm afraid my mind wasn't absorbing information very well at the time."

Griffin explained about the stone that had fallen on Rob's leg, when it should have been the other way around. When he finished, Kathryn's eyes were closed and her mouth was a thin line. Tom asked her if she was all right; she asserted she was. Griffin poured her a glass of water from the pitcher at his elbow, walked around the table, and handed it to her. She thanked him inaudibly and drank several long gulps. Then she looked up again at the policeman, who had perched himself on the table's edge so close to her that their legs almost touched.

She asked him, "Do you think it was someone from Oxford, or at least, someone he knew before, or do you think it was somebody here?"

Griffin hedged, as was to be expected, with phrases like "early days yet," but he did go so far as to say that although they were checking Rob's prior contacts thoroughly, nobody had yet produced a persuasive theory of how a stranger to Datchworth could penetrate the castle, find the muniment room, which could be reached only by a rabbit warren of passages, and get up the spiral stairs to the parapet without any of the members of the household catching sight of him or her.

"So," Kathryn said dully, like a backward child studying a hard lesson, "it was probably someone here."

The policeman made a noncommittal murmur.

Suddenly Kathryn seemed to rediscover her voice, and cried loudly, "But *why?*"

"Ah, yes! Why. Before you arrived, we were hoping you might help us on that, Reverend Koerney. But it looks like you can't. Which means, I'm afraid, that, well . . ."

Meera Patel thought, *The phrase you're looking for, Gee Gee, is, "We haven't got a glimmer."*

Gee Gee, probably reluctant to be that candid, simply spread his hands and shrugged inarticulately.

There was little left to say. Kathryn rose, as did Tom, more courtesies were exchanged, and D.I. Griffin escorted them — or more specifically, Kathryn — to the door.

When they were about twenty paces down the corridor, Kathryn fetched a big breath and announced a touch more matter-of-factly than she was feeling, "Well, I suppose that wasn't so bad. Could have been worse."

Tom looked sour. "Could have been a

147

damn sight better."

Kathryn regarded him with surprise.

Tom explained, "Guy's a jerk. Any idiot could see you were upset. No time for unprofessional behavior."

"What on earth did he do that was unprofessional?"

"Well, I don't know how they do things in Merry Old England, but where I come from, you don't come on to the victim's next of kin."

Kathryn gaped at him, then pronounced with certainty, "You're imagining things."

"You can't tell me you didn't even notice?" he asked in disbelief.

She replied with equal disbelief, "For heaven's sake, Tom! He was being pleasant, that's all! Think about it: I represent the victim's family, for what that's worth, I haven't a motive in sight, and I have an alibi you couldn't break with a SCUD missile, since I was verifiably in New Jersey. Why shouldn't he be nice to me?"

Tom stopped walking and stared at her as though examining a most uncommon phenomenon. "Interesting," he pronounced.

She had stopped, too. "What *are* you on about?"

"You're usually so good at reading

people," he said, shaking his head in perplexity. "Is it possible I'm looking at a case of real, live modesty?"

"Oh, rubbish!" She started walking again. "I know when a man's coming on to me. Derek Banner, for instance, was coming on to me like gangbusters."

"That he was," Tom agreed as he fell into step with her, hoping he'd said it in a sufficiently neutral voice and waiting in some trepidation for her reply.

"Much good may it do him."

Music to his ears! Uttering silent, heart-felt thank-Gods, and being careful not to sound too pleased, Tom asked, "Not interested? Why, what's wrong with him? Seems O.K. to me." *Of course,* he thought, *up to ten seconds ago I was wishing it was Derek who'd been pushed off the tower.*

"O.K. for somebody else," she admitted. "But not for me. I know a bit about him from Rob's emails. He darkens the door of the church only when somebody's getting married or buried, and when Rob told him about me, Derek seemed to think that being a 'lady priest' would be altogether quaint and terribly cute. Rather as if I were a belly dancer, Rob said."

Tom guffawed. "Wouldn't I like to see *that!*"

"Shut up. Besides, I've no fancy to be the Lady of the Manor. Derek is Sir Gregory's heir. Can you picture me, the mad-about-Manhattan girl, stuck in the middle of nowhere, tied to a man who was permanently wedded to an Estate, capital E — in this case a Castle, capital C — and a title to boot, God save us all! Can you see that?"

Tom, who had been seeing precisely that in nightmarish fantasies for the last three-quarters of an hour, sighed ever so gently and said, "No, I can't."

"A place like this," Kathryn continued, "you don't own it, it owns you. You might have the cash to take off a year and sail around the world, but can you do it? No. You're a prisoner. A prisoner of your own wealth, and history, and, oh, how shall I — ? Ah! A prisoner of your own standing in the community. No, thanks!"

"Yeah, I'm sure you're right," Tom agreed, floating along on a sweet river of relief.

The relief lasted until dinner the following day.

CHAPTER 11

APRIL 1997

During the Easter Holidays
Three Months Before Rob Hillman's Death

Rob Hillman was having fun, although an uninformed observer would not have thought so. Rob's brow was knit in terrific concentration and his mouth was a thin, hard line. If his gaze had been directed at another human being, it would have been unmistakably hostile. The target of this aggressive look, however, was a piece of parchment.

On it was written, in a criminally sloppy fourteenth-century book hand, something that might possibly be a hymn in praise of the Virgin Mary. But the person (presumably a monk) who had written it down had had little consideration for those who came after him. Rob was reminded of a remark by Professor Parks at Oxford about a manuscript in cursive script that looked "as though the scribe took a lot of drunken spiders and ran them through a puddle of ink and then set them loose on the page."

Drunken Spider Man, thought Rob, *I have found your grandfather.* Fortunately, bad book hand is easier to read than bad cursive, so it was not more than three minutes before Rob suddenly cried aloud, "Gotcha, you incompetent bastard!"

A particularly puzzling bit of hen scratching, it turned out, was a highly idiosyncratic "g" with a laterally extended tail. Which meant that the bit at the end of line two was in fact "ad virginam." That cinched it.

"Yes. Yes!" cried Rob, thumping the table in triumph. Taking his notebook, he began to write a neat transcription of the opening lines, muttering quietly under his breath. "Why on earth, you little bugger, did anybody ever let you near the scriptorium?"

Jenny, the maid who usually brought Rob's tea, had told the kitchen staff that the American bloke talked to himself. She was in error. Rob talked to the scribes of the manuscripts he read. Sometimes they were his friends; the regular letters of a well-written manuscript elicited Rob's appreciation and even his thanks. "Oh, lovely," he would murmur as his eyes glided effortlessly along the lines. A poor scribe was an opponent, an unworthy rascal who must be defeated. The easy manuscripts were pleasant, but the conquests were more satisfying.

An intrusive clanking heralded the opening of the door. He looked over his shoulder.

"Mr. Hillman? Am I bothering you?"

"Meg, come in; no, you're not bothering me, though four minutes ago I would have bitten your nose off."

"Oh!" she said, taken aback. "Uh, why?"

"Because I was locked in combat with a seriously atrocious scribe and I was losing. However, three minutes ago I made a breakthrough, so now I'm safe to talk to."

She laughed. "I don't believe you. I don't think you'd have bitten my nose off. You're too polite."

He smiled back, but wagged an admonitory finger at her. "Ah, but you've never walked in on me without an appointment before."

"I guess that's true. Well, I have an excuse. A terribly important question."

"Shoot."

"What," she inquired with immense earnestness, "do you want for tea?"

"Ooooo," he emitted through pursed

lips. "That is important." He closed his eyes in concentration, then opened them again. "How about Earl Grey, no milk, no lemon, no sugar, and a tiny little cucumber sandwich? On second thought, not so tiny."

"You got it," she drawled in her best Texas accent, which wasn't very good.

"Not bad," Rob said kindly, "but it still needs a bit of work. Thanks, Meg." He gave her a trace of a wave and turned back to the manuscript.

"You're welcome." She backed out of the room, pulling the heavy door shut behind her. Almost immediately, however, it clanked open again. "But I warn you," Meg said mischievously, poking her head back through a ten-inch opening, "I shall continue to walk in on you without appointments as long as you're at Datchworth. I live here, you know."

Fortunately, the door closed on her last words, so there was no need for him to reply. Rob grimaced, shook his head slightly, and went back to transcribing.

He finished the first stanza of the hymn to his satisfaction and was starting to slog through the second when he remembered that wasn't his job — not at this point, anyway.

He had described the manuscript and transcribed the opening lines, enough to indicate the nature and quality of the text; it was time to enter it into the catalog and move along to the next one. With a tinge of regret he laid aside his late opponent, Drunken Spider Man's Grandfather, and picked up the next manuscript. This one proved to be altogether less interesting; the hand was neither beautifully clear nor beastly challenging, and the text seemed to be a sermon on Saint Mary that would certainly have put its original audience to sleep.

So it was that the clanking of the ancient door came the next time as more of a relief than an intrusion, especially since he was beginning to feel a distinct need for tea. He turned in his chair to greet Jenny, but instead of the thin, plain maid with the nice smile, he saw almost her opposite. The young woman holding the tea tray had a shapely body and a pretty face and had done much to emphasize both. Her smile was definitely not what Rob would have called nice.

"Professor Hillman? I've brought you your tea."

The rural Oxfordshire accent was appropriate to a servant at Datchworth, but the outfit wasn't. Sir Gregory's maids did not wear uniforms as such, but they dressed modestly, and there was nothing modest here. Full breasts in a black lace brassiere pushed visibly against a tight but sparsely knit top of bright fuchsia. The black pants were what his mother would have called "sprayed on." But the principle element of the performance (and it was a performance; Rob had seen enough of them to know) was what she was doing with her full, hot-pink lips. Both the tone of her voice and the quivering smile were unmistakably insinuating.

Rob could think of nothing to say except, "I'm not a professor."

The smile widened. "Is it *Doctor* Hillman, then? I do want to get it right." She tried to set the tea tray down in front of him, but with exclamations of alarm he motioned her away from the manuscripts. "Down there at the end of the table, please. Uh, just 'Mister' will do."

Slightly but perceptibly, she pouted. Rob wondered, as she set the tray down in the spot he'd indicated, if she had been angling for "Call me Rob."

"Thank you very much," he added politely. "Tell me who you are, for despite the fact that you are delivering tea trays, you're clearly not one of the servants."

"Why, thank you," she replied coquettishly, under the impression he had paid her a compliment. She sat on the edge of the table, effectively blocking him from the tea tray, and leaned her breasts toward him preceded by an open hand.

"Julie Crumper. But call me Crumpet. Everybody does."

"Oh!" Rob exclaimed in surprise, shaking hands automatically. "Are you Crumper's daughter?"

"If I tell you I am, will you promise not to hold it against me?"

"Why on earth would I hold it against you?"

She dimpled at him. "That's right, you Americans, you don't believe in all that rubbish about class."

Rob realized with a flash of guilt that she was giving him too much credit; he had his own class system, and had not hesitated to place Crumpet on one of its lower rungs the moment he looked at her. (The butler, her father, Rob had classified as his equal.)

"Um, Crumpet, if you don't mind, I'd like to have my tea."

"Oh! Of course." She hopped up and grabbed the teapot. "Shall I be Mother?"

With polite resignation Rob suffered her

157

ministrations, accepting his Earl Gray and sandwich from her hands while wondering how he could best get rid of her.

She had strolled around to the other side of the long table and poked the corner of one of the older parchments. "What is all this stuff anyway?" she asked.

"Mostly bits and pieces of devotional texts, pages cut out of books of prayers or hymns or such like."

Her cute nose wrinkled in distaste. "Boring! Besides, it doesn't make sense. If they cut out those pages, why didn't they just throw them away? Why hide them in the wall with the silver?"

"They didn't cut them out because they didn't want them. They cut them out to hide them from Cromwell. Like the silver."

It was clear to Rob from the look on Crumpet's face that he had lost her. The teacher in him suddenly overcame his revulsion at her blatant sexuality; he pointed to a chair and invited her to sit.

"O.K., Crumpet, here we go, the English Civil War. What do you know about it?"

Crumpet squirmed. This wasn't the sort of conversation she had been looking for. Still, if this was the only way to get to the man, she would go along with it. With tremendous effort of memory, she produced:

"Sixteen-something. Cromwell thought we shouldn't have a king, so he fought against him and won and chopped his head off. The King's, I mean. Then Cromwell ruled for a while, but people got tired of it and decided they wanted a king back again, so we went back to kings and queens." The look of surprise on Crumpet's face as she finished this speech informed Rob that she had remembered more than she had expected to.

"Good girl," he said, deciding to accept her oversimplifications on the grounds that correcting them might take all day. "So during the war Cromwell's troops and the King's troops were fighting all over the country, and Oxfordshire was for the King, right?"

"Yeah, and all the rich people and the Oxford colleges gave their silver to the King to help pay for the war, but really they didn't give it all, most of them took the best bits and buried them or hid them or something, and that's what they found in the wall here, the family silver that the family didn't want to give the King." Crumpet was starting to preen herself on how well she was doing.

"Bravo, Crumpet. They hid it so the King wouldn't know they'd held out on him, and also so that if Cromwell took the castle, he couldn't find it, either."

"Yeah, but I *know* all that. What I don't know is why anybody would hide a bunch of prayers, for God's sake."

"Ah. That brings us to the other thing Cromwell was against, besides the monarchy. Fancy churchmanship."

"Huh?"

"Cromwell was a puritan. He thought worship should be very plain, very protestant. Everywhere he went, he destroyed stained glass windows in churches and statues of saints and anything he thought was like Roman Catholicism, because he believed the Church of England should be pure and simple."

"Oh, yeah," she was nodding as more long-forgotten history lessons struggled to the surface of her underemployed mind. "Yeah, I remember now. Anything pretty or fancy, he couldn't stand it. So a lot of old church stuff got smashed up. Oh! And not just church stuff, too. Didn't he destroy the Crown Jewels? The old ones, I mean? So we don't have any of Queen Elizabeth's jewelry or anything from the kings and queens from way back in the Middle Ages?"

"Bravo again, Crumpet."

"Yeah, I remember now, that really pissed me off when I heard it. All these nice old things, just because they were beautiful he had to go and smash them. Like he didn't want people to have anything that was, like, fun."

"Exactly."

"But why," asked Crumpet, returning to the original point, "would anybody hide *prayers* from him?"

"Because these prayers — and hymns" — Rob gestured at the spread of manuscripts before him — "are full of references to the Virgin Mary and other Saints, and Cromwell hated that. He would have burned these manuscripts."

"What an asshole!"

Rob could not help grinning, but he said, "Look, Crumpet, thanks for bringing me my tea, and I've enjoyed talking to you, but I really must move on." He indicated a large bundle of manuscripts yet untouched.

She pouted again, and he had to pour a lot of oil over her, but finally he got the heavy door shut after her. To the end she remained flirtatious, making Rob wonder how a woman could be so unaware that her techniques weren't working. Not on this man, anyway. Presumably there were others who would eat it with a spoon. In fact, he decided, there had probably been quite a lot of others who had done precisely that. His own taste in female companionship, however, ran more toward Meg Daventry. Or Meg Daventry a couple of decades older.

With a sigh of relief at ridding himself of the unseductive seductress, he poured himself a second cup of tea, walked across the muniment room to the smaller door, opened it, and mounted the tiny circular stairway to the parapet.

Elsewhere in the castle, the object of his indifference was finding a warmer reception.

"Hallo, Poppet," exclaimed Derek Banner, sweeping her into a crushing embrace and gnawing loudly and comically on her neck. Crumpet giggled and gave every indication of enjoying this activity, but he stopped it to ask her, "How'd it go?"

She stopped giggling and gave him a smug smile. "How do you think it went? He wanted me to sit down and have tea with him and we talked for ages."

Derek looked pleased. "Eating out of the palm of your pretty little hand, was he?"

"Too right he was!" she assured him.

CHAPTER 12

JUNE 1962

Thirty-five Years Before Rob Hillman's Death

She knew that Nigel Daventry had taken her in the backseat of his parents' Bentley, but she could not afterwards remember anything but their laughing stagger toward the car. Nigel had an arm about her waist and his left hand wrapped about the neck of the second champagne bottle, or perhaps the third. Every few steps he had pulled her to a stop and kissed her neck and pulled at the straps of her gown. She had squealed, "Nigel! You wicked boy!" but had not hindered him. About the third stop, he had pulled hard enough that the straps on her left shoulder, gown and bra together, slid down and exposed her left breast. Immediately he put his mouth on her nipple and began to suck.

She just had time to emit a shriek of laughter — Nigel was pretending to be a baby! — when a quiver went through her entire body as though she were a plucked string. She gasped for breath and kept gasping as he backed her up against one of the cars and pressed his body against hers. The pressure against her pubic bone (she would not have known to call it that) began to generate as much wild pleasure as the ripple of Nigel's lips on her breast.

When he pulled away she cried desperately for him not to stop, but he grabbed her by the wrist and pulled her again toward the farthest rank of vehicles parked in the darkness.

"Be better in th' car," he slurred. "Better in th' car. C'mon."

She went as eagerly as he, and they stumbled on. There was no more raucous laughter but their breathing was very loud.

"This one," he said, fumbling with the back door handle and dropping the champagne bottle. The gravel was grassy this far back in the yard, and the bottle landed with a crunch but did not break. Nigel started to pick it up but she pulled at his sleeve.

"Leave it, Nige. We don't need it."

She was right. They didn't need it.

When she woke, she felt cold and uncomfortable and at first had not the slightest idea where she was. It was dark.

She managed to sit up, and discovered that her dress had fallen down about her waist. Her bra seemed to be missing. She attempted clumsily to lift her bodice to cover her nakedness, simultaneously becoming aware that her head was pounding and that she was in the backseat of a car parked with a lot of other cars. In the distance she saw the lights of the house and heard music.

Of course. Her party. Why wasn't she there? She realized she was cold because the car door by her feet was standing open. There was just enough moonlight for her to make out her elegant silver dancing slippers, intact, as were her stockings. But she could see the tops of the stockings, and her garters. Her skirt, she realized, was rucked up about her hips.

Things got worse. She was wet between her legs and she hurt in unfamiliar places. There was a funny smell; she didn't know what it was and this frightened her. She found that she could not remember much of what had happened after they got into the car. Her knowledge of the facts of life was sketchy at best, gleaned from hushed giggling conversations in the girls' rest rooms at school. But it was abundantly clear to her that she had done "it."

You weren't supposed to do *it*. If you did *it*, your parents would kill you. If you did *it*, you got preggers. Then you had to get married.

Her mind hit the word "married" like a fast car hitting a brick wall. There was a silent crash followed by a confused wreckage of thoughts. She couldn't get married. She was *seventeen*, for God's sake.

Carefully she got out of the car. She made an attempt to straighten her gown, pulling the straps back up over her shoulders and doing up the zipper in the back. She began to move through the ranks of parked cars toward the house. As she approached it she could see people on the veranda and in the formal garden, all talking and laughing as if the entire world hadn't just changed. She turned her steps toward the kitchen yard.

Three servants sat on the steps enjoying a cigarette break. They were mostly silhouettes against the light pouring out from the open kitchen door; she couldn't recognize them. As she approached, one of them — a footman, she was pretty sure — saw her, froze to immobility for an instant, then turned to a plump girl and ordered, "Get Phyllis. *Run!*"

Phyllis had saved her. Phyllis had smuggled her up the back stairs through the servants' door to the wide hallways of the family bedroom wing (happily deserted) and whisked her back to the safety of her own bedroom. Phyllis ran a quick bath, encouraged her into it, and plied her with cups of strong black coffee as she sat in the soothing lukewarm water. When she emerged from her bathroom, she saw that Phyllis had laid out a new dress for her.

"Here you go, Miss Clare, yes, step into it, I'll do the zip, don't you fret, you just tell your parents that somebody spilled wine on your green gown, now sit you down, I'll fresh up your hair."

And Phyllis, dear Phyllis, had gotten her through the months that followed. She had found Clare a discreet doctor and comforted her when the news proved to be as bad as she'd feared. She had persuaded Clare that an abortion was nothing but a good way to get killed and further persuaded her to drop the bomb on her parents before Mrs. Banner figured it out for herself.

Wisely guided by Phyllis, Clare had gone first to her father, and begged him for his help.

"Daddy, I'm so sorry. I know it was very bad of me. But I didn't want to embarrass the family, so maybe I could go away somewhere to have the baby, and give it away, and nobody would know. Could we do that? Please?"

John Banner had risen from his huge leather chair and embraced his penitent daughter, loaned her his handkerchief to dry her sniffles, assured her that they would do whatever Clare wanted, and even volunteered — heroically — to break the news to Mummy.

Clare, limp with relief, returned to her bedroom where the faithful Phyllis was waiting anxiously.

"Oh, Phyllis, dear" — she kissed her maid on the cheek — "you were so right. Daddy's going to take care of everything."

The two of them sat down happily to discuss the rival merits of France and America as suitable places to have a secret baby.

If it is possible for a door to open angrily, it did. Mrs. Banner stood in the doorway, terrible as the siege of Stalingrad.

"Out," she ordered curtly.

Phyllis fled.

Clarissa regarded her unsatisfactory daughter with steely eyes.

"Oh, Mummy, I'm so sorry," Clare

rushed, "Nigel got me so drunk, I didn't know —"

"Silence!"

Clare shrank back in her chair.

"Presumably you were not drunk when you spoke to your father in his study just now?"

Confused as she was frightened, Clare just managed to shake her head.

"Then what madness is this about running away to have this child in secrecy and then *give it away?*"

"I — I — just — I thought — well, obviously I can't marry Nigel, and if —"

"Why not?"

"Because he's a pig!" Clare cried, surprised out of her fear. "He got me drunk, he seduced me, and then went off and left me! He's avoided me like the plague ever since. I wouldn't marry him if he were the last —"

"Be silent. Do you know how many miscarriages I had after you were born?"

It was the most intimate utterance Clare had ever heard from her mother, and she gaped, speechless.

"Three," announced Clarissa. "In the end I was forced to give up. I could not give your father an heir. Now *you* will give him one. Nigel Daventry may be a half-wit, but at least he comes from a good family. I shall speak to his parents. I will make it clear to them that we expect him to do his duty as a gentleman."

She rolled on, as oblivious to her daughter's horrified protests as a herd of stampeding cattle to the ground they flatten beneath their thundering hooves.

Clare and Nigel, Mrs. Banner made clear, were to be married in a civil ceremony, utterly private, in Scotland, as soon as it could be arranged. Immediately thereafter friends of both families were to be told that Clare and Nigel, the naughty children, had eloped the week after the party and had been keeping their marriage a secret from their parents because they knew they had misbehaved shockingly.

"Then you will have a son," Clarissa ordered her daughter. "He will be born in wedlock and baptized like a proper Christian in the village church."

Clare knew, looking at her mother's face, that nothing would avail her. That did not stop her trying first pleading, then an attempt at reason, then angry tears. All these things failed her, and so did her father.

"I'm sorry, Kitten," he apologized when she sought him in his study, "but perhaps your mother is right."

So a sulky Nigel had been married in a Scottish registry office to a resentful Clare.

The baby arrived in due course. It was delivered in Banner House, where the newlyweds were living because Nigel couldn't afford to buy a house or even rent a flat, and his parents wouldn't have them. The baby was a girl.

Clare named her Phillipa, remained in bed for the three days recommended by the doctor, arose before dawn on the fourth day, packed a small bag, wrote two brief notes, and left the house before even the servants were stirring.

Phyllis found the empty bed when she entered the room with Clare's morning chocolate. On the dressing table she found an envelope addressed to herself. The note inside read:

Darling Phyllis,
I am so sorry to have to leave you. Thank you for everything.
Love, Clare.

Phyllis ran out of the room and across the hall and threw open the door to the nursery. The nurse, standing near the cradle, was startled into a small outcry, and began to scold in a soft, irate voice.

171

"Heavens, Phyllis, don't you know anything about babies? You shouldn't wake her up with a sudden noise like that — you'll frighten her."

"She's still here?"

The nurse stared. "Are you mad, girl?" Of course she's still here."

Phyllis strode swiftly but quietly to the cradle. Yes, little Phillipa was there, sleeping peacefully after her dawn feeding, not yet ready for her eight o'clock. Tucked into her blankets was a cream-colored envelope, identical to the one in which Phyllis had found the note to herself. This one was addressed to Mrs. Banner.

Phyllis, quaking in her boots, went to her mistress's bedroom.

After hearing the maid's brief report, Mrs. Banner predictably demanded to see Phyllis's note. She scanned it, cast it aside, and opened the second envelope. It was without salutation or signature. It said simply, *You wanted this baby. You can have it.*

CHAPTER 13

SATURDAY LUNCHTIME

Three Days After Rob Hillman's Death

The house was unhappy. Crumper could feel it in his bones.

He had lived at Datchworth all his life; he had been born in the old servants' quarters on the top floor of the south wing. That part of the Castle had been boarded up for years, but all the rest of the house was Crumper's domain. He patrolled its corridors from the busiest to the almost abandoned; he inspected every room from attics to wine cellars. He and the house had spent a lot of time together, and it spoke to him. Today it spoke as if in restless whispers, complaining of violation. Not since Cromwell had it yielded to an occupying force, but now, once again, Datchworth Castle had been invaded.

It would have been easy to blame the police. Certainly they were everywhere; one met them in the halls, one came across them in rooms that should have been empty. They interrupted the servants at their work, taking people off to be interviewed again and again. They were harassing the Family. But Crumper knew it wasn't really the police who were the alien presence.

It was Rob Hillman. Alive, Rob had been sunny, cheerful, friendly. Murdered, he had become an uneasiness in the air, a chill in the marrow of the bones. Crumper, never one to be fanciful, had begun to understand why some people could believe in ghosts. Especially in the ghosts of those who had been wrongfully done to death.

It was Rob Hillman behind Miss Meg's red and puffy eyes. It was Rob Hillman who jangled Mr. Derek's nerves so that he chattered like a fool — which he wasn't — and started at small noises. And it was Rob Hillman who haunted the heretofore indomitable Sir Gregory. Everyone said, of course, that the shock of the news had made the Baronet ill — too ill to greet his guests from America, and so he was keeping to his room. But Crumper had looked into the old man's eyes and seen not illness but something very like terror.

Hickson had seen it, too; of that Crumper was certain. But the valet would not speak of it, any more than Crumper himself would.

Needless to say, not one of the four people who sat down to lunch in the Family Dining Room that day discerned the slightest trace of any of these disquieting thoughts on Crumper's impassive countenance.

Three of the four were so troubled by their own emotions, in any case, that their chief concern was simply to get through the social task before them with courtesy and self-restraint intact. Tom Holder, unburdened by even a nodding acquaintance with the deceased, was the only person who had his antennae out.

He was appreciating the room, a pleasant space made wonderful by a double set of French doors opening onto the terrace. Beyond the terrace was a garden so vast and elegant that Tom knew instinctively that he must not refer to it as the backyard.

Derek was apologizing profusely (too profusely, Tom thought) for the absence of Sir Gregory.

"He really is most completely under the weather, I'm afraid. This business —" Derek seemed to think he had uttered a solecism, and made haste to correct himself.

"Oh, I say, Miss Koerney, do forgive me. I mean, of course, the sad death of your cousin."

"No apology is necessary; I have referred to it as 'this business' myself. And call me Kathryn."

Derek beamed. "How kind of you, Kathryn! I was saying, this — ah — sad affair has shaken my uncle rather dreadfully. He was enormously fond of Rob, you know. As were we all."

Meg, whose demeanor was well arranged to converse with guests despite her tired, red eyes, said, "I wonder if Rob reminded Uncle Gregory of Jerry. I always thought they looked a bit like each other. And then Rob died so suddenly. Like the Accident, you know."

Both Kathryn and Tom sensed the capital "A" in "Accident," sensed immediately that the word had a specific meaning in the family vocabulary. They looked inquiringly at Meg.

She answered the question they were too polite to ask. "I had an uncle Jerry, or at least, I would have had him if he hadn't died before I was born. He was killed in a car crash when he was eighteen; that was in 1972. He was Uncle Greg's and Aunt Sophy's only child, and they adored him.

Which is probably why they took me in when I came along seven years later. They were pretty old to be taking care of a baby, but I needed a home and they gave me one. Here."

It was clear to both Kathryn and Tom that Meg was rehearsing a well-worn story, probably because it offered a bit of pre-packaged conversation, effortless to produce. She looked far too weary for effort. Both of them wondered what she had been crying about while scrupulously pretending not to notice the evidence of shed tears.

"That was nice of them," Tom remarked, wanting to know why Meg had needed a home and again being too polite to ask.

"Oh, the loveliest people ever!" Meg agreed emphatically. "I wish you'd known my Aunt Sophy; she was a treasure, wasn't she, Derek?"

"Oh, yes, best mother a niece and nephew ever had." Derek and Meg exchanged small, melancholy smiles.

Kathryn's curiosity got the better of her courtesy, and she ventured a direct question. "What happened to her?"

Derek replied, "She died of breast cancer in 1994."

Kathryn winced sympathetically.

Tom, also with sympathy in his expression, asked how old she had been.

Meg told him, "Sixty-eight. A lot of people, stupid people, said that was a good old age, as though that made it all right. But we weren't ready to lose her, were we?" She was appealing to Derek, as before, for confirmation. He gave it to her with a silent nod, and a suddenly outstretched hand. They clasped fingers for a moment.

"I hope this is not an overly familiar remark," Kathryn said, "but I must say it's lovely to see cousins who are close." She did not add that it was also painful, given her own current circumstances.

"Ah, actually," Derek corrected politely, "we're not cousins."

Meg jumped in. "He's my uncle."

Tom told her, "You've got a fair number of uncles."

"That's only three," Kathryn objected mildly. She started counting on her fingers. "The late Jerry, the present Derek, and obviously Sir Gregory. Unless there are more?"

"Two. Or one, depending on how you add it up," Meg responded. "The whole set of them goes like this: Uncle Gregory is my great-grandmother's brother. Derek is my grandmother's brother. And my mother had two half brothers, twins, which means that they are both half uncles, and two halves make one. Total of three whole uncles living. And the one that died before I was born wasn't really my uncle anyway, I just call him that. He was actually my first cousin twice removed." An impish smile appeared incongruously under her swollen eyes. "I trust that's perfectly clear?" she asked.

Derek, long accustomed to Meg's uncle monologue, only smiled, but Kathryn and Tom both laughed out loud.

Tom recognized, as he laughed, that the conversation badly needed this lighter note. But it was clear from what had gone before that any further questions about Derek's and Meg's relatives might lead as easily to tragedy as to comedy. He decided to be bold.

" 'Scuse me for changing the subject," he said at just the right moment in the dying laughter, "but now that I'm in England, there's something I've always wanted to know."

"Dear fellow," Derek replied, "we will enlighten you to the best of our ability. What is it?"

Tom asked innocently, "Would somebody please explain cricket to me?"

The maneuver succeeded brilliantly. Everyone cried, "Ah!" and launched into an explanation, three talking at once. Derek and Meg stopped, yielding to Kathryn. She, having correctly divined Tom's purpose, announced sententiously that cricket was a perfectly straightforward game: "You simply start with baseball and then scrupulously remove all the fun from it."

This slur on Britain's national pastime drew, as Kathryn had known it would, outraged protests from Meg and Derek.

"One doesn't *start* with baseball —"

"Just because it's leisurely —"

"One *starts* with cricket —"

"Doesn't mean it's boring —"

"Which is the original of which baseball —"

"Even the quiet bits are full of subtle —"

"Is merely a derivation —"

"Marvels of skill if one only has —"

"And a totally unnecessary derivation, at that —"

"The knowledge to appreciate them."

"Because the original is better!"

Tom and Kathryn were grinning. Uncle and niece looked at each other, then back at their visitors.

Meg eyed Kathryn narrowly. "That was

deliberate provocation, wasn't it?"

The rest of lunch passed in a good-humored effort to teach Tom, as he himself put it, "everything I always wanted to know about cricket but didn't know who to ask."

They were served, flawlessly, by Crumper, who pretended to be deaf except when he was directly addressed. At one point Derek suddenly looked up and made eye contact with him.

"Crumper, is my uncle asleep?"

Crumper permitted the corners of his mouth to turn upward a sixteenth of an inch, to indicate that he perfectly understood the question behind the question. "Not yet, Mr. Banner. Hickson is serving Sir Gregory his luncheon today. Sir Gregory insisted I serve here."

"Ah," said Meg. "Looking after the guests?"

"Precisely, Miss Daventry."

Derek turned to Kathryn, throwing a quick glance at Tom in passing. "As I was telling you earlier, my uncle's feeling awfully rotten about not being well enough to welcome you properly. I expect he's telling Crumper to take pains. Eh, Crumper?" He looked back at the butler.

"That is correct, Mr. Banner."

The pains Crumper was taking became clear after lunch. As they rose from the table, the butler reappeared and begged the honor of showing Miss Koerney and Mr. Holder back to their rooms. Mr. Holder thanked him and Miss Koerney told him he was very kind.

Crumper led his charges back to their wing of the Castle, politely answering Kathryn's questions about the age and style of the various areas they passed through. Tom was impressed by the man's minute knowledge of both the building and the family who had owned it all these centuries. Kathryn, however, took Crumper's easy command of the family history in stride; she would have considered it more remarkable in a household like Datchworth if the butler had not known the hair color and personal habits of every Thorpe and every Bebberidge who had ever drawn breath. Kathryn was far more impressed by the impeccable syntax in which this wealth of knowledge was being revealed.

"Crumper," she said as the butler concluded his explanation of the three different window styles in the hallway they were crossing ("an ongoing clash of wills amongst the then Baronet, Sir Griswold

Bebberidge-Thorpe, his mother, and his wife"), "it's a well-known fact that Americans have no manners, so I'm going to ask you a personal question. Where did you go to school?"

The perfect servant showed no offense, replying smoothly, "Sir Gregory was kind enough to have me educated at Winchester. Now if I may, I would like to show you something."

They had passed the enormous green porcelain vase, which told Kathryn and Tom that they had arrived at "their" corridor, but Crumper had stopped before a door twenty yards short of their rooms. He held it open for them, and obediently they filed in.

They'd entered a charming compartment, full of sunlight and chintz; it would have been about fifteen feet square if it had been square, and it had windows along two walls that were more or less opposite each other, which made for a more open feel than is commonly found in old castles. It was furnished as a sitting room.

Crumper gave them time to exclaim over the double view ("How marvelous!" "Hey, this is nice!") then told them, "It is a well-known fact" — his eyes flickered to Kathryn's and away again, with nary a trace of a smile — "that transatlantic travel is exhausting. It is another fact that sharing meals with persons one has only recently met requires more, ah, effort than does eating with persons more familiar. I thought that perhaps after you have rested, you might like to take tea privately in here."

Tom liked this proposal so much, he was afraid to say so; Kathryn thanked the butler warmly but protested that surely this would create extra work for him?

Crumper assured her that that was not the case; their tea would be brought by Mary, the head housemaid.

"Also," he added, and Tom could have sworn he saw a fugitive twinkle in the man's eye, "every time I see Sir Gregory, as I do quite frequently, he inquires what I am doing to further his guests' comfort."

Tom grinned, "O.K., Crumper, I guess the least we can do is let you further our comfort."

"Please inform Sir Gregory," Kathryn managed to say with a straight face, "that our comfort has been so furthered that we hardly know how to cope."

So it was that Tom and Kathryn, having each enjoyed a deep, delicious sleep before being awakened by Mary's gentle rapping at their respective doors, met happily in the double-viewed parlor a little before five.

"It's late for tea," Kathryn said, "but I needed every minute of that nap. How about you?"

"God, yes. People warned me about jet lag, but a lot of times I work all night and it doesn't faze me, so I thought I'd be immune. Hey!" he exclaimed, catching sight of the tea table. "This is like the first time I came to your house."

On the table was a silver tea service that took Kathryn's breath away. "You flatter my silver. Mine's Victorian. This is Georgian, I'm pretty sure, and twelve times finer. Did I ever tell you that Warby trotted out that ostentatious nonsense without my prior knowledge or consent? I was mortified." "Warby" was Kathryn's housekeeper, Mrs. Warburton.

"Yeah, when I got to know you better I knew it had to be her idea. You hate to look pretentious. You even hate to look rich. That's one of the things," he said, sitting down and reaching for a scone while scrupulously not looking at her, "I like about you."

"Tom Holder, you are the most gratifying friend. Shall I be Mother? Sorry, I'm showing off my British. It means, 'Shall I pour the tea?' "

Tom graciously invited her to do so, and she did, while he sat back and hoped he wasn't audibly purring. He felt just a little sophisticated, like he was going to do all right here in this rich man's house. Rich man's *castle!* Here he was, the pampered guest of a man with a title; he had no responsibilities except to be a friend to the most attractive woman in the world; at this moment, she was pouring Earl Grey out of a piece of silver that belonged in a museum, and offering the tea to him in a flowered cup so delicate that you could see the sunlight through the rim. *What did I ever do,* he wondered, *to deserve all this?*

Despite the lavish surroundings, there was complete ease between them, as if they were older friends than they were; Tom knew it was because murder drives people together where it doesn't drive them apart, and this was the second murder he and Kathryn had shared. Of course, this time was different; this one was Kathryn's by right, and he was in it only because she'd invited him. The first time, it had been the other way around. He liked it better this way, because he didn't have to feel guilty about making up excuses to spend time in her company. Still, maybe he should be doing something to earn his keep.

"Kathryn," he asked, "is there anything you need me to do? I got the idea I was supposed to help somehow, that's why I'm here, but so far I'm just taking up space."

"Oh, Tom, you've no idea! You *are* helping. I need —" she hesitated. "I need a friend."

"So why didn't you ask Celia Smith?"

"Because you're a pro, you're at home with homicide. God!" She grinned at him. "That sounds like a title for a bad TV series, doesn't it?"

Tom smiled, but replied seriously, "You're doing it again. Don't."

"Don't what?"

"Pretend to be cheerful. You conned me into thinking you were O.K. all the way here in the car. Made me think that was just shock at the airport, just a good night's sleep was all you needed. Had me fooled up to when you had to talk about Rob to that English cop. Well, now the cat's out of the bag. So you can stop pretending."

Kathryn sighed. "I keep forgetting about you. You see through people as if they were glass. All right. You want it straight? I asked you and not Celia because I didn't need sympathy. I needed steel. I need to have someone here I can count on to be strong. I feel — I feel safe with you here."

Tom's eyes opened wide. "You think this guy's gonna come after you? For God's sake, Kathryn, if you think it's not safe here, let's get the hell out! I'm flattered that you think I make a good bodyguard, but if you —"

She stopped him with an open palm. "Tom, I am not in the least afraid that this bastard is going to harm me. I want you here when they find out who he is so you can stop me from killing him. Because —" suddenly she was almost sobbing with rage — "because *I want to take a baseball bat and beat him to a bloody pulp.*"

Tom had enough sense to keep his mouth shut and let her decide what to say next. Her eyes were shut and her fingers were mashed half an inch into the uphol- stered arms of her chair. He watched as after a few moments her hands began slowly to unclench and the color crept back into her fingernails.

She continued more calmly, but still with closed eyes and a tight face, "Celia couldn't control me. But with you here, I will behave myself."

"Now *that*," said Tom conversationally, "is the biggest compliment I've probably ever gotten in my life."

She opened her eyes and smiled wearily at him. "Tom, you do understand, don't you, that when I try to make light of it, it's not just because I'm trying to pull the wool over your eyes, it's because I'm trying to escape it? Momentarily, at least. Because otherwise it crushes me. And I can't breathe."

He nodded. "Sure. Just as long as you know you don't have to put on an act for me. So what do you want to do now? Curse the bastard? Smash something? Or escape?"

"Escape, please. And I know just how. As for tracking down the bastard, that's not our job. You and I are just part of the audience on this one. We are not players. Do you find it frustrating?"

"A little," he admitted.

"Well, I hope you won't think it beneath your dignity" — here she dusted the crumbs of scones off her fingers and rose from her chair — "but there is a mystery I should like to solve, and we wouldn't be getting in anybody's way."

"Great! Lead me to it," he said agreeably, getting to his feet. "What's the mystery?"

"Meg's plethora of uncles! I know it

doesn't matter, but I hate being confused about anything, and I like family trees. Could we build one, do you think?"

Tom laughed and declared himself game.

"Follow me, then. I've got some paper in my room."

They sat elbow-to-elbow at an antique writing desk no more than eight feet from Kathryn's bed (*I will NOT think about it,* Tom thought); she had produced a spiral notebook and opened it to a blank page.

"All right, then, we start with Meg." She wrote the name at the bottom of the page, roughly centered. "Her last name's Daventry, so we'll call her parents Mr. & Mrs. Daventry —"

"A brilliant feat of deduction," Tom murmured.

Kathryn hit him on the arm, told him to shut up, and continued, "Until we learn, if we ever do, their first names. Now, Meg said her mother had two half brothers —" She wrote the fraction "$1/2$" twice, out to the right of "Mrs. Daventry." "That means one of her mother's parents must have married twice."

"A small point," Tom said.

"Yes?"

"She said her mother *had* two half

190

brothers. Then when she counted them all up, she said 'three whole uncles living.' "

"Meaning her mother must be dead."

"Right."

Kathryn wrote "deceased" under "Mrs. Daventry," and asked Tom if they were ready to move up a generation.

"Sure. Meg said Derek was her grandmother's brother, which is hard to believe, but why would she make it up? And he didn't contradict her."

"No, he didn't. So we add 'Meg's Granny' here," Kathryn said, suiting the action to the word, "but bear in mind that we don't know whether Granny is Mr. Daventry's mom or Mrs. Daventry's. Do we?"

"Not yet, but I live in hope."

She hit him again and said, "And finally, Uncle Gregory is — didn't she say, the brother of her great-grandmother?"

"That's right."

"Oh! Something's coming back to me. An email from Rob. There's an old woman they call Cruella, and I'm virtually positive she's Sir Gregory's sister. And she's off somewhere wearing a white coat with exceedingly long sleeves."

"You're pulling my leg."

"I pull it not, I do assure you." Kathryn

added "Cruella" and "Sir Greg" to the chart in appropriate places and, after a brief pause, "Aunt Sophy," drawing little connecting lines and leaving blanks and question marks here and there.

"It's this inconvenient business of people having two parents each," she complained.

"Hang on, I think we can get rid of some of those question marks. Derek's the heir, right?"

They discussed possibilities and certainties; Tom pointed to various parts of the diagram; Kathryn scribbled through some of the lines and question marks. They were bestowing slightly tentative approval on the result of their labors when a housemaid appeared at the open door.

"Pardon me, Miss Koerney. Mr. Holder."

"Yes?" Kathryn slewed around in her seat, as did Tom, to look at the maid.

"Mr. Crumper sent me to say that Sir Gregory is keeping to his room, but Mr. Banner and Miss Daventry are going to have supper with him there, and would you" — her glance included them both — "like to have your supper in the Family Dining Room where you had luncheon or would you like to have it in the room where you had tea?"

Tom and Kathryn looked at each other

and asked simultaneously, "Tea room?" They both grinned and turned to the maid, saying, "Tea room!" not quite simultaneously.

The maid, less vigorously trained than Crumper, smiled. "Yes, ma'am. Sir." She started to go but Kathryn called her back.

"I say, are you Mary?"

"Why — yes, I'm Mary."

"Please come in, Mary. We need some help here."

Mary proved to be less omniscient than Crumper about the Bebberidge-Thorpes and all their branches, but she was considerably more willing to chat about the current generations, Kathryn decided, than the butler would have been.

When she left, Kathryn took the much-corrected diagram she had started with, produced a fresh sheet of paper, and on it made a fair copy and presented it to Tom for his approval.

They had done fairly well. There were still some blanks, but there was only one error (they discovered the next day that they had put the mysterious Mr. Daventry in the wrong generation).

Tom and Kathryn's first draft of the Bebberidge-Thorpe family tree looked like this:

THE PREVIOUS BARONET & HIS LADY

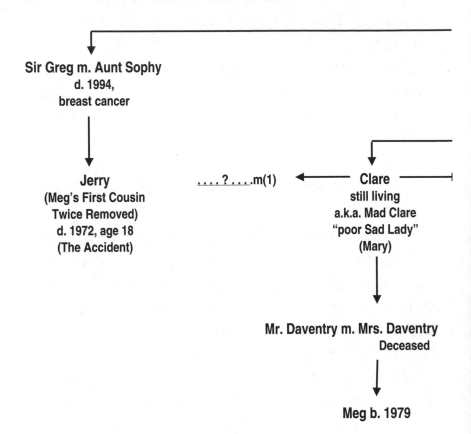

Sir Greg m. Aunt Sophy
d. 1994,
breast cancer

Jerry
(Meg's First Cousin
Twice Removed)
d. 1972, age 18
(The Accident)

. . . . ? . . . .m(1)

Clare
still living
a.k.a. Mad Clare
"poor Sad Lady"
(Mary)

Mr. Daventry m. Mrs. Daventry
Deceased

Meg b. 1979

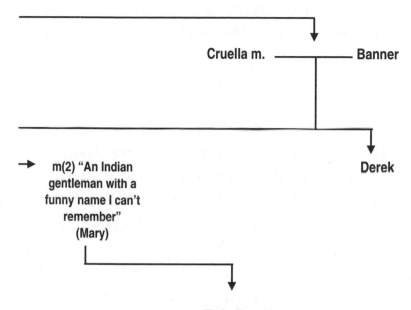

Cruella m. ——————— Banner

Derek

→ m(2) "An Indian
gentleman with a
funny name I can't
remember"
(Mary)

Twin Boys
Mrs. Daventry's Half Brothers
Meg's Half Uncles

★ ★ ★

Thirty miles away another set of data —
known facts and guesses — was under re-
view, but those examining it were considerably less pleased with their results than
were Tom and Kathryn with their family
tree.

"Stop fidgeting, Griffin. Things are bad
enough without your incessant preening."

Gee Gee Griffin immediately stopped
tweaking his cuff links and folded his
hands in his lap. "Beg your pardon, sir. But
may I just emphasize that —"

"Do me a favor and emphasize later.
Let's just go over it first, shall we?" Chief
Inspector Lamp was in a grim mood. The
Reading homicides promised to be a nasty
headache, their only virtue being that they
had temporarily diverted the attention of
the tabloid press from the Datchworth case
("Castle Killer Befuddles Fuzz!"). And the
Chief Inspector had never greatly cared for
Gee Gee Griffin, who, Lamp considered,
would make a better cop if he were less
fond of himself.

"Point number one, from the original list
of eight people in the household who
might have had opportunity to murder
Rob Hillman, you have managed to eliminate two, the gardener's assistant who

found the body and one of the maids. Leaving us with a mere six, namely the niece, Margaret Daventry: the estate manager, Ralph Carlyle: the butler and his daughter — sounds like a smutty joke, that does — and the other two maids. Of which only the Daventry girl appears to have had anything like a personal relationship with the deceased."

"Yes, sir. It was Miss Daventry's idea to get him there in the first place, and she's obviously the most upset. Fits with love affair gone wrong. But . . ."

"Spit it out, Griffin."

"Two things. Her friends that we've talked to say things like she 'had a terrible crush on him,' but they all swear it was one-sided, she got no response out of him. A woman kills her lover, sure, but some guy she just fancies?"

"Sudden rage? Frustration builds up and goes bang? She didn't have to bludgeon Hillman to death, after all. She didn't even have to intend to kill him. Just an angry shove, he loses his balance?"

Griffin was shaking his head. "Doesn't have a reputation for temper. And besides, it doesn't go with the other thing. Miss Daventry keeps insisting it's all her fault. She says it to everybody, all the time. She's said it to me three times. Her fault because Hillman wouldn't have been there except for her. I mean if she really killed him . . ." Griffin shrugged.

Lamp began to think Griffin might be shrewder than he had heretofore appeared. He nodded. "You're right, if she *did* kill him, then running around saying 'it's all my fault' is sheer brilliance, a double bluff and a half. Worthy of a really devious mind. And you don't think she's being devious."

"If she is, she ought to be in Hollywood. Oscars for certain."

Something about the metaphor aroused Lamp's suspicions. He inquired casually, "Does D.S. Patel agree with you on this?"

Sure enough, the faintest pink tinge appeared around the edges of Griffin's manly ears even as he replied, "Yes, sir."

Lamp regarded him for a moment. *You little,* he thought. No wonder Griffin's insights had seemed unusually subtle. The wretch had stolen them from the Family Liaison Officer. Griffin was jealous of her because he was afraid she'd have his job someday. He was right.

On the pearls-before-swine principle, Lamp refrained from sharing these thoughts with his junior officer. Instead he asked, "All right then, Griffin, who's your money on?"

"Banner."

"Ah, why?"

"Because he's frightened. Everybody in the house is jumpy, but you expect that. But Banner is the worst. Scared to death of me. Much too polite. An innocent man in his position would resent the lot of us, he'd be asking us why we hadn't made an arrest yet, when we were going to clear off and leave them alone. But Derek Banner's treating us like some old battle-ax of an aunt he's terrified to offend."

Lamp knew this excellent piece of psychology must also have originated with Meera Patel, but once again declined to rub Griffin's nose in it. He merely nodded and commented, "Which is why you have a small army asking everybody within a ten-mile radius of the Castle if they caught sight of Mr. Banner anywhere in the neighborhood on the afternoon in question."

"Ah, well, two teams, actually."

"Double it. I like the smell of Banner for this. Driving around the Cotswolds, my arse. By himself, if you please. Why do these idiots take *us* for idiots?"

There was silence for a moment. Even

the heir to a baronetcy on one side and a billion on the other could be hauled down to the station and dragged over the coals if they could catch him in a lie. Whether they could wring a confession out of him was another matter.

"Griffin."

"Yes, sir?"

"Find me a motive, dammit."

"Yes, sir, I know, I'm trying. We're going over the printouts of the disk Reverend Koerney gave us, but it's —"

"*Miss* Koerney. Or 'Miz.' 'Reverend' is like 'Honorable.' You refer to your M.P. as 'the Honorable Fred Squat,' but you don't call him 'Honorable Squat.' So the disk isn't helping?"

"I sent a copy of the printouts to Sharkar and Preston with a note to go back to a woman named Chris Foley, one of the dons at Brasenose. Hillman was going on about 'raven' hair and green eyes when they first met, but later it seems he cooled off and he and this Miss Foley settled for just being friends. I know it doesn't sound like much, but sir, *nothing* sounds like much. Whatever the hell this guy did to get himself murdered . . ." Griffin trailed off and shrugged. But the look on his superior's face made him rally. "I'll find it, sir," he declared firmly, setting his square jaw. "I'll find it."

"You do that," the Chief Inspector replied wearily, with a nod that was a dismissal. He watched Griffin's well-dressed back walk out of the office. Meera Patel, Lamp reflected, would have said, "*We'll* find it."

CHAPTER 14

EARLY JULY 1997

Three Weeks Before Rob Hillman's Death

The glorious heat wave was continuing. They'd had a bit of rain the previous day, but that morning had dawned only partly cloudy and a spanking breeze had since cleared the sky. The breeze had died down about lunchtime, leaving an afternoon full of butterflies.

They danced among the blossoms in Sir Gregory's gardens, themselves like flickering airborne flowers. Bees hummed. The Castle, all nine centuries of it, lay in the hot sun like a sleeping cat. Had it been Spain, everyone would have retired for siesta. But the English enjoy such weather far too seldom to sleep through it. The servants had been told to take the afternoon off, and had hauled out their folding lawn chairs and croquet set and were disporting themselves languidly in the large informal garden the Baronet had set aside for their use. The Baronet himself dozed on a chaise longue by his bedroom window.

Meg Daventry had gone riding with friends in the relative cool of the morning, lunched with her uncle, lain for a lazy hour in a secluded side garden clad in a fetching bikini that no one, alas, was around to appreciate, and had begun to wonder how to avoid boredom for the rest of the day before she drove back to Oxford that evening to see the Welsh National Opera.

She decided to go bother her tutor. The man worked altogether too hard, anyway. Wrapped modestly in the beach towel she'd been lying on, she made her way back to her room, showered, changed into plaid Bermudas and a T-shirt in minty pastels, and set out for the muniment room.

The muniment room was part of the rather pretentious embellishments built onto Datchworth by Sir Horace Bebberidge-Thorpe to celebrate the golden jubilee of Queen Victoria. Typical of their time, those additions were a mad attempt to resurrect the Middle Ages, Gothic windows and all. Sir Horace had decided that an ancient castle should *look* like a castle, and had covered up the tasteful Georgian entrance with several tons of Cotswold stone culminating in a round tower and crenellations. Sir Horace's erection, as Derek and

Meg gleefully referred to it, had only two saving graces. Cotswold stone, unlike the gray stuff that renders so many ancient British buildings forbidding, is the color of crystallized honey, a comfort on dull days and a glory in the sun. And in the round tower there was a spiral staircase leading up to a parapet, where one could stroll behind the crenellations and savor a view that stretched for miles. On a clear day one could even see the chimneys of Morgan Mallowan; Meg had joked with Kit about sending smoke signals.

Sir Horace had also decreed that any castle worthy of the name (blithely ignoring that it was he who had resurrected the term "castle" and clapped it on to a building which had gotten along quite happily for several hundred years as Datchworth Hall) must have a muniment room. And so it was that the round stone chamber at the bottom of the tower was fitted out with huge cupboards of ornately carved black wood (more Gothic arches) into which were put all the Datchworth documents, ancient, legal, and miscellaneous, that could be found on the premises. On public days, the Japanese and American tourists were wowed.

This room, for no logical reason, was

three feet higher than the space surrounding it, and thus was reached by a
short flight of stone steps. Up these
tripped Meg Daventry with the nimbleness
of youth. The wrought iron doorknob
turned with its usual loud clank. Meg
burst in on Mr. Hillman and assumed a
stern countenance.

"Up! Up, my friend!" she commanded,
"and quit your books, or surely you'll grow
double!"

"And something, something, something
else, why all this time and trouble?"

He was laughing, and Meg's heart
skipped a beat. *There really ought to be a law
against assigning tutors this gorgeous to im-
pressionable girls like me,* she thought.

Rob admitted she had caught him at a
propitious time. "I've just found a treasure.
Look here."

Meg went to the table and looked down
upon what had clearly been, at one time,
the upper left-hand corner of a page, stiff
and rippled a bit with age. Almost all of
the fragment, which had been painstak-
ingly cut out of its context, was filled with
a capital letter, written in gold and
trimmed with scarlet, and so ornate that
she couldn't figure out what letter it was
meant to be. In the open spaces of the

letter was a tiny scene that must have been painted, in parts at least, with brushes containing a single hair.

Rob had his satisfaction in Meg's audible intake of breath. He handed her a magnifying glass, saying, "It's the Assumption of the Virgin. Check out the angels holding up the cloud."

Meg did as she was told, leaning close over the parchment. "My gawd," she drawled, flaunting her improving Texas accent and her modest knowledge of the medieval, "That is whut ah call an il*lum*inated manuscript."

"Too right, my dear gel," Rob replied, in a wickedly accurate imitation of Derek.

"Oh, you are getting *really* good at that."

"Yes, we're becoming bilingual, aren't we? I could do a backward Henry Higgins and take you to Houston and pass you off as a member of the First Baptist Church."

"Super! And if I pull it off I get a custom pair of boots. Look here, you see that sky out there?" Meg pointed toward one of the narrow windows. "I am unfamiliar with customs in Texas, but in England it is considered a sin to stay indoors in such weather."

"The custom in Texas is to stay as cool as is humanly or mechanically possible in the summer, which means hiding from the sun, not wallowing in it." But he pushed his chair back from the table. "Deadly or merely venial?" he asked.

"Deadly," she assured him. "Lemonade on the terrace? There's shade if you look hard enough."

"You are a wicked temptress and you will burn in Hell for it. Lead me on."

Ten minutes later Rob and Meg were sprawled comfortably in garden chairs at the precise place where a small Georgian addition jutted out from the main pile and cast a shadow across one end of the terrace. Meg was seated in the sun, Rob in the shade.

"I'll say this for you, kid," Rob observed contentedly. "You steal a mean lemonade."

"One of my better-honed talents."

They had crept into the depopulated kitchen and found a large jug of Mrs. Drundle's lemonade in the old green refrigerator. Meg had rummaged in the cupboards and produced glasses; they had poured and run.

Safely removed from the scene of their crime, they relished their cool drinks and chatted of this and that. Rob had long dispensed with the relative formality he exercised in Oxford when Meg came to him for tutoring, a dispensation that pleased that young lady no end, but there were lines that both of them were careful not to cross.

With her maternal ancestors as splendid examples of how to let your life get screwed up (literally and figuratively) by men, Meg approached the opposite sex with a levelheadedness beyond her years. She found her American tutor amazingly attractive, but he was far from achieving tenure, and she wasn't sure how the college higher-ups would react if news got round that a tutor was having an affair with a student. Not that she was afraid of getting into trouble herself, not with the Bebberidge-Thorpe name and the Banner money behind her. It was Rob who was vulnerable, and she had no intention of giving the members of the Senior Common Room the slightest reason not to renew his contract.

From time to time she fantasized about seducing him, but she was not a conceited girl and she never assumed that if she made a serious attempt she would necessarily succeed. There was so little flirtation in his manner toward her that she suspected it was more than professionalism that kept their relationship platonic. Perhaps she was too young for him.

Despite her attempts to be dispassionate toward Rob, however, she felt her primordial female hackles rise when the buxom and scantily clad figure of Crumpet appeared at the opposite end of the terrace and began to saunter in their direction.

"Hello, Meg. Hello, Manuscript Man."

At the age of ten, Meg had begged the then twenty-one-year-old Crumpet, who seemed the epitome of everything jolly, to stop calling her "Miss Meg" and use only her Christian name. Meg wasn't sure how long it had been since she began to regret this democratic impulse.

Crumpet gave Rob a private little smile as she greeted him, unaware that its effect was the precise opposite of what she intended. "So what's new with the manuscripts?"

Rob summoned up his manners and told her he'd found a lovely fragment from a sort of prayer book and he was thinking of taking it to Oxford to show it to his old tutor, as it might turn out to be quite valuable. Crumpet listened to this brief report with an interest both Meg and Rob found surprising, until Rob found himself being given a spectacular close-up view of Crumpet's breasts as she cooed, "Oooooo, that sounds lovely! Can I come and look at it?"

He fobbed her off as best he could without being ruthlessly rude. When she finally turned and ambled off, he turned to Meg and asked, "How on earth did anybody as decent as Crumper turn out a piece of trailer trash like that?"

Meg emitted a whoop of joy. "Trailer trash! What a wonderful term! But as for your question, God knows. None of us has ever been able to figure it out, though a couple of people claim she's a throwback to Crumper's mother, who was apparently the worst mistake Crumper's father ever made."

"The thought of Crumper having a father seems strange. I suppose I assumed that he sprang, fully grown, from the mind of Oscar Wilde or Bernard Shaw or somebody of that ilk."

"Oh, no, we've all got revoltingly real parents around here. Crumper's dad, now officially designated *Old* Crumper, is still to be seen about the place, popping up here and there where you least expect him."

"Retired, I gather?"

"Very. And more than a bit potty. Always muttering about what her ladyship needs, but the last ladyship around here was my

Aunt Sophy, and she's been dead for years. Alas. I believe Uncle Greg would be better, physically I mean, if she were still around."

"Death of a spouse is the number one trauma, according to the experts. But even love can't keep one young forever. And your uncle is getting on a bit."

"How old do you think my uncle is?"

Slightly taken aback by the direct question, Rob hemmed and hawed a little and finally ventured, "Late eighties?"

"Seventy-three."

"You're joking."

"No. It isn't his age, you see, it's his rotten health."

"Crikey," Rob uttered, at his most English. "I hope for your sake rotten health doesn't run in the family."

"It doesn't appear to. Derek and I rarely even catch colds. And Uncle Greg's sister, my great-grandmother, is as healthy as the proverbial horse, which goes to show there's no justice in the world."

"How's that?"

"Poor Uncle Greg is the nicest person you could ever hope to meet, but his sister my great-gran is the Arch Bitch. Her name's Clarissa, but when Derek and I were younger we used to call her Cruella."

"Sounds charming. Do you have to put up with her presence very often?"

"Not at all in recent years, thank God. She's locked away somewhere in the wilds of Hampshire."

"Locked away?" Rob echoed in surprise.

"Yes," said Meg, rather enjoying the effect she was about to cause. "In what they call a 'secure facility,' which as far as I can make out is simply a very posh term for 'home for the criminally insane.'"

CHAPTER 15

JULY 1963

Thirty-four Years Before Rob Hillman's Death

She had never before known power. It was amazing, intoxicating. Champagne was nothing to it. Perhaps that was why, despite her once-burnt-twice-cautious approach to men, she took such a reckless plunge. Her total alcohol intake at the time was only three sips of port. But she was wildly, instantly drunk on power.

There was a good reason for the paucity of alcohol. She hadn't touched a drop since that never-to-be-sufficiently-regretted night when she and Nigel Daventry had created the baby that had ruined her life. The very sight or smell of liquor now seemed distasteful if not positively revolting.

Ellie, her roommate-cum-hostess, seemed to understand; she never pressed Clare to take a drink, and when friends came to visit their flat Ellie wouldn't allow

them to tease Clare about being a teeto-
taler. "Leave the girl alone," she'd tell
them. "It's none of your sodding business
what she chooses to do or not do."

But after four months of this splendid
support, Ellie was now telling Clare it was
time to break the rules and break out the
bottle. "Hooper Van Buren's got a first,
and we're invited to help him celebrate it."

Clare's parents had not thought it important for a girl to develop her mind, so
they had sent her to a school more interested in turning out debutantes than
scholars. When she had run away from
Banner House after the birth of her baby,
she had sought refuge with a school friend
who had managed, despite a similar hand-
icap, to make it into Oxford. Since March
she had absorbed enough of the university
culture to know that a first-class degree
called for a first-class party.

"I'm happy for him, I'll be delighted to
go, but I don't need to drink to celebrate."

"Darling Clare, you don't need to drink
to celebrate, you need to drink to survive
the beastly party."

"What's going to be beastly about the
party?"

"Oh, Hooper's gone all Labour on us,
didn't I tell you? So God knows what sort

of people will be there. Probably half the Junior Common Room of Bloody Balliol. The half that are on scholarships. We'll be up to our arses in communists."

"I've never met a communist. Are they interesting?"

Ellie laughed derisively. "Dearest Clare, they are the most boring people on earth. Soooo earnest. So good, you want to throw something at them."

It did not occur to Clare at that moment that the most entertaining thing to throw at the communists would be herself. That discovery she made that evening, an hour or so into the beastly party. Since she was neither cold nor calculating by nature, she would not have set out deliberately to entice a man for the merry hell of it. But of all the boredoms in the world, the worst is the boredom of the nondrinker at a party where everyone else is loudly and rapidly becoming pie-eyed.

So when Hooper caught her hand and cried, "Clare! I say, just the girl!" and began to drag her through the crowd toward "my friend Shy," Clare decided, on impulse, that she would give this oddly named bloke the full treatment. Then possibly something remotely interesting would happen.

"Shy" turned out to be "Shai," short for Shailendra. He had the mahogany skin and raven hair of the Indian subcontinent, but he greeted her in the flawless accents of Eton. The contrast was highly appealing, as was his exotically beautiful face.

Clare was a pretty good flirt when she had some recently imbibed alcohol on which to float her shaky self-esteem. The steady gaze in Shai's black eyes, however, was too much for her in her present state of sobriety, and she overdid it. As she chatted with him, she began to pat her blond curls, purse her perfect lips, and flutter the augmented eyelashes over her china blue eyes.

He said gently, "Don't do that."

Puzzlement froze the affectations for a moment. "Don't do what?"

"All that phony stuff. You don't need any of it."

The phony stuff melted into honest surprise. "I don't, uh, understand —"

"You are one of the most beautiful women I have ever seen in my life. You shouldn't spoil the effect with that — that —" Finding no words, he mimicked, perching a hand coyly behind his ear, tilting his head, fluttering his eyelashes and pouting.

Clare burst out laughing, not in a simpering giggle, but in honest whoops of merriment, too loud to be ladylike.

"That's better," he nodded with the smallest of smiles.

Clare studied him a second and asked, "Are you a communist?"

It was his turn to laugh. "What on earth makes you ask that?"

She related the warning she'd received about the party.

"Stuff and nonsense," he replied. "World of difference between Labour and Communist. You've been listening to some Tory talking out his backside."

"Careful!" she warned him, with an accusatory finger. "It's a her, not a him, and she's my best friend."

He surprised her again. "What makes her your best friend?"

"What? Why, she, she, saved my life. She gave me a place to live when I ran away from home. She let me stay in her flat without paying rent."

"I'm glad to hear that."

"Why should that make you glad?"

"She's been kind to you and you are loyal to her. I like that. Also —" he hesitated, then continued, "I am glad that you call her your best friend because of the kindness, not because the two of you think alike."

"Whaaa— ?"

"She appears — please don't be offended — she appears to classify people she knows nothing about on a rather superficial basis."

By this time Clare had gotten her jaw closed, and she shot back: "And what makes you think I wouldn't do the same?"

"Because your bubbly Blond Bombshell routine is such an obvious fake. There is a brain behind those baby blues, but you've been told from your cradle that men don't like smart women, so you hide it."

Clare felt as stunned as the woman at the well when Jesus told her everything she'd been doing all her life. But she made a swift recovery. "Do *you* like smart women?"

"Oh, yes," Shai whispered. In the din of the party she couldn't hear the words, but it was obvious what the lips had said.

She was used to being called beautiful. But this man had called her a beautiful woman; everyone else had said "girl."

He had rejected the usual flirtatious games, informed her that her act was phony, and somehow made it sound like a compliment. And he had said she had a brain.

She would have gone with him any-where.

Where she went with him was back to Ellie's flat; Ellie would be at Hooper's till dawn. There would be hours to talk. And talk, honestly, was all either of them intended. Clare was accustomed to boys. She now realized she had met a man. The difference was devastating; all her defenses were blown away. He was at Balliol, for heaven's sake, and true to her flat-mate's prediction, he was on scholarship. That meant he was probably brilliant. But he credited *her* with intelligence, an attitude unprecedented in her experience. The questions he asked her in the taxi indicated he was more interested in getting into her mind than into her bra. Again, unprecedented.

By the time she turned the key in the lock of Ellie's flat, she was both elated and apprehensive almost beyond bearing. Never in her life had she been so desperate to attract a member of the opposite sex, and never had she been less confident of her chances. Clare was afraid he'd think she was a lightweight, a Debbie Debutante. She was afraid she'd say something stupid and he would revise his opinion of her intelligence. But more than anything else she was afraid he'd find out she was married and had had a baby.

She was not alone, either in her excitement or in her apprehension. Shailendra Tandulkar was finding it difficult to believe that this ravishing English rose could be as drawn to him as he was to her. His mother had always told him he was the handsomest young man she'd ever seen, but he had always assumed that that was what all mothers said to their sons as a matter of course. At Oxford the girls hadn't exactly flocked to him. His Balliol mates would try to set him up with their girlfriends' girlfriends, but their efforts had never yet led beyond initial dates into anything like a relationship. Sometimes he thought he was just too damn dark. Over in the States the civil rights movement was declaring "Black is Beautiful," and the young liberal ladies of the Oxford women's colleges gave enthusiastic lip service to this ideal. But after one or two dates they all just wanted to be friends. He knew, however, that he couldn't blame it all on covert racism. His best mates, splendidly color-blind, frequently accused him of being a dull stick. Shai sometimes suspected that he had as much sex appeal as a dictionary.

Dark-skinned, serious, and impatient of the frivolity that his peers spent their leisure time pursuing, he feared he was doomed to be lonely. He did not yet realize that Providence had presented to him a girl whose parents' genteel snobberies had spurred her to find the forbidden faces, the dark faces, attractive; and who had, furthermore, found no real or lasting satisfaction in the superficial (and only) lifestyle that had been offered to her. They looked like a ridiculous mismatch. They were made for each other.

That incredible truth had been stealing into both their brains for some time when he reached for the port bottle Clare had set out for him and poured himself a scant second glass. "You're sure you won't join me? Ginger ale's a bit puritanical once exams are over."

After a moment's consideration she agreed. "Just a finger," she cautioned, determined not to get tipsy, now that being sober had gotten so enjoyable.

He poured, set the bottle down on the table, and sat back in his chair. "I have a confession to make."

Her heart leapt. Something about her?

"I told you I saw intelligence in you. Oh,

by the way, this conversation has confirmed that opinion."

She was deliriously pleased, but murmured merely, "I'm glad."

"But that wasn't all," he continued. "I saw something else that made you different from all the rest of them. But I was afraid to tell you. I was afraid you'd run away."

"I won't run away."

"I know that now." He turned his glass slowly as though to study the ruby liquid in it.

Her mind urged, *Tell me!* But she said nothing. Knowing it would come, she waited for it. (He was right; she *was* different from the rest of them.)

Finally he looked up at her. "I saw pain."

Her eyes widened and her mouth opened, but still she remained silent and waited for him to say it in his own time.

"You've suffered," he said softly. "It shows in your eyes, but not everybody can see it. It takes someone else who has also suffered, I think."

And slowly, slowly, he began to tell her of his childhood. His parents had moved from India to Uganda before he was born. His father had been a pharmacist; he had owned his own shop. But he had become involved in some sort of underground political movement, native Ugandans who were working against Idi Amin. Shai told her about his growing childhood awareness that his mother was frightened. He told her more, he told her all of it, and as Clare sat motionless and listened to the horror, she understood that he was telling the full, ghastly story for the first time.

On the morning that his mother opened their front door to find her husband's right hand and testicles on the concrete step, she had controlled her hysterics, swooped up her young son, and carried him out the back door to their neighbor's house. Three days later they were in England. The neighbor, who was devoutly unpolitical, had done what he could to keep the shop going. From time to time he had sent them some money. They had survived.

Shai, who had told most of the story to his port glass, finally looked up. Clare was sitting across from him, still as stone, tears running silently down her face.

"I'm sorry. I've made you cry."

She shook her head. "No. That is, of course I'm crying for you. That was — I'm so — you've been —" She gave up, knowing there were no words to respond adequately to such a tale. "But I'm also crying for myself. Because now —" She faltered.

Like her, he waited for the words to come at their own pace. They came: "Now I have to tell you my story. Don't I?"

"Not if you don't want to."

She looked at him steadily and said, "That's not true."

He looked back. He nodded. "You're right. It's not true. You do have to tell me." But she knew he wasn't making a demand; he was acknowledging a reality that neither of them could challenge. Like gravity.

So she told him.

By the end, the dawn escape from Banner House, she could hardly speak for sobbing. He left his chair and went to sit beside her, holding and rocking her gently like the baby she had abandoned.

At last she stopped crying, blew her nose once more on the handkerchief he had given her, and braced herself for the terrifying task of looking him in the eye. "Do you think," she gulped, "that I am completely contemptible?"

He took her face between his hands and tried to tell her what he felt, but his shaking voice failed him. So he kissed her.

The kiss was an astonishment to both of them. The unexpected sweetness of the port they tasted on each other's lips was delicious. But it wasn't just that. Blue eyes met black ones. By one accord they closed in another kiss. Gentle like the first, it became hesitant, tremulous, as their lips parted and their tongues moved tentatively to touch each other. Soon it was no longer hesitant.

Five minutes later he broke from her with something like a cry.

"Clare!" he gasped. "Darling Clare! Wonderful woman! I will not do this to you. I will not take advantage of you like that stupid bastard did. You are magnificent, and you deserve better than this."

Since neither of them had anticipated more than the conversation, there had been no romantic dimming of the lights. She could see his face clearly. Gasping for much-needed breath, she stared at him in wonder.

Unwanted by her mother, undefended by her father, Clare had never seen love and strength in one person. She saw it now. The question of lust did not arise. She knew his desire for her was strong and terrible and would look at tempests and not be shaken. This gorgeous, intelligent man, so utterly unlike the bumbling, fumbling boys she had known, had in the space of three hours fallen as wildly in love with her as she had with him. He would not damage her, even though he wanted her with a desperation unmatched in her experience.

In the deep black eyes she saw herself crowned, enthroned. He would do anything she asked. Suddenly, she felt, for the first time in her life, full of power. It was dizzying, intoxicating; it was whole bottles of champagne, magnums of champagne. It was joy and delirium.

She smiled at him. "Silly man," she breathed, reaching for the pearl button at the most strategic point on her satin bodice. "You're not taking advantage of me. You're going to marry me and make me happy beyond my wildest dreams for the rest of my life."

In only one detail did she err. He did indeed make her happy beyond her wildest dreams, an achievement he reached there on the sofa in the following twenty minutes, then twice again in her bed before morning and for years to come, not just in bed but in everything. But it was only for the rest of *his* life.

CHAPTER 16

SUNDAY

Four Days After Rob Hillman's Death

Tom and Kathryn debated whether or not to brave the unwelcome attention of the press hounds at the Castle gates in order to attend worship at the village church; the possibility that they might attract even more attention once inside the church, remote English villages being what they were, turned the decision to a private Eucharist in the double-viewed parlor.

"It's bending the rules a bit," Kathryn admitted, "but I've had a bad week and I think God will forgive me."

Tom earned a smile and a brief hug by responding, "Sure She will."

Meanwhile Sir Gregory's doctor, undeterred by besieging media, arrived at the Castle and after a careful examination certified his patient fit to emerge from his room for supper that evening. As soon as the doctor had left the premises, the patient sent word to the kitchen that what was required was not supper but Dinner. The Baronet, having been tardy in greeting his guests, was determined to make up for it.

Leaving Mrs. Drundle in a happy panic, Crumper sought out the rest of the Family to deliver the news. As he opened the door to their favorite drawing room, he was troubled, though not surprised, to see Mr. Derek execute a nervous start.

And Miss Meg still looked as though she spent much of her time crying. Derek Banner got hold of himself and said, "Ah! Crumper! Only you!"

Affecting the convenient blindness of the perfect servant, Crumper passed on the news about Sir Gregory's health and about Dinner.

When he had left and closed the door behind him, Derek and Meg turned to each other.

"We must make an effort," she said, clearly not feeling like making any effort at all.

"Yes. We must," he replied, as unenthusiastic as she was. "We owe it to him."

"Yes."

Silence fell.

Meanwhile in Crumper's world, the next

item of business would have to be a discreet inquiry into the ability of the American visitors to Dress for Dinner. This British phrase signified more than the donning of clothes; the concern was: would the visitors have brought the *right* clothes? The right clothes being, for the man, a dinner jacket (the upper-class English term for what Americans call a tuxedo) and for the woman, something of equal formality.

Crumper found the visitors in what had been Rob Hillman's room. Miss Koerney was seated on the bed, clearly in somber mode, sorting small piles of clothing; Mr. Holder was watching her from a nearby chair.

Broaching the subject was not difficult; as soon as Crumper employed the word "dinner" Miss Koerney lifted her brows and said, "Ah! Are we dressing?"

"I do hope that would not be inconvenient?" Crumper replied, making it a question.

"Not for me. I was going to dine on High Table at Magdalen, and packed accordingly. But Tom . . ."

Before Tom had time to be embarrassed by either his ignorance or his wardrobe, Crumper interjected smoothly that a gentleman on holiday naturally does not take his dinner jacket, and that he, Crumper, would therefore be pleased to procure suitable attire for Mr. Holder (if Mr. Holder would pardon the liberty) which Mr. Holder would find in the closet of his room when he returned to it.

Mr. Holder expressed a slightly bemused thanks, Crumper withdrew, and Kathryn explained to Tom what had been going on. He expressed his willingness to play along, and Kathryn returned to the business of sorting out Rob's belongings while Tom administered sympathy as required.

Tom found himself looking forward to dinner as an invigorating challenge. After all, he had been in extravagantly wealthy homes often enough not to be intimidated. Admittedly, he was seldom in them as a guest. But Amalie Prescott had once invited the entire vestry to a drop-dead sit-down dinner that had gone, literally, from soup to nuts. He'd heard the expression all his life, but it wasn't until the end of the meal (which had begun with lobster bisque), when everything else was cleared away and the servants had set out the silver bowls of walnuts, Brazils, and macadamias, that he realized he was looking at that rare bird, the source of a proverbial phrase.

He'd gotten through that meal comfortably enough, and not just because he'd been among friends. He'd watched Miss Amalie to see which fork she was using, and he had twice made his ignorance the subject of jokes that had convulsed the people on either side of him. That success under his belt, he figured that he was ready for whatever number of pieces of flatware this baronet chose to throw at him.

Kathryn had tried to tell him something when they met in the hallway to go down to the dining room, but she'd been interrupted by a pretty housemaid who had come, on Crumper's orders, to show them the way. The housemaid acted as if she were dealing with the Bereaved, and Kathryn, obviously hating it, had chatted with the girl and made jokes about getting lost in the Castle until the air of solemnity crumbled under its own weight.

Tom gazed with avid interest at the Family Dining Room, heavily curtained against the still-light evening sky so that it might be transformed by candlelight and silver into something from another age, and at the room's owner, also quite deliberately presented as something from another age. Tom Holder, plain New Jersey cop, sat down in happy anticipation of a rare and enjoyable evening, and caught nary a glimpse of the blow that was soon to turn Mrs. Drundle's excellent food into ashes in his mouth.

It started when their host, frail but genial, had responded to Kathryn's enthusiasm at the sight of the first course, which was fresh asparagus, by telling her to wait until dessert and taste the raspberries; most of the fruit and vegetables consumed at Datchworth were grown on the estate. "Organically, these days, thanks to that young upstart Wales," Sir Gregory added, cheerfully taking advantage of that right which is commonly accorded to the elderly — that is, to say any outrageous thing they please.

Kathryn had instantly thrown a glance at Tom and explained, "Prince Charles is a famously keen organic farmer," and turned back to the Baronet.

Tom was grateful to her; she'd known he wouldn't have a clue who "Wales" was, and she had informed him in a way that made it sound like she was merely explaining a royal hobby to an American who might not have heard about it. He looked at her profile and thought, *God, she's marvelous.* He'd always known she was quick. But the sympathetic tact was new to him — possibly because there had never previously been a need for tact between them.

Sir Gregory was saying, "You should pay a visit to the home farm tomorrow morning, my dear; Derek will be pleased to take you. If you see something you fancy, only speak the word and we'll have it for lunch."

The object of Tom's admiration was responding to this offer with a courtesy slightly more elegant than he had seen her use before and which, he recognized, was perfectly appropriate to their surroundings. It was as though "Upper Class" was a language and she was fluent in it. He felt proud of her, which he knew was silly, but that knowledge didn't stop the feeling.

And then, within two minutes, everything was ruined. Kathryn had assumed a tone of apology; she was telling Sir Gregory that she wasn't going to be at Datchworth for lunch tomorrow. She had met someone on the train to Oxford a few days ago who'd told her to get in touch when she arrived at Datchworth, and she had done so on her mobile phone that afternoon.

"You know him, I believe," she said to the Baronet. "Kit Mallen?" At least it sounded to Tom like "Mallen." And it created a sensation.

"Oh, by Jove!" Sir Gregory exclaimed. "You've met Kit! That's wonderful. A jolly good chap, is Kit Mallowan."

But Derek was visibly not pleased. He attempted to make light of it, saying, "Damnation, prettiest girl" — he pronounced it *'gel'* — "this village has seen in years, and she's off to lunch with the competition." But what he was saying was too close to the truth, and the humor failed to hide his annoyance.

Derek's annoyance, however, was nothing to Tom's. This Kit person was obviously an attractive man of approximately Kathryn's age; if Kit was a friend of the people at the Castle, the odds were good that he was wealthy, too; and since castles and titles surely couldn't be all that thick on the ground, this Mallen fellow wasn't likely to be encumbered by them. Tom sensed danger, and looked at Kathryn. Danger became disaster.

She was blushing.

Bright pleasantries were bouncing around the table like billiard balls. Meg was telling Kathryn how sweet Kit was; Derek was ordering Meg whom he addressed as "Niece," to shut up; Sir Gregory laughed and assured Kathryn that Kit was one of the finest men he knew, then dared Derek to tell *him* to shut up.

As the others laughed, Tom forced a smile, but his stomach had gone leaden, recalling the horrible sinking sensation he'd had at the airport: this time there would be no miraculous reprieve, no request for his aid or his company; Kathryn was abandoning both to go off and have lunch with some rich Englishman.

He stared down at his untouched asparagus, lying in a pool of melted butter in an oval dish, and forgot to watch somebody to see which utensil to use. He picked up the fork which was farthest left and transferred it to his right hand.

"Oh, Tom!" she said.

He looked up.

"Every American should be warned about this," she said with a smile. "I made a complete mess of it when they served asparagus at a dinner at my college." She picked up one green spear with her fingers, muddled the end of it in the butter, leaned over her plate, and bit the tip off.

"Oh, yes, Tom," Derek agreed. "Contrary to what you may think, we're actually savages on this side of the pond. This vegetable, served thus as a first course, is eaten with the fingers."

Tom obediently put down his fork and

followed suit, asking what you did when you got down to the ones that were lying in the butter, you wouldn't be able to keep your fingers clean, and watched politely as Meg demonstrated. ("You plunge right in, get your fingers as buttery as you can, and on the last bite you do this." He watched, as incredibly, she actually put vegetable, butter, and fingertips into her mouth.) But all the while a dull pain grew in him which, he finally recognized, was anger. Kathryn already knew this stuff. She belonged in this kind of place, she was at home here. And she was instructing him in how to behave. He hated it.

Meanwhile, Crumper, unobtrusive as air, moved silently around the table, providing the kind of service that is so perfect, it goes unnoticed. The butler's mind was busy, however, with more than his allotted tasks. He was wondering which of the five people he was serving was having to work hardest to achieve the semblance of a carefree person at an uncomplicated social occasion. He was proud of the showing the Family was making. Sir Gregory seemed his old accustomed genial self; *making an effort for the sake of his visitors,* Crumper concluded. At the same time, the Baronet's niece and nephew had donned their best party faces; *making an effort for their uncle,* Crumper approved. The lady priest, also, was working hard. She made no mention of what had brought her to Datchworth, and appeared intent on being entertaining to her host. At the same time, she was keeping a careful eye on her friend, making sure he was staying afloat, but doing so with exquisite tact. The tact availed her nothing, however, once she had revealed her luncheon date for the next day. Crumper watched sadly as Mr. Holder, who had been the only person at the table not under a significant cloud, became as overcast as the rest of them, until he, too, needed to make an effort to appear more jovial than he actually was. Crumper was impressed with all of them, and only wished he could do something more helpful to them than wait table.

That wish was to be granted the following day.

At twelve-thirty on Monday, Tom was stationed at a window he had searched out that morning. It was at the end of a narrow hallway that seemed little used, and it overlooked the drive in front of the castle. He watched despondently as a vintage MG of a cheerful yellow pulled up to the front door and a very good-looking young man hopped out. Surprisingly, the man looked Indian or Pakistani — much too dark for an Englishman. Not that that mattered. He looked impossibly handsome, disgustingly rich, and obnoxiously young. He disappeared from Tom's view, presumably into the entrance hall. Tom kept his post. In a few minutes, the tall dark stranger reappeared, laughing and talking with Kathryn. They got into the car and drove off, Tom watching them out of sight.

Finally he turned away and proceeded back down the hallway in the direction of one of the broader corridors. Just before he reached it, Crumper walked past, and having caught sight of Tom, stopped, uttered a cordial greeting, and asked if there was any way in which he could be of service.

Tom started to say no, then changed his mind.

"Well," he said, "I guess you could tell me what sort of name 'Mallen' is."

Crumper replied placidly, "A very old one, sir. The Mallowan family has been in Oxfordshire nearly as long as the Thorpes."

"Then why does Kit Mallen look like he comes from Calcutta?"

"I beg your pardon, sir?" Crumper spoke

with as much surprise as he permitted himself to reveal while on duty.

"I was exploring, trying to learn my way around, you know," Tom overexplained, "and I was looking out a window down there" — he gestured — "and saw a little yellow sports car drive up. Guy got out, went into the Castle, came out with Kathryn, so I assume he's Kit Mallen, but he looks Indian. Or Pakistani, I can't tell the difference. What do I know? I'm from New Jersey."

The surprise had gone from Crumper's face. "A very natural conclusion, sir. But an Indian gentleman driving a yellow sports car would be one of the Tandulkar twins. Probably Mr. Harry Tandulkar, as the car is his, but it might be his brother Mr. William, who sometimes drives it. I imagine Mr. Tandulkar came to drive Miss Koerney to Morgan Mallowan for lunch."

Tom assumed Morgan Mallowan was a nearby village, which was a pity, because if he had asked about it, Crumper's answer would have relieved him of some of his misery.

Kathryn, meanwhile, who had hailed her driver as "Will" and been politely corrected, was marveling at God's bounty in having produced not one but two bronzed gods. As they drove, she began to observe the subtle differences in manner which distinguished this one from the one she'd met on the train, even as she enjoyed the soft sunshine and summer greenery of the countryside and wished that her hair was more suitable for riding in convertibles. *God, I'm going to be a mess before we get there,* she worried.

Harry, having thwarted the gaggle of reporters at the castle gates by slipping out of Datchworth by way of the home farm, was offering Kit's apologies. "He'd have come to fetch you himself, but his car is — what do you Americans say? In the store?"

"In the — ? Oh! In the shop!"

Harry complained that he had never been any good at foreign languages, and launched into the sad tale of his first date with an American girl at Oxford; he had gotten entirely the wrong view of the lady's character and intentions when she'd said she'd sat so long in the library that day that her fanny was numb and needed some exercise. (In Britain, "fanny" is a jaw-droppingly obscene slang term for "vagina.") Kathryn admitted that that was a pretty good one, but she didn't want to get bogged down in "divided by a common language" stories, so she asked Harry if he and Will shared a house.

"Not any more. I abandoned the house to Will when I married Dotty."

"But you and, ah, Dotty apparently didn't go far."

"Dotty didn't go anywhere at all. Will and I shared thc Tithe Barn, which is more or less in Kit's back garden, and Dotty already lived in the Dower House, which Kit gave her years ago, and I simply moved in with her there because she didn't want to leave it. I don't blame her; jolly nice house."

"Uh — Kit *gave* Dotty the Dower House?"

"Well, call it a lifetime loan."

"And, ah, Kit loaned Dotty the Dower House, ah, for some reason?"

Harry chuckled. "Well, we all roast him, claiming that he was just trying to halve the number of aunts he had to live with, but the truth is that Dotty is frightfully independent and didn't really want to be a permanent guest in her sister's house."

"Harry, I am hopelessly confused."

Harry allowed that Kathryn could hardly be expected to have the whole family sorted out after one train ride with Kit and Will. He began to lay out the various relationships and domiciles of the people they were going to be lunching with.

Kit, of course, lived in "the Big House." Kathryn had already assumed it must be fairly huge if it had a dower house and a tithe barn. She was feeling a little flutter of excitement. She had known Kit wasn't poor, but it was pleasant to discover that he was, apparently, out-of-the-ordinary rich.

Kit, Harry explained, had inherited from his Uncle Michael whose own son, Freddy, had died in a car crash in the seventies the summer before he was to go up to Oxford.

"Hang on! Would that be the same accident that killed Meg's uncle what's-his-name, not really her uncle?"

"Her cousin Jerry, Gerald Bebberidge-Thorpe, yes."

Harry continued. Kit's father, Michael's younger brother, became the heir at that point, but he had died of a heart attack before his older brother pegged out, so when Kit's Uncle Michael died it all went to Kit. The plan then was that Kit and his widowed mother, who had been living in the Dower House, would move up to the Big House, and Kit's widowed Auntie Fiona would retire gracefully to the Dower House.

Any fool could see, however, that Auntie

Fiona regarded the impending exchange about as cheerfully as if it were her funeral, and in the end, Kit's mother ("a marshmallow, would rather give in than fight, rather like Kit, actually") had announced she was tired of the country anyway, and had taken a flat in London. Which left Kit in the Big House with Auntie Fiona and Aunt Dotty.

"*Aunt* Dotty?"

"Yes," Harry replied with a grin. "I am married to Kit's aunt. But it's not like it sounds; Dotty came as a big surprise to her parents. She was born twenty-odd years after her brothers were, so I am married not to an old woman but to an extremely attractive young one."

Kathryn laughed and offered him her congratulations.

Harry responded with thanks, slowed the car, and put on the turn signal.

They turned off the modest two-lane road they'd been traveling and into a positively self-effacing single-lane track on which the asphalt quickly gave way to dirt.

"Do tell me this is the back way," said Kathryn, ducking as the branch of an overhanging tree whacked the corner of Harry's windshield before taking a swipe at her face.

"I say, I am sorry, I didn't know the greenery had gotten quite so —"

"Aggressive?"

"Overgrown. It is the back way, in fact, or at least the side way, but there's a fabulous view up ahead and I thought you'd like to see it. We've got the time; we're a few minutes early."

The greenery drew back, an open space appeared, and Harry pulled the little car off of the road onto a level stretch of grass.

"Hop out," he commanded. "It's just through here." He indicated a path that disappeared between two large bushes.

Together they picked their way through the exuberant undergrowth, Harry explaining that this was the spot from which all the postcard pictures were taken of the house. Before they had invented helicopters, that is.

Kathryn rounded a dense copse of pale green branches to find herself at the brow of a hill. Below her the ground fell away in endless furlongs of summer grass, and on this huge emerald cushion rested, about a mile away, a vast Tudor palace of mellow pink brick surmounted by a hundred ornamental chimneys.

Kathryn's jaw fell open so far she looked like a rather pretty fish. Her eyes ran over the acres of rosy walls, the mullioned windows, the courtyards and quadrangles, and she thought that she must be looking at the most beautiful house in the world. Then something in her mind clicked and she recognized it. Of course it was the most beautiful house in the world. She had thought so for years; she had twice visited it as a tourist; the picture of it in a book of English stately homes had made her an Anglophile when she was a teenager sitting in her high school library. She laughed.

"What's funny?"

"This is Morgan Mallowan!"

"And?"

"Oh, it's just me being confused again. I thought you were going to show me Kit's house."

"This *is* Kit's house."

Kathryn gaped at Harry, then back at the Tudor palace, then back at Harry again. "But Morgan Mallowan belongs to the Mallowans."

"Oh, didn't anybody explain? The family name is pronounced 'Mallen,' but it's spelled just like the house. The house has kept all three syllables, but the family has been abbreviated to two. Over the years, you know. We English do that sort of thing." He was puzzled because Kathryn's astonishment did not look like the happy kind.

"So Kit 'Mallen' is actually Kit M-a-l-l-o-w-a-n, and he *owns* Morgan Mallowan?" Kathryn had shut her eyes and was reciting this information dully, as though determined to know the full sum of the damage.

"Ah, yes. You don't seem pleased."

"I thought," Kathryn replied carefully, ignoring the implied question, "that the Mallowan family were the Marquises of Wallwood."

Harry was impressed that Kathryn knew how to pronounce the plural of "marquis" in English, but he corrected her again.

"Yes, except that the village is pronounced 'Wallwood' but the family title, though spelled the same way, is pronounced 'Wallud.' And obviously Kit didn't tell you, so I probably wasn't supposed to, but nobody briefed me." He sounded slightly cross.

Kathryn, in dire need of a place to sit down, looked around and saw a well-weathered bench placed to take advantage of the view. She went to it, sat, put her elbows on her knees and her face in her hands, and began to say the word "shit" over and over again, quietly and without emphasis, like a mantra.

Harry sat on the other end of the bench. "I expect Kit didn't tell you because — well, he's always complaining he can never be sure a woman's not interested in him just for the title."

Kathryn's scatological mantra faded into silence. She sat up and sighed. "Well, he's just found a woman who's not interested in him *precisely because* of the title. And the house." She gestured at it. "World's most beautiful prison."

"You Americans," Harry declared, firmly, "are mad."

Kathryn didn't feel like discussing it, so she simply rose from the bench and headed back toward the car, saying, "Well, we might as well be on our way."

It wasn't until they were pulling up at a side door of the house ("Family entrance," Harry said) that an inconsistency struck her.

"You said Kit's car was in the shop."

"Yes. Will was going to fetch you but there was some crisis on the home farm and I was summoned on short notice to fill in. I expect that was why I wasn't properly briefed. About the title and such."

"But what's this rubbish about Kit's car being out of whack? There must be a fleet of cars here!"

"Oh, of course. But Kit's only had one of them altered."

"Altered?"

"So he can drive it. He's left all the others normal, so the rest of us can use them. He ought to have a spare — silly git. We keep telling him so."

Kathryn was so busy digesting this that when Harry set the brake on the MG, she did not immediately make a move to get out of the car. He came around to her side to open the door for her, but she put up a hand to stop him and asked him if he would send Kit out to talk to her.

Harry, now convinced that she was seriously odd, did as she asked.

Kathryn sat still in the car, staring through the windshield but thinking too hard to notice what was in front of her eyes. Her mind had gone back to the encounter on the train. Will had stood in the doorway of their compartment to invite her to come back and join them. Even though it was Kit, surely, who was more interested in her. And Will had risen to tell her good-bye at Oxford. But Kit hadn't. She had never seen him stand.

CHAPTER 17

MID JULY 1997

Two Weeks Before Rob Hillman's Death

Derek was tracing invisible spirals with the tip of his finger on Crumpet's incredible breasts: first the left breast, then the right; first a leisurely, ever increasing circle from the aureole outward and downward, then reversing direction, still slow, around and upward to the nipple, which he would greet with a gentle tap before moving his hand back to the other breast and starting the entire process over again.

The nipples weren't responding with any particular enthusiasm, since every cell in Crumpet's body capable of sexual response was well and truly exhausted. Derek had seen to that.

Crumpet was easier after sex than most of the other women Derek had known. Other women wanted you to talk; they wanted endearments and compliments, some indication that what had gone before was something more than simply the gratification of animal urges. But Crumpet, never all that verbal in the first place, was satisfied if you merely maintained some languid physical homage to her fabulous form. This Derek was more than willing to do; it was a small recompense for the pleasures that had gone before.

For Crumpet was brilliant in the sack, that was certain. Too bad she had the intellect of a Barbie Doll and the morals of a harlot. Derek knew that nearly any man of his class, upbringing, and education, assuming he had ready access to several presentable females (who were not at all bad in bed), would have turned his nose up at Crumpet's vulgar charms. Of course, if the bloke in question were unattached and even slightly randy, he would jump on Crumpet quick as a ferret; but then he would get up, zip his fly, and go looking for someone he wasn't afraid to be seen in public with.

Derek had never, since puberty, been short of presentable women. He was good-looking — reasonably so or remarkably so, depending upon how any given woman responded to his dark, Mediterranean looks. He was also the only son and heir of a fabulously wealthy man, and for good measure there was also the "Sir." It wasn't his yet, of course, and as he was genuinely fond of his uncle Gregory he sincerely hoped it wouldn't be his for a good many years to come. But ever since his cousin Jerry, Sir Gregory's only child, had gotten himself stupidly killed along with Freddy Mallowan, Derek had been the heir to one of the oldest and crustiest baronetcies in the kingdom.

So there had always been girls. Some of them had been pretty bloody marvelous, too, and a few of them, Derek believed, had actually fancied him for himself rather than the money and the status.

But he had come nowhere near selecting the future Mrs. Banner, and meanwhile there was always Crumpet. It wasn't simply that she had the sexiest body this side of a centerfold and that she was such an easy lay as to be a foregone conclusion; he actually enjoyed her blatant, tasteless presentation of herself. Perhaps it was the Italian in him; perhaps old Rufus Banner's lively Neapolitan bride had bequeathed to her grandson some appreciation of unapologetic sensuality, of unembarrassed love of pleasure.

Derek's hand (the one that had been appreciating Crumpet's delicious bosom) slid down until it lay flat on her abdomen. Then he moved it back and forth in tiny rapid movements, rippling the flesh. Crumpet giggled and tried to slap his hand, but he snatched it back and she struck her own belly with a resounding *whap*.

"Oooo, yer a bastard, you are!" she squeaked.

"Just making sure you were awake, dearest Crumpet. Got anything new for me?"

He always waited until after they had sex before he asked. Before the sex she couldn't think about anything else, and besides, Derek didn't want her to get the notion that he was more interested in the information than he was in her.

"Well, if you must know, he's found a fragment."

"A what?"

"A fragment. That's what he said. That's a piece of something, isn't it?"

"Indeed it is, my girl. Did he tell you by any chance what sort of a fragment? I mean, a fragment of what?"

"Some old book. Do books fall to bits, then, when they get old?"

"If they're not taken proper care of. What sort of a book, did he say?"

"Yeah, and I listened really good so I could tell you. Who's a clever girl, then?"

"You are, my sweet," Derek replied obligingly, and kissed her cheek. "So: a fragment from — ?"

"A prayer book. *BORE*-ing! But he said it was valuable."

"How valuable?"

"He wasn't sure. So he was going to ask some old fart he knew in Oxford."

Derek kissed her again and muttered a few appropriate inanities into her hair, but he was thinking about what she'd said. Rob Hillman left Datchworth every weekend to go back to his flat in Oxford. He was probably there now — if he wasn't having tea with the old fart and picking his brains. Derek decided he'd better drive out to Datchworth on Monday evening to have supper with his uncle; by then there might be some more specific information to pick up.

The thought of his uncle brought a twinge of guilt. It sometimes felt like he was plotting against the old man, which of course he would never do. Not *against* him. Not really. It was all for the good of Datchworth, after all, and Derek knew that nothing was closer to Sir Gregory's heart.

Of course Uncle Gregory held Brasenose

in affection, and would enjoy doing something special for the college. Derek felt the same way. As did Meg, in all probability. The whole family has been Nosemen — Meg always said "Nosepeople," but not seriously — for generations. Almost as long as the Mallowans.

But Uncle Gregory was getting most appallingly feeble, and although there was as yet no sign that the weakness in his body had crept into his brain, Derek worried that the old man's judgment, when it came right down to it, might not be as level-headed as it once would have been. Brasenose or Datchworth? Derek could not be dead certain that his uncle would make the right choice.

The problem was that Uncle Gregory seemed to think that Datchworth didn't really need any money; after all, Derek was now the heir and he would bring with him the Banner millions. Derek, being a conservatively reared Englishman, could not bring himself to say to his uncle what he feared. True, John Banner was a lot older than Sir Gregory, and the Alzheimer's made him seem older yet, but the brute fact was that Alzheimer's wasted the brain, not the body, and his father, Derek reflected with mixed feelings, might last for another decade. Dear Uncle Gregory, alas, almost certainly would not.

And that would leave Derek in charge of an estate which was as financially precarious as most of the other ancient estates in the country, with no more Banner money to back him up than the sum his father had settled upon him on the occasion of his twenty-first birthday.

And so he had begun his little game. Crumpet had been easy to recruit, and appeared to be playing her part pretty well. So far it had been innocent enough. But the guilt still niggled at him.

Meanwhile, the gentleman whom Crumpet had stigmatized as an old fart, and who was in fact one of the most agreeable human beings ever to be made a full professor at Oxford, was literally rubbing his hands with delight.

"Oh, just look at you! Aren't you a pretty little thing?"

Rob Hillman was not discomfited by these exclamations, as he knew they were addressed not to him but to the fragment of parchment he had brought for the professor to examine.

"Where's my glass? I know it's somewhere in the chaos here." The professor began to rummage among the papers on his desk, but fortunately Rob spotted the magnifying glass protruding — just barely — from under a notebook on a nearby chair.

"Here you are, Professor."

"What? Ah, brilliant! I should wear the bloody thing around my neck, shouldn't I? Now let's have a better look . . ." He bent over the illuminated capital.

He exclaimed, as Rob had earlier, over the angels holding up the cloud; he admired the color in the Virgin's cheeks, and the intricacies of her lacy halo; he blessed the hand that had preserved her safe from Cromwell; he congratulated Mr. Hillman upon discovering her.

Rob, pleased that his offering had made a hit, sipped his tea and enjoyed the professor's enjoyment; his former tutor's unbridled enthusiasm for manuscripts had figured largely in Rob's decision to specialize in paleography.

When the older man finally calmed down sufficiently to sit, he happily discussed with Rob the probable age and provenance of the fragment, and made suggestions regarding how it might best be preserved and displayed. He was also useful in answering one of Rob's most important questions.

"For insurance purposes? I'd say, oh —" he leaned closely over the brightly painted square, squinting through the magnifying glass. "Couple of thousand. The work's pretty fine, though I've seen better, and so have you. But the angels holding the cloud, as you say . . . yes, a couple of thousand."

At four-thirty Rob took his leave, thanking his former tutor and wishing him a good trip to Denmark, whither the professor was bound the following week. Passing through the outlandish decorative brick facades of Keeble, Rob emerged from the college and began to walk back toward the center of town. He was bound for the specialist framers to whom the professor had directed him; he could just make it before they closed, he thought. He would leave the parchment with them, and they could write to Sir Gregory with a quotation on the cost of having it mounted.

Rob looked forward to taking the tiny treasure, properly framed, back to Datchworth. Of course Sir Gregory had already seen it; Rob had shown it to him at supper the day he'd found it. But the person Rob really wanted to show it to was Kit. Kit had the near-blasphemous sense of humor that is the identifying mark of the well-educated high-church Anglican; Kit would appreciate those angels better than any of the Datchworth family. Rob would take the fragment over to Morgan Mallowan as soon as he could.

Rob had liked Kit from the moment they'd met at Sir Gregory's dinner table. Kit's intensity, his good humor, his command of the English language and his Jane Austen syntax, reminded Rob strongly of his cousin Kathryn.

Hey, there was an idea! Why hadn't he thought of it before? Kit needed to meet a woman who was, as he himself put it, "impervious to both of the beasts." Rob knew that Kit's "Greater Beast" — the house and the title — would not tempt Kathryn. And the "Lesser Beast" would not deter her. Rob decided that when Kathryn came over to England in a couple of weeks, he really ought to introduce her to Kit.

Not far away, in Crumpet's tidy little flat, Derek was getting dressed when the phone rang. Crumpet picked it up and said, "Hullo, Mum." Mrs. Crumper always rang her daughter on Saturday afternoons after tea.

"Hullo, Julie. How're you getting on?" Mrs. Crumper, understandably, never called her daughter by her nickname.

They chatted in a familial, unexcited way; there was not much news to exchange, as Crumpet had been at Datchworth only a couple of days previously. Derek, when he was ready to leave, stole softly over to the bed and silently kissed Crumpet's still naked shoulder before tiptoeing discreetly to the door. Crumpet fluttered her fingers at him in a farewell wave, but did not break the placid rhythm of the conversation with her mother.

But mothers are hard to deceive. When Martha Crumper hung up the phone ten minutes later, she shook her head and said to her husband, "She wasn't alone."

"She's never alone," Crumper replied, trying to keep the judgment and the disappointment out of his voice. "Let's just hope it was somebody other than a certain Mr. Banner."

"There you go again, Crump. I don't see why you object to our Julie making friends with the Family. Times have changed!"

"Changing times have nothing to do with it. I object for the same reason any father would. The man in question is using my daughter for — well, for diversion. Unless —" Crumper sighed. "Unless she's using *him* for diversion. I suppose it could be that way."

"You don't think anything could ever come of it, then?"

"My God, Martha! Derek Banner, marry a woman he calls Crumpet? Besides, my dear, do you really think Julie would enjoy being the mistress of Datchworth Castle?"

It was apparent from Martha's arrested expression that this view of the matter had never occurred to her. She pondered it awhile and said finally, "Well, Crump, perhaps you're right."

"My dear!" Crumper exclaimed, as though shocked at her uncertainty. "I am always right!"

"What you always are, Jim Crumper, is mighty full of yourself!" she replied. But she had to turn away to hide a smile.

CHAPTER 18

SPRING 1972

Twenty-five Years Before Rob Hillman's Death

They didn't want to take him. He was only eight years old, the proverbial pesky little brother. They were the Dynamic Duo, their sights confidently set on Oxford the coming autumn. They were Damon and Pythias, David and Jonathan, complete and content in each other's company. What use did they have for a skinny little freckle-faced brat like him? But he had insisted, he had begged, he had nagged, cajoled, and whined. He had, in fact, been a right royal pain in the arse. And even pain-in-the-arsery hadn't swung it for him; they would still have left him behind, if he hadn't in the end resorted to blackmail.

Sometimes, afterward, he blamed Jerry. After all, Jerry had been the oldest, and should have known better. Should have acted with some modicum of judgment, instead of egging Freddy on. In fact, Kit sometimes suspected that the whole thing had been Jerry's idea in the first place. Would Freddy, left to his own devices, have had the vision, the audacity, the — not to put too fine a point on it — the *balls* to have even thought of taking the Duesenberg without permission? Almost certainly not. But Jerry! It was just the sort of thing he'd come up with. Of course, Kit hadn't seen that at the time, being only eight, but looking back on it in later years, remembering the Gruesome Twosome, he had gradually become certain that it had been Gerald Bebberidge-Thorpe who had instigated that tragic escapade.

But most of the time Kit, in company with the vast majority of the rest of the neighborhood, had blamed Freddy. After all, the buck stopped (to use Kit's favorite American phrase) with the person behind the wheel, and that person had unquestionably been his cousin Fred. The fact that Freddy was new behind the wheel — in fact, they'd been celebrating his getting his driving license — mitigated the blame a bit, but by no means wiped it out entirely. "If you're old enough to drive," Freddy's dad had told him repeatedly, "you're old enough to drive responsibly." They had neither of them appreciated the aphorisms that their fathers had droned at them. Both

Kit's father and his Uncle Michael, brothers in character as well as in blood, had been famous in the family for those little pearls of common sense, recited too often and far too sententiously to appeal to growing lads. But the sayings had lodged in Kit's mind like burrs, and he had the horrid fear that in years to come he would be boring his own children with them. (If he had any children. If he ever found a woman as unmoved by the wheels as by the title, and vice versa.)

Old enough to drive. Old enough to drive responsibly. Freddy, apparently, had been neither. Just old enough to figure out that the time to filch the keys to the Duesy was when Jackson went into the servants' hall for his lunch. When it came to the cars he drove and cared for, Jackson's proprietary zeal and his entirely predictable reaction, should any of those precious vehicles be commandeered by unauthorized teenagers, made their fathers look like puddings by comparison. Provided they brought the Speedster back unscathed, the worst consequence of their dads finding out about the joyride would be a tedious enumeration of all the evils that *might* have befallen them, liberally decorated with statements like "Privilege comes with responsibility; you cannot take one without accepting the other." Jackson, on the other hand, would reduce them to jelly with a torrent of high-decibel rage that would be nonetheless terrifying for being couched in such colloquial rural obscenities as to be incomprehensible.

So the keys had been stealthily lifted from hook number three as the chauffeur in happy ignorance tucked into his celery soup.

"You, Christopher!" the older boys had hissed at him. "Christopher" because they were furious with him; Kit had threatened to grass on them if they didn't take him along. "You sit in the rumble," they commanded witheringly. Thus they exiled him from the grown-up fellowship of the front seat. It was the worst revenge they could wreak upon him. And, of course, it had saved his life.

At first Kit had sulked. Might as well have been left behind after all, stuck way back there where he couldn't even hear over the rattle of the engine what they were saying to each other in front. But after puttering cautiously down to the bend that took them around the first hill and out of sight of the house, Freddy had put his foot to the floor, and they jolted excitingly over the early spring ruts in the drive at a speed Kit's Uncle Michael had never taken the Duesenberg. Or at least not with Kit in the car.

Before too long the bone-juddering ride produced a bounce that lifted Kit clear off the seat, and he let out a whoop of glee. It didn't matter if he couldn't hear the bright chatter of the eighteen-year-olds up front; Jerry and Fred looked like they were laughing more than talking anyway. Kit was laughing, too, as the car burst out of the main gate, slithered through a giant puddle, and took off down the road toward the village.

They never got there. Kit was sure of that much, although he could not later have said with any certainty how many minutes, how many miles, they bounced and jounced and laughed before it ended.

Sometimes — less often, these days — Kit tried to recall what he had seen. But the messages delivered by his eyes were a wild confusion, imperfectly grasped at the time, and more imperfectly remembered. He was reasonably sure that at one point he had seen the sky between his feet. He did not recollect seeing any blood.

But his ears had recorded the event with an awful clarity that even now found its way into his dreams. He had experienced no physical pain, yet the noise was a vicious assault. First, loud over the motor, Jerry shouting, brakes squealing. Then a violent metallic explosion: metal colliding with metal, screeching across metal, crumpling against metal. Things crashed and banged and crunched. Glass shattered.

There was the sky again, but Kit could no longer see his feet. Something round and hard and enormous had attached itself to the small of his back. He remembered clearly that it didn't actually hurt. The only thing that distressed him was the screaming, the terrible, terrified screaming that went on and unrelentingly on after all the other noises had given way to stillness, the soul-searing screams that made him wish more strongly than he had ever wished for anything else, that someone would go to the person who was screaming and somehow render them a comfort huge enough to make them be quiet. It seemed like ages before he realized that the person screaming was himself.

CHAPTER 19

MONDAY LUNCHTIME

Five Days After Rob Hillman's Death

Kit had heard the MG drive up, and he was in the hallway waiting — nervously — when Harry came through the door.

"I say, Kit, she's waiting in the car. Says she wants to have a word with you before she comes in."

"Damn. That doesn't augur well."

"I'm afraid I let the cat out of the bag. You should have warned me she didn't know."

"Which cat?"

"The title. The house."

"Ah. Did you tell her about the chair?"

"For Christ's sake, Kit! She doesn't know about the chair, either? Wait. Come to think of it, she knows now. I said enough for her to figure it out. I can't believe you didn't tell her *any*thing. What's got into you?"

"Hope," said the seventh Marquis of Wallwood. But he didn't sound very hopeful. Harry rolled his eyes heavenward but made no reply other than to hold the door open and gesture for Kit to go out.

Kathryn turned her head to look at Kit as he approached. She could have used more time to gather her scattered thoughts and get hold of her rampaging emotions. *A week,* she thought, *might have sufficed.*

Here he came. He was wearing blue again. The sun caught his red-gold hair. His freckled face looked anxious. Apprehensive. She had been looking forward to exploding at him, to hitting him with her rage as if it were a club. She couldn't do it. It wasn't the sight of the wheelchair that dissipated her anger; she had deduced the presence of the chair before it appeared. What stirred her sudden compassion was the look on his face. How could anyone injure a person so nakedly vulnerable? And he was still the most overwhelmingly attractive man she had ever seen.

"I'm sorry," he said simply. "I should have told you."

"I can see," Kathryn replied in a carefully even tone, "that the temptation not to tell me would have been . . . irresistible. And backed by very sound reasons."

"You are being more understanding than I deserve."

She gave him a long, long look. Unlike Sir Gregory, he propelled his wheelchair with his arms rather than let a motor do the work for him; he appeared to do so effortlessly. She thought his arms must be very strong.

Sitting in the small, open car, she was almost exactly on a level with him. "Don't be too hard on yourself," she said. "If I were in your position, I'm reasonably sure I would jump at the chance to get acquainted with someone without their knowing. It would be very difficult for anyone to try to filter all that" — she waved a hand past him — "out of their response to you."

"Not so much difficult as impossible. I doubt if anyone's ever succeeded."

"And then one day, there I was, there you were, strangers on a train."

"You do understand. But you're still angry. Aren't you?"

"I am trying hard not to shake with fury." She knew instantly that it had been a mistake to say this; it was too honest, and her voice did indeed begin to shake.

Kit was horrified. "Is it that bad?" he managed to ask.

Kathryn began to cry, although she made Herculean efforts not to, although she knew in some dispassionate corner at the back of her mind that she wouldn't be falling apart like this if she had not already been devastated by the death of her cousin. She burst out, "This is stupid! Stupid! I shouldn't care this much! But I liked you, I liked you more than I'd ever . . ." She faltered and covered her face with her hands.

Kit heard the past tense: "liked." As if there could be no hope, now that she knew. He would not believe it. He refused to accept it. With a quick movement he brought his wheelchair alongside the car and laid an unsteady hand on her shoulder. "Kathryn, please. Please don't write me off. It's not as bad as you think. I get around very well. I go to London, I drive my own car, I, well, I'm not sure how to put this politely, but I can *function*. I, um, look forward to being a father. It's just my legs that are useless."

She lifted her face and stared at him. They were both flushed, she from crying, he from embarrassment. His face was so red, she could hardly see his freckles.

"You're talking about the wheelchair," she said in astonishment.

This is turn astonished him. "Why, what else — ?"

At that point Kathryn did explode. "Who the hell gives a flying" — here she used a word that surfaced in her vocabulary very rarely — "about the bloody wheelchair?"

His jaw dropped, and he had to regain control of it in order to say, "Most of the women of my acquaintance. Are you telling me you don't?"

"Oh, for God's sake!" Kathryn cried in disgust. "*All* the women you know can't be idiots! The measure of a man is his mind, not his legs. Surely it doesn't take a genius to see that?"

Kit exhaled a long breath. "No," he said. "Not a genius. But a very unusual woman. If you don't object to the chair, why are you talking about this relationship as if it were dead before it ever got started?"

"You honestly don't know? You must be aware that to anyone with a sensible set of values, the house — and the rest of it, the estate, the title, the position — is a much more serious encumbrance than a wheel-chair."

Will you marry me? Kit had to clamp his mouth shut to keep the words from popping out. What he did permit himself to say, softly, was "Thank you, God."

Kathryn could not pretend that she

didn't understand. She smiled — a bit wearily — at the compliment, but shook her head stubbornly. "Don't go thanking God yet. You have no idea of the strength of my objection to your real encumbrance."

"What's the worst part of it? The title? The money?"

She waved a dismissive hand at him. "Money's not a problem. I have money myself. Though not, it is becoming increasingly obvious to me, nearly as much as you have. But my money is — how shall I say this? — loose. I could give it all away tomorrow if I felt like it. You couldn't do that with yours."

"That's right. I need it to maintain the house. And the estate."

"Which means I'm free. And you're not."

Kit studied her a moment. "How free are you, really?" he challenged.

"What do you mean?"

"You say you could give it all away tomorrow if you felt like it. Why don't you?"

"Because I enjoy it."

"What about, 'Sell all you have, give it to the poor, take up your cross and follow me'?"

Kathryn winced slightly. After a moment

she began thoughtfully to rub her nose.

Kit ventured a little smile. "Have I hit a nerve?"

Kathryn sighed. "Oh, boy, have you. I get along most of the time by ignoring that verse."

"And you a priest! I'm shocked!"

It was back; she felt it again, just as she had on the train: the vitality, the humor, the energy that hummed through him like an electric current, that danced in his eyes and tickled the edge of his mouth and charged the air between them.

She looked at him, at the red hair, the blue eyes, the freckles, the mouth that quivered as it pretended not to smile. She began to think — she began to fear — that she had met her match.

Lunch at Morgan Mallowan was a little late that day, since it took the guest of honor a while to rearrange her face and her hair to the point where both were ready to present to strangers.

At Datchworth, however, lunch was served precisely on schedule, and the food was excellent as always. Aside from those two points, it was a disaster.

Crumper had come to that conclusion early in the meal, as he moved around the table invisibly providing all that was needed. Miss Meg, to judge by her appearance only, was feeling marginally better; her eyes were less red and puffy, and she was getting a bit of her color back. She seemed dull, however, and disinclined to talk. Mr. Banner, on the other hand, was talking too much, trying to hide his nervousness and only succeeding in making it more obvious. Mr. Banner had a severe case of fidgety hands; his fingers toyed with the flatware, rubbed at nonexistent spots on the glasses, and moved from his napkin to his tie to his hair and back again. And when Miss Meg dropped her salad fork on the edge of her plate, he jumped.

Worst of the three, however, was the American guest, who had the look of a man who had just attended the multiple funeral of everyone he loved. Mr. Holder had good manners, and he was trying hard; he made responses of a general and innocuous nature to Mr. Banner's edgy chatter; he asked a few polite questions of Miss Meg perhaps in an attempt to draw her out; but his heart was not in it. Crumper knew why.

Finally the meal was over. Those who had lunched rose from the table, thanked those who had served, exchanged temporary farewells, and began to go their separate ways. Crumper had come to a decision. There was nothing he could do for the Family. So he waited a well-judged moment, then set off in stately pursuit of the melancholy guest.

Tom had gotten as far as the entrance hall; there he had come to a halt and stood, no more dynamic than a figure in wax, staring out the open front door onto the gravel of Sir Gregory's drive. The gravel was white and winked in the sun.

"Ah, yes," said Crumper quietly, pretending to read thoughts he knew that Holder was not having. "It is a lovely day, isn't it? Much too nice to stay indoors."

Tom had started at the butler's unexpected voice, but he recovered enough to utter some vague agreement.

Crumper rolled on. "When I'm free after lunch, as I am today, I sometimes like to go for a spin, particularly in this sort of weather. I thought today I might pop over to Morgan Mallowan in the old Rolls-Royce and see if Miss Koerney would like a ride back to Datchworth. If you don't think it too presumptuous of me to ask, would you like to join me?"

Sir Gregory would have been shocked into an early grave to hear his butler being so familiar with his guests, but then he didn't really know his butler. Crumper was two people. One was the perfect servant, stepping miraculously out of another century to attend to the needs of a gentleman of the old school, in the manner to which that gentleman had been accustomed in his youth.

The other Crumper was a real live human being with a job he enjoyed, a good sense of the ridiculous, and an impressive ability to read people. This last quality was telling him that the American bloke didn't need a butler, he needed a friend. And since Jim Crumper's qualities also included a kind heart, he was doing something unusual, though not quite unprecedented. He was stepping out of character.

Tom was not at all affronted, but he was very surprised. He was also tempted. "Why, thanks, Crumper. I don't know, though . . . does she *need* a ride home?"

"I don't really know; but the Tandulkar lads might be busy about the farm, they usually are on a summer's day; and His Lordship's car is in Oxford for repairs and he doesn't really like to call upon Her Ladyship's chauffeur."

"I got the first bit all right, but who are this lord and ladyship?"

Damn, thought Crumper. *He doesn't know. This is going to make it worse, not better.* Reluctantly he answered, "The gentleman who is called Kit by his friends is Christopher Mallowen, Lord Wallwood. His aunt, the dowager marchioness Lady Wallwood, also lives at Morgan Mallowan."

This information did not seem to distress Mr. Holder. Mr. Holder, in fact, was jubilant. Once again Providence had flipped his life like a coin. "Yes!" he cried, pumping the air with his fist. He laughed, "She doesn't know that. I *know* she doesn't know that." He thought a moment and grinned. "But I guess she knows it now!"

Upon Crumper an unlikely light dawned. "Does Miss Koerney have an aversion to the nobility?"

"Don't know, but she sure as hell has an aversion to *being* one." Tom was still grinning. "My name is Tom, by the way."

The butler grinned back. "Mine is Jim, but I prefer Crump."

"Well, Crump, old buddy, let's go for a ride."

Down the hall in the parlor set aside for the police the mood was considerably less merry. Chief Inspector Lamp had come to

Datchworth to assure the Family that everything possible was being done to solve this tragic affair and that progress was being made; he had then gathered his colleagues together and asked them why nobody was doing anything and nothing had been accomplished.

Detective Inspector Griffin was understandably defensive; a great deal, he assured his superior, was being done. The residents and staff of the Castle had been repeatedly questioned. Teams were working in Oxford gathering information on Rob Hillman, Derek Banner, Meg Daventry, and even Julie Crumper, the butler's daughter, who lived in Oxford, slept frequently with Derek, was in the Castle on the afternoon in question, and was one of the eight people who could not be ruled out as to opportunity.

"And aside from the fact that the heir is banging one of the serfs, you have discovered what?"

"The victim was a homosexual," announced Griffin, proud of himself.

Lamp's eyebrows rose. "And?"

"Beg your pardon, sir?"

"Does he like rough trade? Has there been a lover's quarrel?"

"Uh, not that we've been able to discover, sir. You'll remember I told Sharkar and Preston to go back to a don at Brasenose College called Chris Foley, because Hillman's emails made it clear there was a sexual attraction there, at least at first, then later it supposedly settled down into just being friends. Well, guess what? Chris Foley is a man. He admits to being Hillman's lover last autumn, but he claims that, quote, 'the flames died down' before Christmas, and since then, well, sir, this is the exact quote." Griffin flipped open a small notebook and read: "We were wonderful friends, wonderful. But the dear boy *would* sit home by the fire and I *must* have the night life or I shrivel up and die, do you understand? Just *die*. So we decided to kiss and part. All very amicable, I assure you."

"And you have found evidence to the contrary?"

"No, sir. Friends of Foley's, other homosexuals, back him up, but then they would. But also people at the college confirm that Hillman and Foley were great mates, sat together at most meals, always laughing, they say. No sign of any quarrel. And I have to say that Foley seemed pretty straightforward," Griffin admitted, unaware of the pun. "Very upset, didn't seem to be hiding anything."

"Alibi?"

"Practicing with the Bach Choir. About a hundred witnesses. Airtight."

"And of course you asked Foley and all his, ah, homosexual friends, if Hillman had found a new love interest in the last six months?" There was a slight ironic emphasis on "homosexual" but it sailed right past Griffin.

"Of course, sir. Nobody admitted to knowing about one."

"So in short, you burrowed down this promising rabbit hole and found not a bleedin' thing of any relevance to the case, am I right?"

"Uh, yes sir."

"Griffin," said Lamp with a sigh. "Let me tell you something; it may be useful to you in the future. A great many gay people have amazingly dull personal lives. Try to keep your lurid imagination under control."

Since Lamp's further questions elicited the information that apart from the gay red herring, absolutely nothing of interest had been discovered, Griffin was feeling acutely underappreciated when his superior summed up: "So basically, if we don't come up with a motive, we're nowhere.

Anybody got any bright ideas? Hell, if you'd had a bright idea you'd have spoken up by now. I'm ready for dumb ideas. Let's hear it. Really stupid ideas, anyone?"

Meera Patel cleared her throat. Lamp shot a glance at the dark Asian face of his favorite Detective Sergeant and Family Liaison Officer. The perfect marriage of beauty and brains, Patel was ambitious, Lamp knew, but she was completely lacking — thank God — in that vanity that made George Griffin insufferable. She spoke. "I just had a thought."

"Wonderful, somebody's had a thought," Lamp drawled sarcastically, careful to disguise his mild partiality. "You have the floor."

"Money is always a good motive, but Hillman didn't have any, so we've been looking elsewhere. But what bothers me is that there's a huge amount of money connected indirectly with Hillman. It would be a great motive if we could just figure out the connection."

"This huge amount of money being . . . ?"

"The silver they found here last February. Hillman was here to work on some old manuscripts that weren't supposed to be particularly valuable, or at least not financially valuable. But the manuscripts were found hidden with some pre–Civil War silver that the Family talks about as if it were the Crown Jewels. One piece, they say, is priceless."

"But the silver's all in London," Griffin protested impatiently. "It's being pawed over by experts and insurance people. None of it's here, it hasn't been here since sometime in March. Hillman never even laid eyes on it."

He was met with a fleeting dagger glance that reminded him that it was unwise to speak dismissively to Meera Patel. But she replied not to Griffin but to Lamp. "My thought was that Hillman might have discovered something in the manuscripts that has to do with the silver. That would prove it was fake, perhaps, or stolen?" She shrugged. "You said you wanted to hear dumb ideas."

"So I did. You're suggesting Hillman might have been killed to keep him from spilling the beans?"

Meera waved a hand. "It's just that there's not much else to suggest."

Lamp considered a moment. "I agree. Duncan, start on the silver. Find out where it is, talk to whoever's messing about with it and whoever found it and anyone else that can tell you anything at all about it.

What's it worth? What happens to it when these experts are through with it? Is it insured, and by whom? I want to see the policy." He stood up. "And I suppose I'd better go to the university and see if I can dig up someone who can read medieval manuscripts."

CHAPTER 20

The Monday Before Rob Hillman's Death

The door of the muniment room was wrenched open and Rob Hillman came flying out, making an instant's contact with the top step but leaping over the others. He hit the flagstones at a run and sprinted down the corridor. At the end of it, he all but skidded into the turn, ducked through a low archway, opened another door, took a narrow flight of upward steps two at a time, flung himself across an irregular lobby, and pelted down another corridor.

He reached the old library and stumbled breathlessly to the shelves in the north alcove. His eyes swept over the book titles with a hungry gaze while his fingers pitter-pattered frenetically over the spines like dry raindrops.

"Robinson, Robinson, I know you're in here," he panted feverishly; "I saw you just the other day, where are you — oh that's right, you're not blue, are you, like *my* Robinson, like everybody else's Robinson, no, you've got a custom leather binding and you are — burgundy, that's it, you are claret, you are some damn wine color — *ah!*"

He pulled a gold-tooled leather volume from the second shelf with less care than it deserved or than he normally exercised with books. Striding over to a window for better light, he pawed through the pages until at last he found what he was looking for.

Still breathing in great gulps of air, he cradled the book in his left arm and ran his right forefinger down the columns of text, drinking in the words, the amazing, wonderful words.

"Yes! Oh, by God, yes!" he shouted, clasping the open volume to his chest as if it were a lover and dancing joyfully around the room until he got dizzy. Collapsing on an overstuffed Edwardian chair, he began to chortle quietly.

"Calm down, Hillman," he ordered himself. "Calm down. Your employer is a very fragile old man. You do not want to give him a heart attack."

After a while he succeeded in following his own advice. At least the physical manifestations of his excitement waned. Inside him there was still a little boy jumping up and down and waving his hands.

But it was a relatively sedate young man who walked out of the library and made his way back to the muniment room in a manner altogether less precipitate than his previous journey.

Back in the muniment room he placed the elegant leather-bound volume on the table where he worked, opened it once more to the crucial page, and began to read aloud in Middle English. The mellifluous syllables fell easily from his lips; Rob could read fourteenth-century English as effortlessly as he could read the *New York Times*.

He read seven lines from the book, then moved his eyes to the manuscript that had sent him storming up to the old library. He continued to read, without missing a beat, and as he listened to the regular, unbroken pattern of emphasis and rhyme, unchanged from book to manuscript, his heart once more began to thump so loudly that he could both hear and feel it.

He continued reading until he had finished both columns of verse on the manuscript page. Oh, God, it was so sweet!

He'd been handling it with his bare

hands before he'd realized what it was. He went to the end of the table and picked up an old leather briefcase from the floor, rummaged through it, and pulled out a plastic food storage bag sealed with a twist-tie. He undid the tie and removed from the bag a pair of thin white gloves. He put these on, picked up a plain manila folder, and with care bordering on tenderness picked up the piece of parchment and laid it in the folder. He closed the folder, removed the gloves and stuck them in his pocket, and set forth to show Sir Gregory a prize beyond — surely — the Baronet's wildest expectations.

Calm, Hillman, calm! he told himself as he skipped down the steps from the muniment room. But it was no good telling himself to be calm. His heart was singing and his brain was dancing jigs. He couldn't wait to see Sir Gregory.

Unfortunately, as it turned out, he had to wait, and there was nothing he could do about it. Sir Gregory was unable to come down to lunch; the Baronet was keeping to his room. Crumper relayed this information apologetically to Rob, who tried not to look as disappointed as he was, excused himself from the family dining room, went back to the muniment room, locked the manila folder away in one of the dark Gothic cupboards, and pocketed the key. Then he went back to his beautifully laid-out lunch and ate it without tasting it.

After lunch he went up to his room for his mobile phone and attempted to call Derek. He got Derek's message service. Rob swore mildly and hung up. Then he entered Meg's Oxford number; again a recording. He uttered a cry of mock anguish.

The discovery was hopping around inside him like rabbits. He felt as though if he didn't tell somebody about it pretty soon, he was going to explode. He couldn't go back to work on the other manuscripts. Instead, he changed into shorts and went out for a run.

The gardens were glorious in the sunshine, but England's humidity renders warm summer days uncomfortably steamy. Rob, drenched with sweat, slowed to a walk as he skirted the kitchen garden.

"Blimey! The man's got legs!"

He turned to see Crumpet lounging on a cushioned bench wearing a halter top and amazingly short shorts. He grinned at her. "Speaking of legs, my dear girl!"

She smiled, lifted the limbs in question, and waved them in the air. "See anything you like?"

Rob passed a hand over his forehead, pretending to feel faint. "Too rich for my blood, fair lady!"

Crumpet lowered her legs and sat up. "You're in a very jolly mood. Found something nice?"

Rob, reflecting that the girl wasn't half as stupid as she looked, nodded. "Uh-huh."

"Oooo! Tell, tell!"

She wasn't the audience he would have preferred, but it had been three hours since he'd come upon the manuscript and he still hadn't been able to find anybody he could tell about it.

"Crumpet, sitting in the muniment room even as we speak, is a fragment of —" He stopped. This was wrong. Let alone it was pearls before swine, since she couldn't possibly comprehend the parchment's significance, it was also disloyal. Derek or Meg he might have told before he got to Sir Gregory. But not Crumpet. He shook his head. "Sorry, Crumpet, I just can't. I have to tell Sir Gregory first; he's not well today, so I can't see him yet."

Crumpet pouted for a second. "All right then, so don't tell me. But I guess," she said, eyeing him carefully, "that you've found out it's worth a lot of money, right?"

"Money?" Rob repeated blankly, as though he were unfamiliar with the word. Then he laughed and shook his head again. "No, Crumpet, I wouldn't say it's worth a lot of money. I'd say there's not enough money in the world to buy it. It's beyond price."

Her mouth made a little round "o" as this information sank into her brain. Then she rose from the bench in a sudden hurry, declared that if he wasn't going to tell her she wasn't going to talk to him, and flounced off in the direction of the kitchen entrance.

Rob chuckled, and having caught his breath, finished his run, returned to his room, and took a welcome shower.

Derek, meanwhile, was lying on a towel in his back garden in Oxford, toasting himself to the color of mahogany, when the tiny telephone at his side began to chirp. He picked it up and told it hello.

"Derek, it's me!"

"Hullo, Crumpet; something's happened?"

"Yeah, I just talked to him. He's banging on about that bloody fragment again, only now he's found out how much it's worth."

"And?"

"He says it's priceless. He said there's not enough money in the world to buy it."

"Jesus," Derek murmured.

"So what now?"

Derek took a deep breath. "All right, Crumpet. Here's what we're going to do. We're going to save that thing for Datchworth."

Crumpet laughed. "You sound like that thing they say, you know, do it for Harry and Saint George and England and all that crap."

"Crumpet, dear girl, sweet, sexy, wonderful girl, this is no laughing matter."

"O.K. O.K., I'm not laughing. So how do you think you're going to do this?"

"Not me, Crumpet. We. *Us*. We are going to do it together."

"Are we now?"

"Yes. Now. First you must understand, this is very important: we are *not going to steal it*."

"Well, of course we're not! Don't be bloody daft!"

"We are going to relocate it. Temporarily."

"Speak English, will you?"

"The fragment is on the table in the muniment room where Rob does his work. It's been mounted between two little pieces of glass, like a sandwich, and it sits on a little stand. Have you seen it?"

"Yeah, it's gorgeous, like jewelry or something."

"Yes. So you know what it looks like. Great. Now, for the time being it's in the muniment room, because my uncle said that Rob should be able to enjoy it while he's at Datchworth because he found it. The idea is that when Rob goes back to Oxford the thing will go to my uncle's desk, in his library, but meanwhile it's on a big table that has stacks and stacks of papers and manuscripts all over it. I think there's a pretty good chance Rob won't notice if it's missing. Or at least, not for a while."

"All right, then, when are you going to nick it? Oh, pardon me, relocate it?"

"I'm not going to do it. You are."

"Me?" Crumpet screeched. "You're out of your effin' mind, you are! What if I get caught, eh?"

"You won't get caught." He explained to her how it could be done. It was a simple plan and he'd had months to work on it, so he was able to make it sound so easy that a child could pull it off.

Crumpet wavered. "Well, I don't know. It does sound a bit of a lark, kind of James

Bond, you know, but . . ."

"If anything goes wrong, you know I'll take the blame for it. You won't be in any trouble at all. Please do this for me, darling. Do it *with* me. We need this thing for Datchworth, Crumpet. We need it."

The first person plural had its effect, as he had known it would.

Crumpet capitulated.

CHAPTER 21

1977

Twenty Years Before Rob Hillman's Death

She had always known she was not wanted at home; that was why they had shipped her off to school. Of course they said it was so she could learn how to be a proper lady, but any idiot could tell that was a lie. They hadn't shipped Derek off, had they? At least not until he was old enough for Eton. But *her* they had sent away practically as soon as she could talk.

School hadn't been so bad, at first. There were lots of other girls there in the same boat she was. Their parents obviously didn't want them, either. And there was lots of stuff to do in London, more than at home. They were always going to the zoo or the museum with the big dinosaur skeletons and the pretty rocks.

The headmistress was awful, of course. There was a rule, somebody said: you couldn't be a headmistress unless you were such an awful person, nobody would let you do anything else. One of the girls had whispered this in the dorm after lights out; her big brother was at Harrow, and he had written it to her in a letter. They'd all giggled, of course, but then Matron had come in and made them be quiet. That girl with the letter didn't know how lucky she was. She had a brother, and he cared enough about her to write to her.

Most of the teachers were pretty nice, though. Pippa could tell they all felt sorry for the girls because their parents obviously didn't give a toss about them. Some of them felt so sorry for you, you could get them to do things they really weren't supposed to do, like let your chums bring you sweets in the infirmary when you were sick.

So for seven years it wasn't so bad. Not at school, anyway. The rotten bit came when she had to go home. Because then, no matter how hard she tried, it was, "Phillipa, sit up straight. Phillipa, eat more quietly. Phillipa, there is a spot on your dress; go upstairs at once and change."

Of course Derek got told off, too, especially when Grandmother saw him looking all scruffy. But there was a difference, somehow. Pip didn't know how to put it into words. The thing about laps was the only example she could ever think of.

"Grandfather, can I sit in your lap, too, like Derek?"

"*May* I," Grandmother's voice interrupted. "One asks permission by saying 'May I', Phillipa, not 'Can I.'"

"Grandfather, *may* I sit in your lap?"

Grandfather had looked at Grandmother.

Grandmother had said, "No, Phillipa, that is for babies. You are too old now. You must sit in a chair like a young lady."

But Derek got to be less of a baby, and he still got to sit on Grandfather's lap. In fact, Derek got bigger and bigger, and still, there he was, sitting on Grandfather's lap.

One summer day she had gotten up her nerve. "Grandmother, Derek is still sitting on Grandfather's lap."

"Don't be tiresome, Phillipa. You have been told. Sitting on laps is acceptable for babies, for very small children only. You are much too old."

"But Grandmother, you said I was too old when I was four and Derek was three. But now I'm six and Derek is five. So why isn't he too old, too?"

She had been sent to her room for three days for "answering back." They brought her meals to her on a tray, and they let her out only to go to the bathroom.

A month later they had sent her off to school. That was when things started getting better. Except of course for the holidays, when she had to go back home again and watch Derek get all the attention. All the *good* attention, anyway. The only nice times in the holidays were when she and Derek got to go to Datchworth. Uncle Greg and Aunt Sophy were super.

Then when she was thirteen everything went really horrible. Absolutely putrid. The Hastings School only had grades one through seven. After that one had to go somewhere else. So they sent her to Stiles Academy. It was awful.

To begin with, it was in the middle of nowhere in Kent, and there was *nothing* to do. No zoos, no dinosaur skeletons, just a lot of new subjects she couldn't stand and school trips to boring Canterbury. She never did see why all the teachers got so worked up about Canterbury; it was only a dull little town with a stupid big church, that was all.

But worse than school trips that weren't fun anymore, and teachers that were not nearly as nice as the ones at Hastings, was that the other girls were a lot of cows.

Making friends had been easy at Hastings. Sometimes, of course, one's friends got to be big fat pains in the bum; then one just stopped going around with them and made some other friends.

But at Stiles, the girls were different. They would be friendly one day and the next day they would turn their backs; learn one's secrets and then blab them all over the school. One of the older girls started calling her Phillipa simply because she didn't like it and wanted to be called Pippa. Then somehow Phillipa got short-ened to "Philip-ah," then suddenly people were calling her "Flipper." Whenever they saw Pippa they would encourage her to jump out of the water and turn a somer-sault, and promise that if she did it well they would throw her a fish.

They started this in her first year, and they never stopped. In the spring of her second year, shortly after the Easter hol-iday, she went back to her room one day and saw a big square box on her bed, gift wrapped. The tag on it said *Happy Late Birthday*. (She had turned fifteen in March. Her grandparents had given her a check.)

She'd had a bad day. Her French teacher had had a go at her for not handing in her prep. Her chem teacher had put her on detention for talking in class. And the last class of the afternoon had been with the history teacher Miss Edgeware, who was *always* a rat-bag.

So when Pippa saw the prezzie on her bed, she thought it was the only nice thing that had happened to her all day. Afterwards she wondered how she could have been so dumb. She unwrapped it.

It was a beach ball. There was a piece of paper taped to it that said: *For balancing on your nose.*

That was when she decided to run away. Like her mother, Pippa had a brain behind her long eyelashes, and this decision was not a mindless reaction against unbearable circumstances. It was a calculated attempt to change those circumstances.

She had been trying for the better part of two years to get her grandparents to send her to a different school. Her grandmother always claimed that Stiles Academy was a perfectly good school, full of girls from good families, and Phillipa should be grateful to be there. Of course her grandfather just said that he didn't know about such things, and Phillipa should try to understand that her grandmother was only trying to do what was best for her and it was always difficult to get used to a new school and eventually she would make some nice friends.

Persuasion had failed. Stronger measures were clearly needed.

She began, very carefully, to plan. The check she'd been given for her birthday was surprisingly large; she suspected that her grandfather had managed somehow to keep her grandmother from knowing the amount until it was too late. There were six weeks before half-term, when she was to be allowed, for the first time, to travel home by herself. Some school authority, probably a teacher, would be down at the tiny local station sorting girls onto the right trains. Pippa would be put onto the two-car slow train that rattled across country to Guildford; there she was to change to a Portsmouth train that would let her off at Haslemere. At Haslemere she would be met by her grandfather if he was feeling brave or by one of the staff if he wasn't, and driven to Banner House.

Perfect.

She had weeks to plan, and plan she did. Whenever the chance offered, she would go to the library and read the classified advertisements in the London papers. She got the *London A to Z* and studied the major streets, learned the names of the different boroughs, and memorized the patterns of the Underground. She discovered there were books especially written for students who wanted to visit London and live cheaply. She got hold of one.

She did everything she could to be ready when the time came. She thought she was. All in all, it was an excellent plan. It was not her fault that everything went wrong.

A few of the other girls were also traveling on the train to Guildford, but she was careful to avoid them; when they got to Guildford station she went into the ladies' and stayed there for an hour. When she came out there was no one there who could recognize her among the scores of other students from other schools, all scurrying around to make their connections, no one who would know that this particular schoolgirl had no business to be getting onto the train to Waterloo.

At Waterloo she caught the tube across the river to Embankment. Out on the street she looked for a large pharmacy and found one after only a short walk. She bought a can of black spray-on hair dye and a package of proper black dye she could use later when she had found a place to stay. She found a public loo; it stank even worse than the one at Guildford station, but she was excited and determined and she ignored the stench. In one of the stalls she took off her school uniform and stuffed it into her backpack. She used the black spray on her honey-brown hair, getting some on her bra, but that didn't matter. Then she got out a pair of jeans and a plain blue pullover and put them on. Coming out of the stall she saw herself in the mirror and giggled.

She found a cheap café, ordered tea, and opened her backpack again. She took out a piece of school notebook paper and an envelope she had brought for the purpose, and wrote a note to her grandparents. She'd been working on the wording for weeks.

Dear Grandmother and Grandfather,

By the time you get this you will already know I have run away. Don't try to find me, you would be wasting your time. I kept trying to tell you Stiles is awful, but you never listen to me. I just can't stand it any more. You HAVE to let me go to another school. I'll DIE if I have to stay at Stiles.

She went on to describe what they must do: find a "nicer" school — it had to be in

London — enroll her there, and put an ad in the Personals column of the *Times* saying, *Pippa, we agree,* followed by the name, address, and phone number of the school. When the ad appeared, she would phone the school to check that it was all arranged, and then she would go directly to the school.

She found a pillar-box and posted the note, smiling to herself as she imagined her grandmother's reaction. She went back to the tube station and took the District Line east to a shabby neighborhood full of cheap lodgings; there she took out her map and began to make her way toward the first of three hotels she had chosen as possibilities. She didn't want to stay in a slum, but it would take time before her grandmother gave in, and she simply had to have enough money to last until that happened.

Arriving at the first hotel, she gazed doubtfully up at the dull facade that looked more like a prison than a hotel. Out of its somewhat grimy doors came a girl dressed almost exactly like herself, but (Pippa judged) about four years older than she was. Pippa summoned her courage and asked her, "Are you staying here?"

The girl stopped, looked Pippa up and down, and smiled. "That I am, sweetheart.

What do you need?"

She had crooked teeth and frizzy hair and an Australian accent. Pippa asked if it was a decent place to stay, and within a minute the friendly Aussie was looking at Pippa's short list of hotels.

"No, you don't want to go to the Hudson. Their prices have doubled since last summer, and they're not worth it. My God, girl, the Ripley! You go there, you get raped in the halls. Now, this place is a bit of a dump, but the loos are clean and the prices are right. Want to check it out?" she asked, cocking her head back in the direction from which she'd come.

So Pippa had gone with her gratefully. The girl's name was Janine, and over the next forty-eight hours she became Pippa's best friend. Janine never questioned Pippa's dyed hair or her obvious youth or in fact anything else about her; she just showed her how to survive in London on next to no money at all.

On the third day of their acquaintance the two girls went out on a pub-crawl. "You let randy blokes buy your beer, then you slip out when they go to the gents'." The unaccustomed beer went instantly to Pippa's head, but Janine kept the "randy blokes" from taking advantage and Pippa had a roaring good time. They came in late and staggered, giggling, toward the elevators. As the last possible second, however, Janine leapt out of the closing doors, crying that she needed to check the desk for a message.

The only other person in the elevator with Pippa was a tall, good-looking boy about Janine's age who pressed the stop button between the fourth and fifth floors, took a blackjack out of his pocket, and hit Pippa efficiently on the head with it.

It seemed like a long time to Pippa before she became dimly aware, through the pain and darkness, that Janine was calling her name. She came to on the floor of the elevator, looking up at Janine's horrified face.

"Oi! Pippa! My God, sweetie, what happened?"

Pippa became aware that her head was being cradled by one of Janine's hands. Also that her head hurt worse than she would have thought possible. Janine was uttering sympathetic noises but the concern remained in her voice. As Pippa managed to sit up just enough to see the contents of her handbag strewn all over the elevator floor, she heard Janine mention the word "hospital."

"No!" Pippa objected, then winced at the sound of her own voice. In an urgent whisper she repeated, "No! *No*. The hospital might call the police."

"Well, of course they would! What's the matter with —" Janine broke off. "Oh, I see. Poor kid, you don't want your parents to find you, do you?"

So Janine had figured her out, and had been nice enough not to give her any grief about it. Pippa began to cry at the same time she realized she was about to throw up. She tried to warn her friend, but when she opened her mouth it was too late.

"Jesus, Pippa! Here, have a tissue. Look, luv, I know you don't want to move but if you want to keep your parents and the police out of it, we've got to get you out of here. When the super sees this mess he's going to think you just got drunk and puked in the lift and he'll toss you out of the hotel. Unless you tell him you were attacked and then he'll call the cops and an ambulance and Christ knows what-all. Come on, my room's closer."

Pippa soon found herself in Janine's bed, her face wiped clean with a warm washcloth, her splitting head laid, thankfully, on the pillow, a couple of strong prescription painkillers washed down her throat with some hastily made tea. Janine patted her and soothed her and assured her everything would be all right; eventually the painkillers did their work and Pippa drifted off to sleep, with Janine's comforting voice assuring her that everything would be better in the morning.

But it wasn't.

"So I thought you looked all right for the night and I thought I'd go sleep in your room, so I looked for your room key, I *knew* I'd picked up everything off the floor of the lift and put it back in your bag, of course the bastard took your wallet, but I couldn't find your room key, so I went up there on the off chance you'd left it unlocked, and Pippa, love, the door was open and your whole room was trashed, he obviously took your key . . ."

Her money. Oh, God, her money!

He had found it, of course, he'd pulled all the drawers out of the tiny bureau and dumped their contents on the floor.

Pippa wept for most of the day, at least when she wasn't again sleeping off her injuries with the help of Janine's painkillers. Janine helped her clean up her room; Janine got food from a take-away and brought it up to her; Janine brought her a copy of the *Times* and didn't ask why she wanted it; Janine spent the next several days taking care of her more solicitously than Pippa had ever been cared for in her life.

By the time Friday came around, when Pippa needed to pay the next week's rent or leave the hotel, two things had happened: Pippa had reached the point of panic and desperation (the ad hadn't appeared in the *Times* yet) and she had bestowed upon Janine the unquestioning trust that a well-loved child normally bestows on her parents.

Pippa had been working her way tearfully through Janine's box of tissues for forty-five minutes before the older girl finally said hesitantly, "I don't know, I wasn't going to suggest this, you're a bit young, but I don't know what else . . ."

Janine had a friend who'd done it last summer to earn some extra cash. The friend had loved it. It had been perfectly safe; they'd treated her well; they'd respected her decisions absolutely about what she did and did not want to do. The friend had worked for six weeks and earned almost four hundred pounds *and* she got free room and board while she was there. On second thought, however, Pippa was probably too young. . . .

Pippa had to work hard to convince Janine to give her a chance at it; Janine gave in finally because, she admitted, she didn't really know what else Pippa could do except go home. Pippa shuddered at the thought.

The woman at the house in Mayfair was, surprisingly, a lady. She was as proper as a headmistress, and the right age for one as well, but she dressed more elegantly and spoke less sternly. Her name was Mrs. Cavendish, and she would have been right at home at one of Pippa's grandmother's luncheons.

She explained to Pippa that she gave private parties for gentlemen. Most were visiting London on business and did not know anyone in town; Mrs. Cavendish provided "polite, proper, and pretty" young ladies to be their dates at the parties.

Without ever using so vulgar a term as "brothel," Mrs. Cavendish was able to convey to Pippa most emphatically that her establishment was no such thing. And it was quite safe; the guests were thoroughly vetted and if one of them behaved in an improper manner, said something to one of the girls that made her uncomfortable, he was promptly evicted.

Pippa was younger than the other girls,

Mrs. Cavendish admitted, but . . . The woman gave Pippa a confiding smile and said that she wasn't going to ask any awkward questions, but she herself had run away from home when she was very young. . . .

"I don't want you to make a decision now, dear. You're tired and upset and you've had a dreadful time these last few days. Why don't you stay a couple of nights with us? You can rest up and meet the other girls; if you'd like to go to one of the parties, we can get you a nice dinner dress and you can come and see what it's like. If you don't care for it, you can leave after ten minutes and go back to the flat where you'll be staying. There will be absolutely no obligation."

Pippa was not a complete fool. She knew it sounded entirely too good to be true. She suspected that Mrs. Cavendish, in sheltering an underage runaway, would be breaking the law, and the woman would not be taking such a risk if she wasn't hoping to profit from it. Also, Pippa realized at some point toward the end of Mrs. Cavendish's smooth speech, that the sick feeling in her stomach had nothing to do with her headache but with the dawning understanding that she had been very professionally set up.

On the other hand, Pippa didn't see any alternative other than crawling back to Banner House in disgrace, and she thought she'd rather die than do that. So, warily, she accepted Mrs. Cavendish's invitation.

A summons was sent by telephone to somebody named Marilyn, who turned out to be a platinum blonde in her early twenties. She had an American accent, an unfashionably voluptuous figure, and a kindly disposition. She exclaimed in horror at the story of Pippa's misfortunes, and bore her off to an elegant block of flats not far away. Pippa looked around for Janine as they left Mrs. Cavendish's house, but was both relieved and unsurprised to see no sign of her.

Marilyn had a super flat, bang up-to-date and exceedingly posh. Pippa was urged to take a long soak in the tub while her hostess rustled up some supper. The bathroom had marble everywhere and the tub was huge.

Pippa was suspicious of everyone at that point, but it is difficult to maintain a clenched mind when one is up to one's earlobes in warm water and scented bubbles. As she began to relax a little, Pippa decided she would feel stronger if she looked more like herself, so she shampooed the dye out of her hair, working gingerly around the lump on her head. After the bath she dressed in the best casual clothes she had with her, and emerged from Marilyn's small spare bedroom, ready to engage the enemy with cool, implacable civility.

Marilyn bustled solicitously about her, asking Pippa if she needed anything for the pain, inquiring what she'd like to drink with supper ("It's just an omelet and salad, hope that's all right?"), and generally being perfectly lovely, but it availed her nothing until, halfway through the meal, she looked sympathetically across the table at her reticent guest and remarked, "Well. So you are the latest victim to be rescued by Mrs. Cav from the Melbourne Muggers."

It was clear from Pippa's blank stare that she hadn't a clue what Marilyn meant.

"That's what we call them. Vicious bastards. We don't know if they come from Melbourne, of course, we just call them that because of the Australian accent that the female uses, and even that might be a fake. We've got a real Aussie in the house, nice girl, name of Chrissie, she's from Sydney; Chrissie's heard the female Mugger talking a bit, and she thinks the accent's not the real thing. What's she calling herself this week, the female Mugger I mean?"

"Janine," Pippa replied faintly.

"Well, don't you worry, honey. Mrs. Cav's as good as her word. You don't want to stay here, you don't have to stay. You don't want to party, you don't have to party. I mean, Christ! You're a child! No offence. The only reason Mrs. Cav takes girls from that Australian reptile and pays her a commission, even when she knows what the Muggers do to the girls to make them desperate enough to come here, is that Mrs. Cav knows that if *she* doesn't take them, the Muggers' next stop is somewhere less respectable and less nice, and down the line from there until you get to places where they beat the girls and stuff them full of drugs. Lucky for you that you're pretty enough and posh enough that the Muggers brought you here first. And I gotta say, dear, you look a hell of a lot better with that black crap out of your hair!"

Pippa laughed, which made her head hurt, but from that moment onward, her life began to improve by leaps and bounds.

In the long run it was not the luxury or the money that seduced Pippa. Nor was it the promise of an easy life, free of boring schoolwork and nagging teachers. It was the kindness.

Marilyn had started calling her "little Sis" by the next morning; she introduced Pippa to some of the girls in the other flats (the entire building, it seemed, was owned by Mrs. Cavendish). Marilyn and two of her chums took Pippa out to lunch. All were friendly and jolly and all seemed to be glad to have Pippa around. It had been almost two years since anybody had been glad to have Pippa around.

They talked to her enthusiastically about the life they led and encouraged her to give it a try; Mrs. Cav was a wonderful boss, more like a mother; she allowed every girl to "go at her own pace"; no girl was ever forced to get "more involved" than she wanted to. Of course some of the girls were right cows, you had to expect that, but most of the girls were nice and the ones who weren't had their own little crowd and left you alone. Mrs. Cav saw to it that everybody stayed polite to each other. And you had all day, every day, just to do what you pleased!

And so, by easy stages, Pippa entered into a life of genteel prostitution. It was four months before she actually had sex with one of the "gentlemen"; Mrs. Cav made sure it was one of the regular guests, vouched for by the other girls as mild-mannered and gentle and patient. The encounter was a success; Pippa, liberally relaxed with champagne, actually achieved an orgasm.

In the early weeks, Pippa had checked the *Times* every day to see if her grandparents had put in the advertisement she had demanded. Then, one particularly enjoyable day (two of the girls took her shopping), she forgot to check the paper. Soon there was another day when she forgot. By the time Mrs. Cav spotted the ad many weeks later, Pippa had stopped looking.

She had concluded that her grandmother refused to be bent to the will of a child; she assumed that the police, possibly even private investigators, had been dispatched to find her. The fear that they might succeed was the only shadow across her bright, newfound life.

She received a message to see Mrs. Cav in her office. The older woman handed Pippa the newspaper with the ad circled in red. "Your grandparents," she said, "want you to think that they've relented." Pippa, having found Mrs. Cav every bit as motherly as the other girls had led her to expect, had long since confided in her employer her plan to escape Stiles Academy and go to a "nicer" school in London.

Pippa stared at the tiny bit of newsprint, then looked up at Mrs. Cav. "They're going to be waiting for me with cops and psychiatrists and maybe even men in white coats, aren't they?"

"I should think so."

Pippa smiled with unholy joy. "Let them wait!"

After she had been at Mrs. Cav's for a little over a year, Pippa discovered she had fallen prey to the occupational hazard of the world's oldest profession. She was pregnant. Mrs. Cav, ever supportive, offered to get her an abortion; the house would stand the cost. Pippa pondered the offer for a moment; she wasn't sure she liked the idea.

"Well, my dear, you have another month or so before you decide. Let me suggest you talk to the other girls who've been in your position. See what they say."

This Pippa did. She pondered all her options. After two weeks she had come to a decision.

On a sunny day in May 1979, John Banner received a telephone call from the police. A healthy infant girl, about ten days old, had been left in the ladies' room off the lobby of the Angel Hotel in Guildford.

Unknowingly following the example of her mother Clare, Pippa had left two notes. One was to the management of the hotel, telling them whom to call about the baby. The other, tucked into the baby's blanket and addressed to "Mrs. John Banner," was in an envelope sealed with wax. The management delivered this missive intact to Mr. John Banner, who in turn delivered it likewise to his wife together with all the proofs of identity Pippa had left in the baby carriage. These included such things as the books and schoolwork she'd had in her backpack when she'd run away and letters she'd received from her grandfather while she was at school.

Later the police confirmed that the handwriting on the school papers matched that of the notes found with the baby. Mrs. Banner had allowed them to have pieces of the letter to herself; she cut these out with scissors. She never allowed anyone — neither the police nor her husband — to see the entire message.

Pippa had written:

Dear Grandmother,
    This is my daughter. I know you

don't want her but you didn't want me either, and you kept me anyway. I think you just like to have someone around to be horrid to. I am not going to let you be horrid to my daughter. I want her to know who she is which is why I'm not just giving her up for adoption. Her name is Margaret Sophia Bebberidge-Thorpe Daventry, and I want her to be called Meg. I want you to ask Uncle Gregory and Aunt Sophy if they will take her. If they won't, you can find a nice loving home for her some place else but she must keep her name. I want you and Grandfather to settle 100,000 pounds on her. Put it in a trust and make Uncle Gregory and Aunt Sophy the only trustees. You must not be a trustee yourself or Grandfather either. You must not try to keep her yourself. I don't want you even to ever speak to her because you are a poisonous old bitch and you make everybody miserable. If you don't do everything I say you will be sorry because I will have you killed. I know you don't believe that but you should. I have friends now who know how to get someone killed without anybody finding out. All it takes is money and I have plenty of that, no thanks to you. Don't try to find me, you can't. But I'll always be able to find you. So just do as I say or you'll die.

Your granddaughter Pippa.

CHAPTER 22

MONDAY MIDAFTERNOON

Five Days After Rob Hillman's Death

"I didn't know he was in a wheelchair," said Tom to Kathryn.

"Neither did I," she replied.

They were sitting in the backseat of a 1936 Rolls-Royce that was wending its way through the hedgerows back from Morgan Mallowan to Datchworth. Behind the wheel "Crump" had reverted to Crumper, conveniently deaf servant, so that Tom could talk to Kathryn privately.

Not that anybody was doing much talking. *Does the wheelchair make a difference?* Tom wanted to ask, but was afraid to. Something, certainly, had made a difference. Derek she had dismissed indifferently and without hesitation. Had she dismissed Kit? Tom couldn't tell, but whatever had happened, Kathryn was obviously not feeling indifferent about it. That was bad. Also she didn't seem to want to talk about it. That was worse. She just looked at the scenery, or pretended to, lost in thought and looking troubled.

Back at the Castle Crumper held the car door open for Kathryn while making a sympathetic face at Tom to show they were still friends. Tom grimaced back and followed Kathryn into the Castle.

As they approached the big vase that marked their corridor, Kathryn resurfaced. When she spoke, however, it was without animation. "The Mallowans and Bebberidge-Thorpes are intermarried, did you know that? And I've met Meg's half uncles. I'd met one of them already, on the train with — on the train. But I didn't know who he was. Would you like to expand that family tree?"

"Sure." Tom would have liked anything that kept him in her company; he had begun to fear that she was going to shut herself up in her room without a word.

"Thanks. It's just that it would give me something to think about besides — besides Rob. Will — one of the half uncles — was talking to me about Rob."

Tom waited for the next sentence, and when it didn't come, ventured, "Um, should I ask? Or not?"

She shook her head. "Sorry. My mind's wandering. Where was that chart?"

They sat at the table in the double-viewed parlor, nearly elbow-to-elbow. But the fizz had gone out of it for Tom. He had never seen her like this, never tried to talk to her when she was a thousand miles away, never had to deal with her when it was so obvious that she was paying attention to him only with an effort. That alone was not good for the ego; knowing the reason behind her inattention made it worse.

"Starting at the top," she said, taking a pen and writing on the chart they'd previously constructed, "We now have a proper name for Cruella. It's Clarissa, and, just as Rob said, she's in a very posh "secure facility" somewhere in Hampshire; nobody knows for sure why she's there, except, presumably, for Sir Gregory and Derek, who put her there. There is lurid talk about a granddaughter who vanished in mysterious circumstances, but saner heads say nonsense, the girl just died in childbirth. The child in question being Meg. Oh, these putative Daventrys are not Meg's parents; Mr. Daventry was Mad Clare's first husband, and Meg's name is Daventry because nobody knows who her father was."

Kathryn was making alterations to the chart as she spoke, rearranging Daventrys and printing over Meg's name: "Phillipa

(No Husband)" and directly under Phillipa: "DIED IN CHILDBIRTH? MURDERED BY CLARISSA???"

"Add another line there. Crumper thinks she's still alive."

"Really? Why?"

"Well, Clarissa and her husband both claim she died in childbirth, which is why they had baby Meg on their hands for all of twelve hours before they handed her over to Sir Greg and Aunt Sophy, but Crumper says a few people thought it was weird that there was never a memorial service for her. Not down in whatchacallit, Surrey, where the Banners live, or here at Datchworth either. No body, no coffin, no grave ever appeared in the local cemetery in either place. Not so much as a jug of ashes."

"That *is* curious. But if Phillipa's still alive, why do her grandparents say she's dead?"

"Dunno. Crump thinks it's something to do with avoiding scandal. Meg was born out of wedlock, that's for sure. So maybe Cruella bribed Phillipa to go away quietly and not make any more trouble."

Kathryn obediently wrote under *Phillipa* QUIETLY DISAPPEARED?

Kathryn had already crossed out *Cruella* and substituted *Clarissa*, filling in the blank for her husband's first name with *John. An Indian gentleman with a funny name,* et cetera, was scribbled through to be replaced by *Shailendra Tandulkar,* and *twin boys* expanded into *Harry Tandulkar* and *Will Tandulkar.*

"You say you've met both of them?" Tom asked.

"Yes, they were both at lunch. It was rather a family occasion. Will and Harry — who suffer endless grief for sharing names with the young princes, as you can imagine, but they point out that their mom, that's Mad Clare, thought of it years before Charles and Diana did, and besides, Harry, this Harry, is the older one and Will is the younger. Where was I? Was that a sentence?"

"I don't think so, but who cares?"

"I do, normally," Kathryn said, and then added quietly as if to herself, "but 'normally' died a sudden and violent — Never mind."

"Did you find out why they call Mrs. Daventry-Tandulkar Mad Clare?"

"I did. And let me tell you, the rest of the family might be rather staid, but this line" — Kathryn actually achieved a small smile — "is a rip-roaring melodrama from start to finish. Clare got married to Daventry when she was seventeen, for heaven's sake, just in time to legitimize Phillipa. She then decamps, leaving poor old Pip, I should say poor *young* Pip, because she was three days old, to the tender ministrations of her Grandmother Cruella. Eventually Pip, who apparently couldn't stick it as long as her mom, runs away from home at fifteen, and a year and a bit later leaves a baby, our Meg, in a hotel rest room with instructions to turn her over to Sir Greg and Aunt Sophy. Then, as we've already established, Pip either dies in childbirth or is mysteriously murdered by Cruella or is alive and well and living God knows where, depending on who you're talking to."

"Great stuff. But weren't you going to tell me about Mad Clare?"

"I'm getting there. Clare, last seen abandoning Pip, divorces Daventry and instantly marries one Shailendra Tandulkar— isn't that the most marvelous name? Then Clare promptly produces twins Harry and Will, in that order. I know the order because Harry harps on it. Now it gets interesting."

"Lay it on me," said Tom, pleased to see her beginning to enjoy herself.

"Out pop Harry and Will, and instantly Cruella, who is *way* past it, produces Derek; everybody in the county openly agrees that she did it because she couldn't stand the thought of the Banner billions, much less her brother's baronetcy, going to 'some half-breed Indian,' as Harry himself puts it. Clare and Shailendra don't give a damn because they're lost in love's young dream and they're card-carrying socialists anyway and don't want their kids to be corrupted by wealth. Apparently they tried like the devil to get Phillipa away from Cruella, but Cruella had more money and therefore better lawyers, and the upshot is that Harry and Will have never even laid eyes on their big sister, wherever she may be, assuming she's still alive."

"Do you remember where you're supposed to be going with this?"

"Patience, dear fellow. When the boys were thirteen their father caught a rare blood disease and died almost within days; Clare had the most sensational nervous breakdown in the history of psychiatric medicine and according to many people has never fully recovered, hence 'Mad' Clare. Meanwhile, just as the decent members of the family were trying to figure out what to do with the boys until their mom was able to take care of them again, this famous Accident occurred that killed Sir Greg's son and heir, Gerald, Meg's Uncle Jerry who isn't really her uncle, *and* his best friend Freddy Mallowan, son and heir of Kit's Uncle Michael, Marquis of Wallwood, and put Kit simultaneously in line for the title and in a wheelchair for the rest of his life. Kit needed to go off to Eton, and Sir Greg, bless him for a democrat, suggested that the twins be sent to Eton with him, to look after him and help him get around in the chair and such. They told me this at lunch; my own private reading is that Harry didn't like it because he felt like a servant, but Will has the same sweet disposition Kit does and they wound up as best friends. Will and Harry are now joint estate managers for Kit. Now, get this."

Kathryn started sketching a diagram of the Mallowans at the bottom of the page. "See here, Dorothea, the middle-age afterthought? Kit's aunt, just a bit older than he? She ups and marries Harry. So Harry isn't only Meg's uncle, he's Kit's uncle as well. By marriage at least. Don't you love it?"

Tom, murmuring appreciation, studied the diagram while Kathryn began to make a clean copy of it. He told her about a few details he had gleaned from Crumper on the drive to Morgan Mallowan; after Kathryn had added those, the Bebberidge-Thorpe and Mallowan family trees looked like this:

BEBBERIDGE-THORPE FAMILY TREE
THE PREVIOUS BARONET & HIS LADY

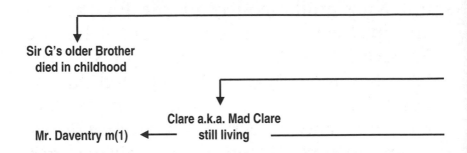

Sir G's older Brother
died in childhood

Mr. Daventry m(1) ← Clare a.k.a. Mad Clare
still living

MALLOWAN FAMILY TREE
(MARQUISES OF WALLWOOD)
5TH MARQUIS & HIS LADY

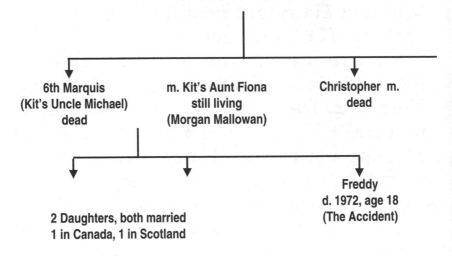

6th Marquis
(Kit's Uncle Michael)
dead

m. Kit's Aunt Fiona
still living
(Morgan Mallowan)

Christopher m.
dead

2 Daughters, both married
1 in Canada, 1 in Scotland

Freddy
d. 1972, age 18
(The Accident)

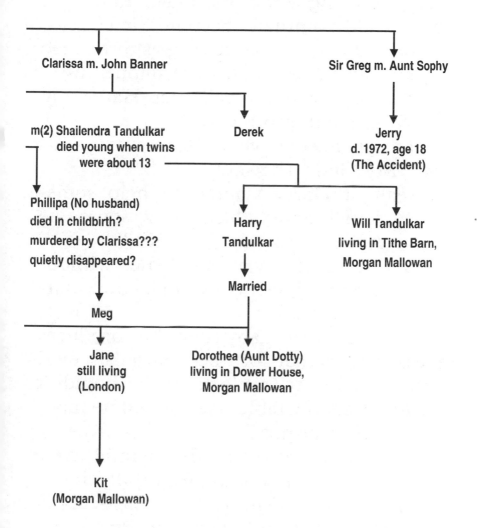

Clarissa m. John Banner

Sir Greg m. Aunt Sophy

m(2) Shailendra Tandulkar
died young when twins
were about 13

Derek

Jerry
d. 1972, age 18
(The Accident)

Phillipa (No husband)
died in childbirth?
murdered by Clarissa???
quietly disappeared?

Harry
Tandulkar

Will Tandulkar
living in Tithe Barn,
Morgan Mallowan

Married

Meg

Jane
still living
(London)

Dorothea (Aunt Dotty)
living in Dower House,
Morgan Mallowan

Kit
(Morgan Mallowan)

After a moment Tom remarked that if Derek fell down a dark flight of stairs before producing a son, the older Tandulkar twin would eventually become Sir Harry.

"Yes; Derek, apparently, was produced specifically to keep that from happening."

"But have you noticed that Harry's in line from another direction?"

Kathryn looked where Tom was pointing. "My God," she said.

"Yeah, if Harry wanted to help somebody to fall down those dark stairs, he might do better to start with Kit."

"But hang on. Even if Kit dies without issue, Harry doesn't become the marquis."

"No, but any baby boy he produces does. The father of the marquis could count on a pretty comfortable life, couldn't he? More comfortable than the estate manager of the marquis."

Kathryn scowled at the family tree. "Well, I admit that's all frightfully interesting, but although I don't particularly care for Harry, I don't immediately see any profit in finding motives for Harry to do away with Derek and/or Kit. Do you imagine that if we perused this thing a trifle longer, we might discover a good reason for Harry to do away with a visiting

American? Because, after all, it's my cousin . . ."

Tom shook his head. "I just can't see anything here that could possibly tie in to Rob."

Kathryn sighed. "Neither can I. Well, it's not our job, it's Inspector What's-his-name's."

"Griffin," said a voice.

Tom and Kathryn turned, startled, to see the Detective Inspector standing in the open doorway. Kathryn apologized and invited him in; Griffin came, followed by Sergeant Duncan. "Have you found out anything?" Kathryn asked.

"As a matter of fact we have," D.I. Griffin said, sounding a trifle cross. "Can we sit down?"

Kathryn hopped up from her chair beside Tom and started to play hostess, ushering Griffin and his colleague to the overstuffed seating around the coffee table. Tom joined them, observing that the Detective Inspector's attitude toward both of them had altered, and not for the better.

Griffin went after Kathryn first; this Chris person whom she had said her cousin was interested in —

"Only initially," she corrected him. "It turned out platonic."

"All right, initially. Chris Foley. He's a man."

"So?"

"You *knew* that?"

"I assumed it."

"Why didn't you tell us your cousin was a homosexual?"

"You didn't ask. It didn't occur to me. I didn't think it was relevant."

"It didn't *occur* to you?"

"No it didn't." There was an unmistakable touch of frost in her voice. "Many people regard a person's sexual orientation as a very minor piece of information, not worth mentioning in most circumstances."

Griffin may have been about to say that in a homicide investigation everything was relevant, but a rare flash of insight seemed to warn him he was going to lose this argument whatever he said. So he turned to Tom. "How about you, Chief Holder? Did you regard what you do for a living as a minor piece of information not worth mentioning?"

So they had checked with New Jersey. Tom approved. It would have been sloppy of them not to have made inquiries about their American visitors. But he was not about to congratulate Griffin, because Kathryn was irked at the guy. He spread his hands and deliberately repeated two-thirds of what Kathryn had said. "You didn't ask. I didn't think it was relevant."

"Not even as a matter of personal courtesy?"

"I thought it would be more courteous to stay out of your hair."

Griffin, balked of prey, seemed uncertain how to proceed. He was saved the bother by the sudden appearance of Derek in the doorway.

"Kathryn, my dear! Tom! I came to ask if you'd enjoyed Morgan Mallo—." He had spotted the policemen, and the change in his expression was almost comical.

"Oh, come in, Mr. Banner," said Griffin with false courtesy.

Mr. Banner did so, obviously reluctant. The frustrated Detective waited until Derek had found a vacant space in the chintz and dropped into it, then said to him querulously, "Nobody tells me anything, Mr. Banner. It gets annoying."

Derek assumed an expression of surprise and hurriedly assured the Inspector that he, Derek, would be happy to tell him anything that he might possibly —

"Then why don't you tell me," Griffin cut in, "why you've been walking around on hot bricks ever since this happened?"

Derek goggled speechlessly; Kathryn and Tom exchanged glances; Derek found part of his voice and began to croak, "Why! Of all the — ! Am I supposed to be cool as a cucumber while police crawl all over the house insisting there's been a murder, all the while, I might add, failing to turn up a murderer or even a feeble excuse for a motive or even —"

It was the right speech, but it was days too late, as even Derek himself seemed to be aware; he began to falter. He was spared the effort of thinking up anything else to be indignant about, however, because again someone appeared in the doorway. It was Crumper.

Every person in the room immediately recognized that something, somewhere, was very wrong. It was all too clear that Crumper was preserving his decorum only with the exercise of iron will; he was pale, he was rigid, and his fists were clenched.

"Detective Inspector," said the butler, "your presence is required downstairs. Mary will show you," he gestured.

The policemen were out of the room in a matter of seconds; Derek, Tom, and Kathryn had risen instinctively but were making no attempt to leave. Rather, they were looking at Crumper, who, having stepped back to let the police pass, had entered about eighteen inches into the room, his fists still clenched. The butler was looking at Derek, and it was clear he was laboring for words. Finally, he managed to convey a great deal in three syllables. He said apologetically, "Sir Derek."

There followed two seconds of frozen silence before Derek uttered a desolate cry of "No!" and ran from the room. Crumper, who appeared to have tears in his eyes, turned and sprinted after him. Kathryn and Tom followed suit.

At the door of Sir Gregory's library there was a scene. Griffin's cohort from upstairs was forcibly preventing a frantic Derek from entering the room. Derek was putting up a mighty struggle to get past him, shouting, "He's my uncle, damn it!"

Kathryn stole up behind the struggling pair and peered through the open door; Tom approached quietly and stood looking over her shoulder. On the far side of the library they could see an enormous desk; slumped across it lay the unmistakably dead body of Sir Gregory Bebberidge-Thorpe. At dinner the previous night his wit and determined good cheer had disguised his frailty; now his hair seemed instantly to have thinned to mere wisps, and the skin of his hands had gone virtually transparent. D.I. Griffin was nosing around the corpse with an air so eagerly curious and so completely ungrieved that Kathryn felt a little sick.

Derek and the Sergeant were still wrestling with each other.

"I'm sorry, sir," the cop kept saying, "I can't let you in," and as both he and Derek were being equally stubborn, it is uncertain how long the fracas would have continued if it hadn't been for Crumper.

The butler touched one of Derek's struggling shoulders and said, "Sir Derek. Sir Gregory would expect his heir to behave with dignity."

The fight went out of Derek instantly. He lifted his hands from the lapels of the policeman and stood still. The policeman in turn released his hold, and Derek stepped back. When he spoke, however, he was far from calm.

"I *insist* that you allow me to go to my uncle."

"Sir, I'm sorry, but your uncle is dead."

"*I know that, you blithering idiot!* Why won't you let me go to him? You have no right —"

Crumper threw Tom a glance, a mute cry for help.

Tom stepped forward and laid a firm hand on Derek's arm. "Derek, he can't let you into the room. He has to keep you out here. There was a homicide in this house five days ago. An unexpected death must be treated as a possible crime until proven otherwise. And the place where it happened has to be treated like a crime scene, no civilians allowed."

Tom went on, calmly explaining to the stricken young man all the common-sense facts that Derek's mind would already have recognized if it hadn't been experiencing a tidal wave of emotions.

Crumper took the opportunity to inform Sergeant Duncan that an ambulance had already been summoned but that Sir Gregory's doctor, who had also been called, was likely to arrive first. Duncan turned to relay the information to D.I. Griffin. Kathryn went down the hall to where a pair of Chippendale chairs flanked a china cabinet; she picked up one of the chairs, brought it back to the tense group by the library, set it behind Derek, and urged him to sit down. Tom added his persuasion vocally and physically, pushing Derek gently toward the chair until the backs of his knees hit the edge of the seat and folded under him. Kathryn turned to the Sergeant and assured him that they would keep Derek out of the library and he was free to assist D.I. Griffin if he needed to. She then assured Crumper that she and Tom would look after Derek if Crumper needed to convey the news to Meg and other members of the household. He thanked her in a shaking voice and walked rapidly away.

It was a long afternoon. Tea, in the English sense of a light meal, simply did not occur, but countless cups of that comforting beverage were consumed by those who waited in the hallway outside Sir Gregory's library. It was delivered by Crumper, who moved discreetly among the group of watchers as their number gradually increased. The Vicar joined them, as did Kit Mallowan, both summoned by Crumper. More chairs were mustered, and the hall became crowded, but Derek would not leave his post and none of the others would leave Derek.

The only time the new Baronet left his chair was when running footsteps coming from the main entrance announced the arrival of Meg, who had been in Oxford. She called Derek's name and he strode to meet her; they held each other and wept. Kathryn, watching them, felt herself welling up, and then saw that Kit, who had wheeled his chair next to hers, also had silent tears running down his cheeks. She took his hand. Tom, meanwhile, was trying his best to be supportive to Crumper, who he suspected was almost as devastated as Meg and Derek.

Some slight alleviation to the misery had arrived with Sir Gregory's doctor, a familiar figure who could be trusted (unlike the police) to be sensitive to the Family. Sure enough, after several minutes in the library under Detective Inspector Griffin's watchful eye, he emerged to inform Derek that as far as he could determine, Sir Gregory had suffered a heart attack. "I can't find any sign of violence, Derek; I know it's hard for you to lose him, but we've always known he could go at any time. But at least he wasn't — well, uh, it wasn't deliberate, is what I'm trying to say."

But Griffin continued to hold his fort until the force's own doctor arrived. In time she did, and confirmed the opinion of her colleague. No signs of foul play; probably natural causes, evidence consistent with coronary arrest. All of this was well received, right up until the point when she concluded, "Of course, under the circumstances, there will have to be a post-mortem."

Derek, who had risen to listen to her report, sank back into his chair with a groan and covered his face with his hands. Meg put her arms around him and buried her face in his shoulder.

Finally, after what seemed like half a week, the police allowed the niece and nephew to enter the library and commune silently with the body of their uncle.

Kathryn had ascertained, with a quiet question to the Vicar, that he intended to stay "all day and all night if necessary." She had watched him with Derek and Meg, he had touched them, embraced them, encouraged them to hold hands as they sat and waited. He had not uttered a single traditional pastoral atrocity, such as "Don't cry," or "It's God's will." Kathryn had concluded that priests in the Church of England were getting better training in grief counseling than they used to, and further concluded that her professional services were not going to be required. Kit and Crumper, though still somber, seemed to have recovered their composure.

Kathryn excused herself, went up to her room, and changed her luncheon outfit for shorts and sneakers. She went down to the entrance hall and out the open front door. She turned left onto the gravel drive and walked around the Castle until she got to the side where the yellow police ribbon still staked out the place where her cousin had fallen to his death.

She sat on the grass verge of the drive in the shade of a tree; it was nearly seven p.m., but thanks to England's semieternal summer evenings, it was still broad daylight. She stared at the empty space where Rob's body had lain and immediately began to cry without restraint.

The sobs had abated but the tears were still falling when she became aware of the crunching of gravel and the sound of a small motor. From the rear of the Castle appeared Kit in a motorized wheelchair with huge, fat, soft tires like black balloons.

He lifted a hand in greeting and called, "Wonderful contraption, don't you think?"

"It is indeed," she agreed, wiping her cheeks and sniffing. "Where did you got it?" Now that he was closer, she could see the ravages of grief on his face, belying the cheerful words.

"Borrowed it. It's Sir Gregory's outdoor chair. Rolls over gravel like a tank, wades mud puddles like a jeep, leaps tall buildings with a single bound."

As usual, Kit made her laugh. He rolled the chair over to where she was sitting under the tree and stopped beside her, thoughtfully not blocking her view of the yellow tapes. Now that he had made his entrance, so to speak, he dropped the levity, and for a while they talked quietly about their losses.

"We shared a certain frustration," Kit explained, tapping the arms of the wheel-chair with his forefingers. "It spanned the age gap."

Kathryn nodded and made a listening noise. "You will miss him, won't you?"

"God, yes."

They were silent for a few minutes. Then Kit said softly, "Kathryn, do me a little favor."

"Sure, what?"

"Stand up."

Puzzled but willing, she stood. Kit put his hands on the arms of the chair and pushed himself up about ten inches. Then with a swift movement he brought his right arm up, caught the branch above his head, and pulled himself up to his full height. He put his left arm around Kathryn's waist and pulled her suddenly to him.

She had been right when she had surmised that his arms must be strong. He held her tight, waist-to-waist, their faces level and almost touching. He waited a second for some move or murmur of protest, but aside from a little gasp of surprise she was still. He kissed her.

Unlike most of the kisses Kathryn had experienced, this one began hard, insistent, passionate, then slowly, over the space of a full minute, relaxed into a gentle caress of lips and tongues. Kathryn could feel, below her waist, his body's proof of his assurance to her that he could "function." She herself was fiercely aroused, and returned the pressure.

When they drew slowly away from the kiss, Kathryn asked breathlessly, "Isn't your arm getting tired?"

"Yes, but other parts of me are very, very happy."

She laughed, and so did he. He began to scatter kisses on her face, whispering, "Tonight, Kathryn — come back with me tonight."

"Yes, oh yes," she responded without an instant's pause for thought.

Neither of them had heard the footsteps on the gravel. Neither of them saw Tom Holder come around the corner of the Castle and stop, his heart contracting so painfully at the sight of them that he threw up both hands to his chest as though to shield it from further injury.

CHAPTER 23

A WEDNESDAY IN LATE JULY 1997

Thirty Minutes Before Rob Hillman's Death

"Oh! Hullo, Dad." Crumpet had come around the corner of a hedge in the servants' garden, and had been surprised to see her father sitting in a chair in the sun with his sleeves rolled up and his shoes off.

"Hello, Julie." Crumper lowered his newspaper. "I thought you'd gone back to Oxford."

"Uh, changed my mind." She waved a vague hand. "Nice day and all, you know."

"I see."

"Don't need to ask your permission, do I?"

"Of course not," Crumper replied mildly, wondering why his daughter was so defensive. Hiding something again, it appeared. "Shall we see you at tea, then?" He smiled. "I think your mum might have time to stir up some of her orange biscuits." He hoped it wasn't horribly obvious that he was making an effort.

"Thanks, Dad. That'd be nice. See you in a bit, then." She started to continue down the path, but turned back, crossed swiftly to his chair, and planted a kiss on his forehead.

This unaccustomed display of affection threw Crumper a little off balance. Had she done it deliberately, he wondered, knowing it would have that effect? Was she trying to keep him from asking what was going on? Certainly she wasn't her normal self. It wasn't just the hint of guilt; his daughter was normally languid, as if rapid movement were a waste of energy. But now she was being positively brisk.

Crumpet swore softly under her breath as she hurried along. She *would* have to run into her dad! She was nervous, and her old man had spotted it, she knew. Nothing ever got past him.

She arrived at a small door on the south side of the Castle, looked around to ensure she wasn't observed, slipped a key from her pocket, unlocked the door, and went in. The musty hallway was dark. She went to a tiny window for enough light to read her watch. Five minutes late. She swore again.

She put the key back in her pocket,

reached into her capacious shoulder bag, and pulled out a mobile phone. She punched three buttons for a prepro-grammed number, and waited impatiently while it rang.

"Hello?"

"I'm here, in the back hall. I know I'm late, I got held up. Is he there yet?"

"No, not yet. I haven't seen him."

"Thank God. I was afraid I was going to get yelled at."

"Darling Crumpet, when have I ever yelled at you? I'm going to ring off now. Stay there till I ring again, O.K.?"

"O.K., but it'd better be *soon*. I don't fancy crawling around on the bloody floor all afternoon."

They had decided that in case she was discovered loitering, she was to pretend to be looking for an earring she'd dropped.

"Crumpet, you're my hero. I shall *bathe* you in champagne for this. Bye now."

Derek rang off, and Crumpet switched off her phone and got down on the floor. At least it would be convincing that she was having trouble finding something small on the worn flagstones. The only light switch in the hallway was cunningly hidden behind a huge old armoire, and Crumpet, being neither staff nor Family, would not be expected to know how to find it.

She was dressed for the sun outdoors, and she was soon wishing she'd brought her cardy. Or a cushion to sit on; her bottom was freezing, sitting on the old stones. Of course, a cushion would have ruined it; if she heard footsteps coming or a key in the lock of the door, she was going to roll onto her hands and knees and start patting the floor.

After what felt like hours, her phone purred quietly (she had turned the ringer volume down).

"Yes?" she whispered.

"Yes. Go! Now!"

She turned the phone off and scrambled to her feet. She hurried around the bend in the hallway; the passageway widened, and well-spaced lights in wall sconces brightened her way. She reached the steps of the muniment room, ran up them, and opened the heavy door as quietly as was possible. Derek had not failed her; Rob Hillman was nowhere to be seen. Quickly she moved to the long table and scanned the piles of manuscripts, file folders, notebooks, and other scholarly clutter.

There it was, glowing like a jewel among the dull papers: a small square, intricate and brilliant in gold and scarlet and blue, sandwiched between two pieces of glass, held upright by a stand of black wood.

Crumpet hesitated. Was she supposed to take the stand, too, or just the fragment? They hadn't discussed it. She thought a moment. If she left the stand where it was, Rob might notice it. He'd know instantly that the fragment had been taken. Better to take the stand as well. She knew from experience that people frequently don't notice if something is missing altogether.

She pulled a hand towel out of her shoulder bag, picked up the fragment by the corner of its stand, and wrapped the towel around it. She had started back toward the door before she had even finished wrapping, and with equal care and haste tucked the impromptu parcel into her bag before pulling the door open and making good her escape.

She tried not to walk too fast down the corridor, but she was terrified somebody would see her before she got out of the Castle. If someone did see her, she was to say she was looking for her dad, but she was afraid she looked too nervous, too excited, not to arouse suspicion.

Around the turn into the narrow dark hallway, she broke into a tiptoed run, fumbling in her pocket for the key. Outside, with the door locked behind her, she looked around. If her father saw her again, the game would be up; he'd see through her in a minute. She headed away from the servants' garden, around toward the terrace. Behind a yew hedge, out of sight of the house, she again pulled her mobile phone out of her bag and punched the three digits.

"Yes?"

"Got it!"

"Good girl! Excellent girl! Where are you?"

"Between the terrace and the woods. I'm pretty sure nobody's seen me. But I want to get the hell out of here."

"Do that. The White Hart at five?"

"Can't. Ran into my dad going through the garden and got hooked into tea with my folks. Couldn't say no, could I?"

"No, I guess you couldn't. Never mind, we can — *what the* — ?"

"Derek?"

Silence.

"Derek, what's happening?"

No reply.

"Derek, damn it! Tell me what's going on! *Derek!*"

She heard two brief clicks, then the dial tone. Derek's phone had been switched off.

CHAPTER 24

WINTER 1995

Two Years Before Rob Hillman's Death

There were two telephones on the desk in Sir Gregory's library. The black one was the house telephone; Sir Gregory rarely used it. Persons who wished to speak to him generally came to do so face-to-face; if the Baronet wished to summon anyone in the household, he preferred to use the old bell rope by the fireplace, a relic of former days which it amused him to keep in working order.

The white telephone, an altogether more modern machine with a wireless receiver which the Baronet could hold to his left ear while maneuvering his chair about the room with the controls on the right armrest, was the family telephone. The only people who had the number were Sir Gregory's six living relatives, and only two of them, Derek and Meg, used it regularly. Since they were well acquainted with the old man's habit of retiring to his bedroom every night at nine, it was a bit of a surprise the instrument rang at precisely that hour.

The nightly handover, as Sir Gregory referred to it, was in progress; Crumper had ascertained that Sir Gregory required nothing more of him that evening, and opened the door for a stately exit; as frequently occurred, Sir Gregory's valet Hickson was upon the threshold preparing for an unobtrusive entrance; the two men nodded cordially to each other, Crumper held the door open, Hickson entered, Crumper exited, and Hickson began to ask his invariable nightly question: "Are you ready to go up, Sir Gregory?"

The unexpected ring cut him off in midsentence. Sir Gregory murmured a mild "My word!" and rolled his chair back to the desk. He picked up the receiver. "Yes?"

Derek's voice, shrill with agitation, assaulted his ear with a babble of apologies and explanations. "Oh, Uncle . . . so sorry . . . my mother . . . I can't . . . I couldn't . . . she's mad . . . I never . . . she said . . ."

The old man's heart sank. He had been afraid of this ever since Dotty Mallowan had announced her engagement in January. He did his best to pour oil over his nephew's distress; they reached an agreement, and the baronet switched off his telephone.

"Hickson."

"Yes, sir?"

"Tell Crumper immediately, please, that Derek is arriving at Oxford station at eleven thirty-seven and will need to be met. When he arrives here he is to be brought to my room. You will awaken me at eleven forty-five and help me into my chair so that I am able to receive him."

"Yes, sir." The valet turned toward the door.

"Oh, and Hickson?"

"Sir?"

"See that there's brandy in my room. And a fire."

The brandy, as Sir Gregory feared, turned out to be well and truly necessary.

He got to bed only fifteen minutes late, but he scarcely slept before Hickson entered a scant two hours later to wake him. It wasn't that he needed to consider what to tell Derek; Sir Gregory had seen this conversation coming for years, and he had his speeches well rehearsed. But the impending task of delivering them made his heart grow cold.

Before he could say anything to Derek, however, he had to listen to him.

"She was raving mad about Dotty marrying Harry Tandulkar. The things she said about him! And Will, too. I don't want to tell you what she called them."

"You don't have to; I've heard it myself. She calls them 'those filthy niggers.'"

Derek winced. "Yes, sir. I think that was what made me snap. I told her I was going to the wedding, and she needn't waste her time trying to talk me out of it."

"I can imagine," Sir Gregory said dryly, "how well that was received."

Derek closed his eyes. "She actually started to throw things at me, vases and things. I was afraid she was going to have a heart attack. She stopped throwing and I stopped ducking, and then I began to make out what she was screeching at me. I was no son of hers, she said; she was going to disown me. Disinherit me. Cut me off without a shilling. I thought it couldn't get any worse. Then —" He faltered. "Then she started saying there was only one way I could redeem myself, prove I was her son. She said —" Derek shook his head. "You won't believe me."

"Try me," the old man said gently.

"She said I was to kill Harry Tandulkar

before the wedding. I was so gobsmacked I couldn't utter, just stared at her with my mouth hanging open. Then she — she actually started suggesting ways I could do it. That was when I left, just walked out of the room, walked out of the house, got in my car, and started driving. When I turned onto the A-Three, I realized I wasn't in any condition to drive, I was shaking so much; I got off at Guildford and caught the train."

Derek had been pacing all the time he was relating this ugly tale. Having finished, he dropped into the chair opposite his uncle and wiped his face with one hand. "I know it's an ungodly hour for you, Uncle, but I was desperate to see you. I knew you would be able to help somehow. I'm sorry I —"

"Don't apologize. You did the right thing in coming to me. I have feared for years that it might come to this, and now it has. The situation requires action. And Derek, it will also require courage."

Derek looked at him with some trepidation. "What are you saying, Uncle? What must I do?"

"You must put your mother in a home for the criminally insane."

"Uncle!" Derek exploded, incredulous.

"You can't be serious! I mean, just because she's flown off the handle, you can't honestly think she would do anything — anything really — I never — really, Uncle!"

Sir Gregory sighed. He had expected this reaction. He set himself to persuading his nephew first, that he was entirely serious, and second, that Derek must immediately take steps to see to it that his mother was confined.

Sir Gregory tried his best for several minutes and got exactly the reaction he anticipated. Derek backtracked, began to claim that it wasn't all that bad, his mother had just had a worse-than-usual temper tantrum. Sir Gregory allowed him to talk himself out, and a brief silence ensued.

It was broken by a long sigh from the Baronet, who said sadly, "I was afraid, Lovely Boy, that you would need convincing. I am sorrier than I can tell you."

"Sorry for what?" Derek asked, puzzled.

"Sorry that I can only think of one way to convince you. I must demonstrate to you the sort of person your mother is."

"Demonstrate?"

Sir Gregory closed his eyes for a few moments as if gathering strength. Then he began.

"I've always been convinced that your mother detested, shall we say, the personal aspects of marriage. She was duty bound, of course, to give your father an heir, and that was an age when we did our duty. She managed to produce poor Clare, of course, but after that there was a very long dry spell."

"She sometimes rants about miscarriages."

"She claims three."

"Claims?"

"All three occurred so, ah, early that there were never any visible signs she was pregnant. She said she was. She said she miscarried. And after this had happened three times, Clarissa said she was giving it up. She established her own bedroom, down the hall from your father's. Then years later the Tandulkar twins were born, and suddenly your father had an heir — two heirs — who were sons of a black immigrant. Your mother made no secret of her feelings. She flew into a rage, said dreadful things, your father told me. The phrase 'filthy niggers' dates from that time."

"Uncle, *you* don't think — I mean — just because Will and Harry are half-Indian . . ."

"Of course not! Anyone educated at Eton is a gentleman, provided he behaves like one. At any rate, shortly after that your mother went abroad. You know, of course, that you were born in Italy. Eight months after your mother's departure, your long-suffering father received a telegram from her and came posthaste to Datchworth, nearly incoherent with joy. Clarissa had been safely delivered of a baby boy. In Rome, it was. She hadn't told him when she'd discovered she was expecting, because, she said, she didn't want to disappoint him again. A few weeks later you were brought home in triumph and displayed to both sides of the family with what I have always thought was unattractive smugness on the part of my sister."

Derek was looking alarmed. "Sir! You don't mean you think I'm — that's to say, if I was born eight months after she left, it must have been my father, I mean, before she went —"

Sir Gregory looked immensely sad. "Lovely Boy, I'm not suggesting your mother became pregnant on the Continent."

"Thank God!" Derek said with feeling.

"It's worse," Sir Gregory managed to say.

"How the devil could it be *worse?*"

"I'm suggesting your mother never became pregnant at all."

"But how —" Derek stopped as the full import of his uncle's words struck him and rendered him temporarily speechless. His mouth moved but no words came out.

His uncle clenched both hands tightly on the arms of the wheelchair and continued, "When you recover your tongue you are going to say you don't believe me. I don't blame you. Even I had no suspicions at first, and I believe I have as low an opinion of your mother's moral worth as anyone who knows her. But then the maid who had gone to Europe with her — indeed, her only companion for all that time — was dismissed out of hand. Clarissa accused her of stealing a diamond necklace."

Derek was staring at his uncle with mulish incredulity, but he was too shaken to speak.

Sir Gregory continued. "I thought it was a bit smoky, to say the least. If the girl was a thief, why wait until they got back to England? Why not grab the necklace and simply escape into the wilds of Italy? At the time, I was a couple of years into the Sirdom, my father having died in 1964. I had money and resources and nobody to tell me what I could or could not do with them. So I hired a private detective.

"He followed the maid to London and found her. She was living far too handsomely for an unemployed domestic, and though it was clear she resented his questions, she appeared to hold no resentment against my sister. The charge of theft had not been true, she said, but she shrugged it off as a misunderstanding. I found another private detective. His name was Bendini; he had been born in Naples and brought to England as a teenager. He was, of course, fluent in Italian, and I sent him to Rome."

Derek was shaking his head just perceptibly back and forth and he was silently and repeatedly mouthing, "No."

Sir Gregory's mouth was a thin line and his old eyes sagged much more than they usually did. He pressed a button on his wheelchair and it hummed quietly over to his dresser. With some difficulty the Baronet inserted a finger between his buttoned pajama collar and his withered throat, fumbled a moment, and pulled forth a fine gold chain upon which hung a single key. This he inserted into the lock of the top left drawer.

From the drawer he removed a thin, flat,

brown box like a miniature suitcase. He laid it on the desk, opened it, and extracted a folder labeled "Italy." Navigating over to his nephew's chair, he placed the folder in Derek's nerveless hand. "Mr. Bendini's report," he said gently.

Derek stared at the folder like a bird transfixed by a snake. His hands, completely unbidden, opened the folder and picked up the first of several sheets of paper.

It was all there. Every horrid, soul-shattering detail. Since his father's mother — Derek corrected himself — since *John Banner*'s mother had been from Naples, Italy had been the logical place to look for a baby. The family of his birth had been, for Italians, unusually light-skinned. His mother — Derek corrected himself again — *Clarissa Banner* had chosen well. *I matched*, thought Derek desolately. *Nobody ever suspected. Except Uncle Gregory. Who is not my uncle.*

The Baronet watched, not bothering to wipe the tears from his face, as Derek's world fell horribly apart around him. By the time the last page was read and laid back in the folder with a shaking hand, Derek had been crying quietly for a quarter of an hour. At one point his entire body had begun to tremble; Sir Gregory had fortified him with a double brandy, and the trembling had eventually stopped. The tears had kept flowing.

Derek looked up at his uncle — *not* his uncle — dazed, lost.

"Take those papers," said Sir Gregory with quiet command in his voice, "and put them on the fire. Do not hesitate. Do it now."

Entirely willing, Derek stood up. Or tried to. Swaying, he grabbed the chair arm. He steadied himself, and with clenched jaw put one foot in front of the other until he stood by the fireplace. He took the loathsome pages from the folder and threw them in a bunch into the flames. Then he ripped up the stiff card folder and threw it after them.

"Now hear me, Derek —" Sir Gregory began.

"That's not even my *name!*" cried the young man in anguish.

"Don't be silly!" the Baronet barked, forcing himself into a sternness he was far from feeling. The boy had to be pulled back from the brink. "You were baptized Derek St. John Bebberidge-Thorpe Banner in St. Paul's, Greyswell, by the Bishop himself. That is your name. You are my nephew and my heir, and I will attest to that before any court in the land. A year from now I want you to have forgotten that you ever saw those papers."

"Then why on *earth*," cried Derek, "did you show them to me?"

Sir Gregory sighed deeply and sagged in his chair. One excruciating hurdle cleared, one more to go.

"Because," he said, "I haven't got that kind of evidence" — he gestured toward the curling, blackening pages in the fire — "the kind of evidence that would stand up in court, about — the other thing I need to tell you. And I *must* convince you. I must."

"Convince me of what?"

"That your mother, my sister Clarissa, will go to any length whatsoever, however outrageous, however illegal, however immoral, to get what she wants. To get her way. Do you believe that?"

Derek stared into the fire. The pages had all turned to ash and were dematerializing among the burning logs. He drew two deep breaths, one after another. He turned back to his uncle and said, "Yes. I believe it."

"You agree she could be dangerous?"

Derek closed his eyes a moment. "Yes," he replied. "She could be dangerous."

"Then sit down, Lovely Boy, pour yourself another brandy, and I will tell you a nasty story about a golf club."

Derek did as he was bid. He leaned forward in his chair as he listened to Sir Gregory unfold another terrible tale. This time, however, nothing inside him rose in protest. It was all too horribly credible. As his uncle had said, the evidence wouldn't stand up in court; it was circumstantial. But it was compelling. As Sir Gregory carefully detailed a series of events spanning half a century, Derek found himself believing every word.

Sir Gregory stopped speaking and looked at his nephew.

His nephew looked back at him, man-to-man, and nodded. "Yes, sir. You were right." He was silent a moment; Sir Gregory waited.

Derek steeled himself and continued. "She needs to be — confined. But dear Uncle, what I don't see is how on earth we can commit her to a home, as you suggested. We'd have to tell doctors, police —" He broke off, appalled at the very thought.

Sir Gregory replied, unruffled, "I agree with you; that would be unbearable. That is not what I am suggesting."

"Then what shall we do?"

"I think we can achieve what is necessary without scandal. After all, she would not like to see our families' names in the vulgar press any more than you or I would."

"Naturally, sir, but do you really think you can persuade her?"

"I think 'blackmail' might be a more accurate term than 'persuade,' but yes, I do."

Derek laughed. He was surprised he remembered how. Feeling minutely better, he listened as Sir Gregory explained his plan, which was both simple and audacious, and then he shook his head in admiration. "I say, sir, that's amazingly clever."

"I confess that I have been working on it — only in my mind, you understand — for several years now. Ever since I was certain. Ever since I got that DNA report."

"Well, I think it's bloody brilliant."

As he and his uncle discussed how to proceed, Derek was chasing an elusive thought at the back of his brain. It was, amazingly, a positive thought — it was making him feel better — but he couldn't quite pin it down and it was beginning to distract him. Suddenly he realized it was not a thought, but an emotion. He felt relieved.

What the hell, he asked himself, *have I got to be relieved about?* Then, as he looked at his uncle, his dear, wonderful uncle, he suddenly knew.

That woman wasn't his mother. He didn't have to love her anymore.

"Anything wrong, Lovely Boy?"

Derek gave himself a mental shake and apologized, "Sorry, Uncle. Guess the old brain's so full, it's stopped working."

"Speaking of old brains . . ." said Sir Gregory.

Derek's eyes flew to the clock over the mantel. "Dear God, Uncle, I do apologize! Let me ring for Hickson."

As they waited for Sir Gregory's valet, Derek attempted to thank his uncle, but the old man would have none of it.

"Hush, Lovely Boy. You — and of course little Meg — have been the joy of my declining years, and I would never allow a mere accident of birth to take you away from me. Besides, the best thing my worthless sister ever did was present me with an heir I could be proud of, and frankly I don't give a damn where she got you."

Naturally Derck was utterly unmanned by this speech, and felt the unwelcome tears start in his eyes again. Sir Gregory, too, was a bit dismayed at his own forth-rightness; English gentlemen were normally more temperate in their expressions of affection.

Fortunately for the both of them, Hickson arrived at that moment to escort the Baronet to his room; all they could do — all they *had* to do — was bid each other a hearty good-night.

As Sir Gregory's chair carried him smoothly toward the library door, however, Derek was struck by a troublesome thought. "I say, Uncle!" he called.

The chair stopped and rotated slightly in Derek's direction. Derek opened his mouth but hesitated, flicking an uncertain glance at Hickson. Sir Gregory's valet was nearly as well trained as Sir Gregory's butler; in half a second he was out of the room with the door closed behind him.

"What is it, Derek?"

"Well, you said I should forget —"

"Indeed you should."

"But there are two other people who know and might not forget."

"Well spotted, lad, but there is no cause for concern. I myself attempted to make contact with the maid after I found out — after I received the report from Italy. I went to the flat my first detective had found. I spoke with the girl's mother, Glady Slocum. She had inherited the flat upon her daughter's death two months previously."

"How did her daughter die?" Derek dreaded the answer.

"Mrs. Slocum told me that the coroner had ruled it a suicide." There was a brief pause before Sir Gregory added, "Mrs. Slocum didn't believe it."

Derek covered his eyes with one hand and muttered, "Jesus."

"As for the detective I sent to Italy," Sir Gregory said with a sudden touch of cheer, "that's an altogether happier story. Mr. Bendini abandoned this dreary climate for sunny California, where he was able to purchase an extremely posh Italian restaurant which serves, I am told on good authority, the most expensive spaghetti in San Diego."

Derek couldn't help but smile, but he also couldn't help but wonder how a private eye could afford to buy a posh restaurant. Did private detectives make that much money?

Sir Gregory saw the unspoken question in his nephew's eyes. He smiled seraphically and said, "Just because I don't like my sister doesn't mean I can't learn from her. I thought, however, that California was a safer distance than London." Then he raised his voice and called, "Hickson! I'm ready now."

As the door opened, the Baronet set his chair in motion, threw a last fleeting smile at his bemused nephew, and said, "Good-night, Lovely Boy."

CHAPTER 25

MONDAY

Five Days After Rob Hillman's Death
Three Hours After Sir Gregory's Death

Tom was back in the double-viewed parlor, having retreated from the unendurable sight of Kathryn and Kit's embrace in the driveway. He had given up trying to read the newspapers and magazines provided by Crumper that morning, and had taken to pacing back and forth across the room from one set of windows to the other. He had left the door wide open, and he glanced at it every fifteen seconds. She had to show up sooner or later.

Finally he thought he heard the faint squeech of sneakers on the stone floor of the corridor. He stopped pacing and looked toward the door. Here she came — and went. She was walking right past the parlor, not even looking in.

"Kathryn!"

She reappeared in the doorway. "Ah,

hello, Tom," she said too casually. "I've been outside. Any more developments?"

She didn't wear much lipstick, so it needed a good eye to see that it was smudged. Tom had a good eye. He wished he didn't.

"Aside from the fact that they've taken Sir Gregory away, I don't know and I don't care. Look, Kathryn, why don't we get out of here for a while? Derek and Meg sure won't want us tonight. Let's get that little car and you can take me to one of these English country pubs everybody talks about. I'll buy you supper."

It was clear from the look on her face that he wasn't going to get the answer he wanted.

"Oh, Tom, that's so kind of you, but I sha— I won't be needing supper. Kit's invited me —"

"Oh, for Christ's sake, say the goddamned word!"

Kathryn's jaw dropped and her eyebrows climbed halfway to her hair.

Tom answered the question she was too stunned to ask. " 'Shan't.' You can speak the King's English to me, I can translate. I'm not stupid."

Kathryn could not imagine where this unprecedented hostility had come from.

After an open-mouthed moment, she walked to the nearest of the chintz-covered chairs and sat down.

"Tom," she said carefully. "Please understand. I picked this stuff up at Oxford. 'One would not wish to offend' instead of 'You don't want to piss anybody off.' Everybody at my college talked like that, not just the ones who were upper-class, but also the ones whose grandfathers were miners. One picked it up" — she made a little grimace to acknowledge she was doing it — "without even noticing. Then when 'one' got home to Texas, 'one' had to drop it like a hot brick, or the family would think you were trying to be better than your roots."

"*One* sure picked it up again in a hurry, didn't *one?*"

Kathryn glared at him. "Tom, stop and think a minute. Then when you've figured out what you're really mad about, tell me."

"I don't have to think, I already know. The la-dee-dah accent is just the tip of the iceberg. Back in New Jersey, you don't put on airs. You're smart as hell and you've got more college degrees than most people have had hot dinners, but you always act like a regular person, not like you're better than other people."

Kathryn, now well and truly offended, demanded, "Who on *earth* are you accusing me of acting better than?"

"It's more like, getting ready to be better than."

"What the hell is that supposed to mean?"

"Oh, all this crap about how you don't want to be tied to a castle and a title, no you're above all that, it doesn't interest you. Bullshit! It was just Derek that didn't interest you; show you a man you find halfway attractive and you're all set to go for a bigger castle *and* a bigger title!"

There was just enough truth in this accusation to sting Kathryn's overzealous conscience, which meant that she became very angry indeed. "Where in *hell*," she demanded in a seething voice, "did you get the idea you can pass judgment on me?"

From the still-open door came the sound of Detective Inspector Griffin clearing his throat.

Two startled faces turned instantly to look at him, froze, then turned an even darker red than they had been before.

"I'm sorry to interrupt," he said.

Tom turned his back, stalked over to one of the windows, and leaned heavily on the sill, his head down.

Kathryn managed to say, "You needn't apologize. I think an interruption was sorely needed. What do you want?" She thought that sounded rude, and corrected herself. "How can we help you?"

"I didn't actually come for help, Reverend Koerney. I just came to let you know how things stand."

"How kind of you. Please sit down."

Griffin chose a chair alongside Kathryn's rather than one facing her, a bit of unnecessary familiarity Tom had no opportunity to disparage, simply because he did not see it; he had not moved from his position slumped over the windowsill. Gorgeous George pursued what he took to be an advantage, leaning toward Kathryn and speaking in a quiet, confidential tone, unaware that she had no emotions to spare for him and precious little attention.

"Well of course, the death of Sir Gregory will have to be gone over quite carefully. It may have been natural causes; he was old and ill, obviously. But if, ah, if —"

"You're saying," Kathryn interrupted bluntly, "that if Sir Gregory was murdered it might provide you with the break you've been looking for in my cousin's murder."

Gee Gee Griffin discovered it wasn't nearly so easy to be manly toward a woman if she wasn't prepared to be womanly. "Uh, yes," he stammered. "Uh, yes, that's so. But on another track entirely, we were interrupted earlier and I didn't get a chance to tell you that we'd already opened up a new line of inquiry regarding Mr. Hillman's death, and Sir Gregory's, uh, sudden passing won't stop us from pursuing it. The difficulty has always been in finding a motive. We're checking out a new possibility."

Kathryn's attention sharpened. "Can you tell me what it is?"

"I don't see why not," the Inspector replied. "We are looking into the idea that your cousin may have come across something in the manuscripts having to do with all that old silver that was found last February. And that what he discovered was something that somebody else didn't want to have known. I admit it's a long shot . . ."

"I think it sounds clever of you, Inspector. I assume you'll need someone to read the manuscripts for you?"

"Oh, yes, and there's the hitch, at least temporarily. This is not the best time of year to locate somebody who can read that stuff. All the experts at Oxford are on holiday."

"I can read medieval manuscripts."

"Can you now! I wonder — it's a bit irregular — but I don't think Chief Inspector Lamp would object. Would you, ah —"

"I'll come now, if you like."

Griffin said that would be splendid, and Kathryn walked out of the parlor without a backward glance.

Tom knew without looking around that she was gone; he could hear her talking to Griffin as they walked down the hallway back toward the main body of the Castle. He began, slowly and deliberately, to hit his head against the upright between two windows, uttering a savage litany of every profane expression he knew. He had repeated himself about three times when his shoulders began to shake, and he realized with horror that for the first time since his childhood he was crying.

Griffin, meanwhile, had listened to Kathryn explain that she was not in her cousin's league when it came to deciphering the handwriting of the thirteenth and fourteenth centuries, because for her it had been a sideline to her studies and not the main focus. The Inspector was rapidly getting back in charity with her, and ventured to lay his fingertips on her shoulder as he assured her they would be deeply grateful for even the slightest assistance.

Kathryn had not previously been permitted to enter the muniment room. They had allowed her to sort through the collection of clothing and other personal items in Rob's bedroom after both room and contents had been submitted to severe scrutiny, but the muniment room was still classified as an extension of the scene of the crime.

Entering it now, she looked around with keen interest. At a cheap table which had clearly been brought in for the purpose, a policeman and policewoman were looking through files. The man closed a file, put it on a stack of other files, rose, and carried the stack over to a row of ornately carved cupboards that stood against the far wall. One cupboard was open; the man placed the files in it and returned to the table with a similar stack. Fifteen feet away stood a long, substantial library table that matched the cupboards. On it were a few ancient-looking books, several large, flat boxes with labels on them, and a clutter of papers.

Kathryn felt gratified and slightly excited to be in the previously forbidden room; here was the inner sanctum and she was needed. But when she was invited to take the chair at the long table, it struck her that it was Rob's chair; this was where he had worked; he would never work again. She clamped a lid on her emotions and listened to Griffin.

"We've looked at every piece of paper on this table," he was saying, "and we've been careful to put it all back exactly as your cousin had it. Frankly we couldn't make heads or tails. It's not just all the old stuff, we can't even read the notes he made."

"Notes?"

Griffin pointed to a three-ring binder of pale blue, and as Kathryn hesitated, said, "Go ahead."

She picked up the notebook and opened it. In a matter of seconds she announced that this was a stroke of luck.

"It's Rob's transcriptions. I may not have to look at manuscripts at all."

"Trans— ?"

"It's a record of his work. See here: at the top of the page is the number he's assigned to each manuscript, Datchworth one, two, three, et cetera. Later he would have worked out a more sophisticated system, but to begin with he was just numbering them as he worked on them. See the dates in the lower right corners of the pages, here? They're chronological."

"What's this stuff?" Griffin was pointing

to the first paragraph on the "Datch-worth 1" page.

"That's the description of the manu-script itself, and its binding if it has one: its size, the material and color of the binding and how it's held together, whether the pages are paper or parchment, the type of handwriting, the age of the thing. I was al-ways complete crap at this part, but Rob could do it all."

This was not the sort of language Griffin expected from a lady minister, but he could see she was concentrating hard, so he hid his smile.

"Then here," Kathryn pointed, "in rela-tively plain English, is a description of what the writing actually is; Datchworth One, for instance, contains prayers to the Virgin Mary, most of them in Latin. Sort of thing Cromwell would have burnt without a second's thought. Provided, of course, he could read it. After that comes the transcription; you simply write down in legible modern letters what the manuscript says. These transcriptions aren't complete; apparently Rob transcribed enough of each manuscript to get a feel for it, then moved on to the next one."

"That's not a modern letter," Griffin ob-jected, pointing. "Neither is that."

"Those are medieval letters that later fell out of the English alphabet. Those two are an 'eth' and a 'thorn,' both signifying the sound 'th,' and that thing there, an 'a' and an 'e' mashed into one letter, is called an 'ash.' "

"I'm sorry I asked. The point is, can you read this stuff?"

"Certainly. But I don't have to. You're looking for something to do with the silver. All I have to do is look at this bit here, where he says what the manuscript contains, prayers or whatever. If Rob found anything about the silver, it will be right here, under the manuscript description. I should start at the back, shouldn't I?"

She had already flipped through the notebook until she reached blank pages, and was now moving back through the ones containing Rob's neat writing. "This last one should be dated — yes, last Wednesday." There was a perceptible quaver in her voice. Resolutely she continued.

"It's a hymn to Saint Cecilia." She flipped back a page. "Booklet of prayers to various saints." She flipped another page. "Polemical sermons against Luther and John Knox. What fun." Another page. "Sermon on the Assumption of the B.V.M. Oh, now we're back to Tuesday." She looked up at Griffin. "I'll look at all these; if there's anything about silver, it should be obvious. But on second thought, this seems to me very unpromising. I can't believe Rob would have found out something about the silver and not mentioned it to anybody. And obviously you've talked to everybody in the entire Castle, and if any of them had said anything —"

"Pardon me, Inspector."

The policewoman who had been going over files at the smaller table was standing slightly behind Griffin. As he turned, she handed him a plain manila folder, saying, "This was in a section marked 'Lunchroom Extension, 1978.' "

The Inspector asked, "This was in the cupboard whose key was missing?"

Kathryn went back to flipping through Rob's notebook on the grounds that whatever else was happening in the room would be considered by the police as none of her business. But after three seconds Gorgeous George whirled back to her with a smile as wide as God's mercy.

"Kathryn!" he exclaimed, forgetting himself. "Oh, I do beg your —"

"Oh, call me anything you like! Just tell me you've found something that's going to help."

"I don't know. But this was found in a very peculiar place, which suggests it was hidden."

"What is it?"

"You tell me. *Please* tell me." He placed the open manila folder carefully on the table in front of her.

Inside the folder was a single sheet of what appeared to be very old parchment, on which there were two columns of writing.

Kathryn scanned the first few lines:

Þis helply wyf was Dalida yclept.

A-nightes whiles softe hir spouse yslept,

Gre De she wolde hir body in aparaille

Brighte and gay þe bet for to bigyle

Þe lechoures þat dwellen in þe toun.

"Can you read it?" he asked.

"Easy-peasy." She started to read aloud, producing pleasant, mellifluous sounds that were completely incomprehensible.

"What language is that?"

Kathryn, who was beginning to catch his excitement, looked up at him solemnly and said, "It's English, Jim, but not as we know it." A smile lurked at the corners of her mouth.

Griffin started to say his name was George, then realized she was doing a take-off of Dr. McCoy's line from Star Trek. He decided he had to solve this crime in the next hour so he could take her out to dinner.

He gave her his best grin. "Old English, is it? And call me George."

"Middle English," she corrected, not calling him anything at all because George was a name she didn't like. "Sounds fourteenth century, maybe fifteenth, and it's a narrative, a story of some kind."

"Looks more like poetry."

"That's because all the best stories at that time were written in verse, not prose. Did you do the *Canterbury Tales* in school?"

"A couple of them. Ah, you're right. I remember now. So what is this story about, and why do people keep hiding it? I'm assuming this is one of the manuscripts that was found with the silver."

Kathryn glanced at the next few lines. "I think I can tell you why it might have been hidden from Cromwell. It looks like a fabliau."

"What's a fabley-oh?"

Kathryn chuckled. "It's a fancy academic word, medieval French, that scholars use to prove to themselves how knowledgeable they are. Basically it means 'dirty story.'"

Griffin laughed delightedly, and Kathryn decided she might have to forgive the man for his awful taste in color coordination. She asked him to give her a minute to read the thing properly, and he obligingly backed away. But he kept an eye on her as she read. This was the first indication, aside from Hillman's sexual preferences, that the utterly blameless and ordinary murder victim had done anything remotely furtive or even interesting, and they desperately needed a break after five pointless, clueless days. Especially if, as seemed likely, the old man really had died of natural causes and wasn't the second victim.

As Kathryn perused the manuscript, Griffin heard his name spoken in an exchange outside the room. He went to the open doorway; at the foot of the steps, talking to the bobby on duty, was the estate manager.

"Did you wish to speak to me, Mr. Carlyle?" asked the Inspector as he descended the steps. He thought the man looked agitated.

"Indeed I do, Detective Inspector. I've just found this thing where it should not be. It is supposed to be either in the muniment room or in Sir Gregory's library."

Griffin looked at the small, beautiful object Carlyle was holding up for his examination. "What is it?"

"It is an illuminated capital cut from a medieval book of prayers; Rob Hillman discovered it some weeks ago amongst the manuscripts he was examining for Sir Gregory. He took it to Oxford and had it mounted as you see it."

"Where did you find it?"

"Outside my office there is an old hat-and-coatstand which has a sort of storage compartment as its base. Weeks ago, before all this sun, my wife left her brolly in it and this morning she asked me if I could bring it home before she forgot where it was. When I picked up the brolly, this was under it. Perhaps it's not important, but it seemed so odd —"

"Oh, yes, Mr. Carlyle, you did well in bringing it to me," said Griffin as he took the jewel-like object and examined it eagerly. "Valuable, is it?"

"Yes, Inspector. We've insured it for two thousand pounds."

Griffin's interest died. In parts of England people got killed for sums of money that wouldn't get you a cup of tea, but he was pretty sure that Datchworth Castle was not one of those places. He thanked Carlyle, then added, "Actually, I was planning to speak to you about something else. When Sir Gregory died, he appeared to be looking at some household accounts."

"Yes, Inspector. He asked me yesterday to bring him some papers."

"Could you be more specific?"

"He wanted to look at anything having to do with repairs and alterations to the fabric of the Castle over the last few years. I assumed it had something to do with the rebuilding of the wall that had to be repaired when the silver was found. I thought perhaps he might be comparing costs or some such thing."

"Did Sir Gregory normally look over papers of that kind?"

"Not in the time I've been here."

Griffin's interest was rekindled. He said

to the bobby, "O'Rourke, escort Mr. Carlyle to Sir Gregory's library and see that he's admitted." To Carlyle he said, "Could I ask you to look at those papers? They're still on the desk as they were when Sir Gregory died."

"I would be happy to help, Inspector, but what am I looking for?"

"To begin with, anything that might startle a frail old man into a heart attack. Aside from that, I suppose, anything at all that catches your interest."

Carlyle agreed cordially and went away with O'Rourke. Griffin did not immediately return to the muniment room, however, because another of his officers was hurrying down the corridor toward him with a piece of paper in his hand and a satisfied look on his face.

"Thought you'd like to see this right away, sir."

Griffin took the paper and read it. "Yes!" he hissed through shut teeth. "Get Banner — get *Sir Derek* here now. I don't care if he's planning the funeral. Drag him if you have to."

"Yes, sir!" The man strode away looking even more satisfied than he had before.

Griffin skipped up the steps and re-entered the muniment room. Finally things were happening. Now all he needed was for the beautiful Kathryn to come through.

She was still reading the manuscript. He approached the table and she glanced up at him a moment to say, "It's certainly a fabliau, but more than that . . ." She shrugged. "I'm still working."

He let her work. He stood still and watched intently, willing her to find something important, something he could use. Because he was watching her so closely, he saw the moment when she stopped moving, indeed, stopped breathing. He couldn't see her face, bent low over the manuscript, but every part of her suddenly froze. Then there was a small, sudden movement of her head as she looked back at a point farther up the page; then down again to the place where she had been before.

"What is it?" he asked urgently.

She put up a hand, showing him a flat palm, but did not take her eyes off the parchment.

He bit his lip and gave her the silence she wanted. Over at the small table, both the woman and the man had stopped going through files; like their superior officer, they stared at Kathryn in hushed anticipation.

Finally Kathryn looked up at the Inspector, and he saw that the expression on her face looked almost like fear. Or possibly awe.

She swallowed. "Do I understand correctly that you have been pursuing a connection between the manuscripts and the silver principally because the silver is worth a fortune, and where there is money there is motive?"

"Yes!" he cried. "There's something there about the silver?"

She shook her head. "Forget the silver. Forget all the silver in England. This —" She started to tap the manuscript with her finger but abruptly drew her hand back so as not to touch it. "This is worth more. I know people who would give you the Crown Jewels for this and call it a bargain. If you wanted to find something worth killing for, Inspector, you've found it."

CHAPTER 26

Minutes Later

When Kathryn left the muniment room her emotions were running high. She had just participated in the most sensational literary discovery of the twentieth century and, very probably, given the police the information they needed to find her cousin's killer; now her urgent agenda was to locate two men, one to make peace with and one to make love with. She couldn't enjoy the latter until she had done the former, so Tom came first.

He wasn't in the double-viewed parlor. Repeated knocks at his bedroom door, followed by pleas to be let in, produced no response, so she opened the door slowly, calling his name. He wasn't there, either. She went back to the entrance hall, where she saw a familiar face.

"Meera! Have you seen Tom?"

"About forty minutes ago he was with Crumper."

"Where?"

"They were going into the servants' wing."

"Thanks!" Kathryn gave her a smile and was hurrying toward an archway in the northeast corner of the hall when the policewoman called after her.

"Kathryn! Is there any way I can help?"

Kathryn made a sound that was somewhere between a laugh and a groan. "Thanks, Meera, but either I don't need help or I'm beyond it." She broke into a jog.

The door to the servants' wing had been one of the borders of Kathryn's wanderings around the Castle; she'd never been through it. It would have been a solecism to intrude on the staff's privacy. As she stood before it, irresolute, it opened and she silently thanked God as another familiar face emerged.

"Mary! I'm looking for my friend, Tom. A while ago he was with Crumper heading this way. Is he in there?" As she said this, Kathryn upbraided herself for not first noticing — and responding to — Mary's reddened eyes; it should have dawned on her that the staff would be upset by the sudden death of their beneficent employer. She was too preoccupied with her own inner turmoil. She was being selfish.

"I'm sorry, Miss Koerney, but he's not in the servants' hall, nobody is. We're all busy trying to —" she waved an inarticulate hand, lacking the directness to say, "cope with this disaster."

"I'm sorry, Mary, I shouldn't be bothering you, I know it must be terribly difficult for you." Kathryn wanted to put a sympathetic hand on the maid's shoulder, but didn't know if the gesture would be regarded as too familiar. "It's not important," she lied.

Mary looked at this American woman who spoke to the servants in exactly the same manner that she used with the Family, and saw that, contrary to what she had just said, it was very important. "You come in," Mary said. "You can wait in the hall and I'll find Mr. Crumper and ask him where your friend is."

Mary did eventually locate the butler, who told her that Mr. Holder was in the Crumpers' own flat. But before she could get back to the servants' hall to pass on this information, Kathryn had departed on an unexpected mission of mercy.

She had been sitting in a chair drawn back from the long table that was already set for the staff's supper when she was surprised by the entrance of an elderly man.

He was dressed neatly in an outdated black suit and he was all too clearly in a high state of agitation.

"Oh!" he exclaimed, startled at the sight of a stranger where strangers were rare. "And who might you be?"

Kathryn, feeling like an intruder, apologized for her presence, and explained that she was a guest in the house and had been told by Mary to wait there for a few minutes.

The mention of Mary's name appeared to comfort the old fellow slightly, but his disapproval was still obvious. Kathryn, seeking to mollify him, identified herself further.

"My name is Kathryn Koerney. I am the cousin of Rob Hillman, who died here last week. Sir Gregory kindly invited me to stay for a few days while the police sorted out what happened to my cousin."

The old man managed to force the agitation from his face long enough to announce formally, "I am Crumper."

"Crumper?"

"Yes, miss."

"The only Crumper I know is the butler."

"That would be my son. He is butler to Sir Gregory. I am butler to Lady Bebberidge-Thorpe."

Kathryn, behind her blank face, was thinking furiously. Who on earth would Lady Bebberidge-Thorpe be? She tried to summon up the family tree she and Tom had constructed. The only woman to whom that designation would properly apply would be the wife or the widow of the Baronet. Sir Gregory's mother, obviously long deceased, would have been Lady Bebberidge-Thorpe; so would his wife, but she was dead, too, mourned by Meg and Derek as "Aunt Sophy."

Kathryn decided it was pretty safe to say, "I don't believe I have met Lady Bebberidge-Thorpe."

"You wouldn't be allowed, if I may take the liberty of saying so, miss." The wrinkled face, already laboring to mask the agitation it had worn when Kathryn first saw it and the disapproval that had then joined the agitation, now had a further burden; it had to hold back what Kathryn guessed was a very long-established anger.

Despite the other emotional fish that Kathryn had to fry, her curiosity was aroused. She asked delicately, "And who, if I may be pardoned for asking, would not allow me to meet Lady Bebberidge-Thorpe?"

Old Crumper sniffed, a wordless expression of disdain. "I couldn't say, miss, but there are others could tell you if they would."

Kathryn, overwise in techniques for getting people to talk, opened her eyes wide and said not a word. It worked.

"But they won't. Oh, it's all right for them. Him in his chair and everybody feeling sorry for him, not to speak ill of the dead. And that young wastrel, Mr. Banner, Sir Derek I should say. Not a bit of natural feeling in *him*."

This speech, not unnaturally, unleashed a storm of speculation in Kathryn's mind, which she managed to hide successfully behind a face full of sympathetic concern. "You believe it's not right," was all she said. It was all she had to say.

Old Crumper pulled a chair out from the table and sat facing her. "I can tell you, miss, it's very wrong indeed. Keeping her a prisoner, like, in her own house." The old man had decided in Kathryn's favor; she had no business being in the servants' wing but at least Mary had put her there, and besides, he needed an ally. "Especially now," he continued. "Didn't anybody think about her? They did not. Left it to me to tell her Sir Gregory had passed on. She's upset something terrible, I can tell you."

"Of course she is," Kathryn agreed, feeling her way. The first and obvious possibility was that the old man was crazy. He was certainly Crumper's father, though; she'd had time to discern the resemblance through the wrinkles. And another possibility, far from obvious but growing on her by the minute, was that he was telling the unvarnished truth.

After all, this family seemed to have a habit of dispatching their inconvenient womenfolk, didn't they? Clarissa had been sent off to that "secure facility" in Hampshire, and Meg's mother — obviously another disgrace to the family, having a baby with nary a husband in sight — she, too, was conspicuously absent amidst a swirl of rumor. It would have been entirely consistent, Kathryn was beginning to think, for them to have swept Aunt Sophy under the carpet if she had somehow put herself beyond the pale. For a brief instant she wondered if, like poor Clare, Sophy had simply gone mad. The thought occurred, only to be instantly dismissed. *This is not Jane Eyre, Koerney; get a grip! There's no disgrace in nervous breakdowns these days, and besides, they talk about Clare's nervous breakdown quite openly. And clearly Sir Gregory didn't need to get rid of her so he could marry the governess.*

Old Crumper, meanwhile, had begun to wring his hands. "Miss Koerney, I don't know what to do. Lady Bebberidge-Thorpe is so upset, so upset I've never seen her. She sent me to fetch Mr. Ban—Sir Derek, I should say, but I don't think he'll come. He never does. Sir Gregory never came, either. Heartless, I call it."

In Kathryn's mind Tom Holder and Kit Mallowan had faded into unimportance. No man stood a chance with Kathryn when there was an abused woman nearby; the priest and the feminist in her came roaring to the rescue.

She leaned toward the old man and said, "Crumper, take me to her. I can help. My job, in fact, is talking to people who are upset. I'm good at it."

He needed very little persuading.

Derek, however, was a different matter. In the muniment room, Inspector Griffin had given up his hope of a quick confession. He had thought, at first, that Derek was going to crumble. Certainly the new Baronet had turned pale and sick-looking when Griffin had begun their conversation with, "Would you mind telling me, Sir Derek, what you were doing last Thursday afternoon at teatime on Hawley's Hill, northwest of the village, with a pair of binoculars pointed at this house?"

Derek, nowhere near a chair, had sat down on the edge of the long table and closed his eyes.

"I'm waiting for an answer," Griffin said sternly.

None came. Derek sat silent, his eyes still closed, his skin pasty underneath his tan.

Mecra Patel left the corner where she had been silently standing; she picked up Rob Hillman's chair and brought it around the table to Derek, gently encouraging him to sit in it. As he did so she said, "You'll feel better, you know, after you've told us about it. I promise you, Sir Derek. It's all going to come out anyway. Might as well get it off your chest." She was patting his shoulder in a motherly way.

Griffin watched this performance with mixed feelings. Personally, he didn't care much for Patel — too damn reserved for his taste — but he had to admit the woman knew her job.

Still, it might have gone either way, but for the chance angle at which Patel had set the chair. The illuminated capital, sitting at the end of the long table where Griffin had put it, was now in Derek's line of vision. Derek saw it when he was looking around miserably trying to find somewhere to put his eyes.

He gasped. "Where did you find that?"

Griffin's eyes narrowed. "Hidden in a very odd place," he replied.

But Derek only stared at the brilliant little square and offered no further comment or question. Griffin decided to push.

"Sir Derek," he said, "I wouldn't think a man in your position would need to steal something worth only two thousand pounds."

Derek gaped at him. "Two — *two thousand?* Where did you hear that?"

"Carlyle. He should know. He handles the insurance policies."

Derek stared incredulously at the Inspector and then back at the scrap of parchment. He began to make odd noises that eventually resembled laughter. He laughed until tears rolled down his cheeks, took his handkerchief out of his pocket, wiped his face and blew his nose, and then explained how he had persuaded Crumpet, whom he referred to as "Miss Crumper," to assist him in stealing it. "Then when she heard Rob was dead she panicked and hid it somewhere. I told her I didn't want to know where."

The confession was transparently true but Griffin was still puzzled. "It's obvious you thought it was worth a lot more than it is, but why did you want to steal it? Whatever it was worth, it would have been yours sometime in the near future."

Derek sighed. "Kit Mallowan's uncle — you've met Kit, haven't you? His late uncle, the sixth marquis, went to Brasenose College, Oxford. So did Uncle Greg. Our family and the Mallowans have all gone to B.N.C. since the turn of the century. Kit's uncle left the college a huge chunk of money in his will. Uncle Greg wanted to do something for the college as well, but our pockets are not as deep as the Mallowans' so it couldn't be money. Uncle Greg got the idea that if Rob Hillman found anything really remarkable in the manuscripts, we would give it to the B.N.C. library. I tried to talk him out of it because Datchworth needs every asset it has, we shouldn't be giving away things that might help maintain the estate. But I couldn't get him to see it that way. So I got Miss Crumper to chat Rob up and keep an eye on him so she could notify me right away if he found something really valuable." Derek shook his head. "Obviously there was some sort of mix-up. Miss Crumper says Rob told her the fragment was priceless, in fact he said 'beyond price.' "

"Ah!" said Inspector Griffin, as several pieces of the puzzle fell into place. After a moment he said, "Sir Derek, you were watching the parapet so you could notify Miss Crumper on her mobile when you saw Rob Hillman. I assume she was waiting nearby until she know the coast was clear and she could then come into this room to steal the fragment, correct?"

"Yes, that's right."

"I don't suppose you saw Hillman fall, did you?"

Derek shook his head. "He, ah, he went around the west side where I couldn't see him. I kept watching to make sure he didn't come back and go down to the muniment room again while Miss Crumper was still there. Then she phoned me and said she'd got the thing and was safely out of the house. So then I didn't need to watch anymore. So I got back in my car and went back to Oxford."

Griffin kept after him for a few minutes, but nothing more was to be elicited from Derek. Finally Griffin said, "All right, you can go now. Of course we'll have to check your story with Miss Crumper."

"Of course. Remember, though: she didn't want to do it. I, ah, put pressure on her. Any blame for this goes on me."

Griffin promised to treat Miss Crumper gently, and Derek left.

Kathryn, meanwhile, was sitting in a large, sunny, round room in the south wing of the Castle, wishing she were less impulsive. The moment Crumper Senior had ushered her into the presence of Lady Bebberidge-Thorpe, it was apparent that when he had said she was very upset, he did not mean she was weeping and in need of comfort. The woman was, on the contrary, mad as a wet hornet.

Not that she was openly angry; on the surface she was acting the perfect lady.

"How do you do, Miss Koerney. You must forgive me if I seemed startled when Crumper announced you. I am unaccustomed to visitors."

She spoke in the exaggerated upper-class accent of the Royal Family and was, Kathryn judged, about the same age as the Queen. The years had been a bit kinder to Sophy, however, than they had to Elizabeth; Lady Bebberidge-Thorpe was as slender as a girl, and her face had the bones a woman needs to maintain beauty long after youth has flown.

Like her butler, she was dressed with a formality that seemed slightly dated; Kathryn felt self-conscious in her shorts and sneakers. She decided she might make points by apologizing for them.

"I hope *you* will forgive *me*, Lady Bebberidge-Thorpe, for calling upon you dressed in such an inappropriate manner. I only put on these clothes so that I could sit on the ground on the west side of the Castle near the place where my cousin died. It was a way of paying my respects."

"Ah! You are the cousin of that young man who fell from the parapet."

Superficially it was a polite enough remark. But something in the inflection wasn't quite right; Kathryn sensed it without being able to name it, and it was not a pleasant sensation. She wondered how Aunt Sophy, that "treasure" so beloved by Meg and Derek, had become this frigid, hostile creature.

She ventured to say, "Lady Bebberidge-Thorpe, Crumper informs me that you are upset over the death of Sir Gregory —"

"I appreciate your sympathy, Miss Koerney, but I don't need it. My brother and I were never close."

"Your brother?" Kathryn asked, wondering how complex the family tree could get before it toppled under its own weight.

"Sir Gregory."

Thoroughly baffled, Kathryn said, "I'm sorry; I thought Sir Gregory was your husband."

Lady Bebberidge-Thorpe made a noise that in a less elegant person might have been called a snort. "Heavens, no!"

"But the only Lady Bebberidge-Thorpe I have heard of is Sir Gregory's wife."

"That was Sophy; she died several years ago. They called her Lady Bebberidge-Thorpe, but they were wrong. I was next in line after Richard, my older brother, died in 1937. But they denied me my birthright and gave it to my younger brother, simply because he was male. But here in private, no one can stop me from using my rightful title."

A slow, cold snake slithered up Kathryn's spine. "Lady Bebberidge-Thorpe," she said in a voice that was barely audible, "may I be so forward as to ask you to tell me your Christian name?"

The aged beauty lifted her plucked eyebrows. "That is a curious question, Miss Koerney; I might even say an impertinent one. However, since you wish to know, my name is Clarissa."

CHAPTER 27

A Few Minutes Earlier

The private flat of James and Martha
Crumper was a far cry from the servants'
quarters of old. Their sitting room had
French doors facing south-east onto a mini-
garden of their own; these doors were standing open to welcome the evening breeze that
was springing up to dissipate the day's heat.
It was altogether pleasant, but it was utterly
wasted on Tom.

The Crumpers, of course, were in the
main house dealing with the family crisis;
Crumper had seated Tom in his own
chair, plied him with Earl Grey, and told
him to make himself at home. He had
then hurried apologetically away. The tea
grew cold as Tom stared sightlessly out at
the garden.

How could he ever apologize? He would
have to explain what had driven him to
such fury. And how could he do that

without revealing how he felt about her? It would end their friendship. They would become distant, cordial acquaintances. He couldn't bear it.

Finally he stood up. He had to see her. He had no idea what to say, no idea what disastrous turn the conversation might take, but he had to see her. He walked out of the flat and promptly discovered that he didn't know where he was. He had been in a daze when Crumper had led him through the servants' wing to the flat. Rather than get lost inside, he opted for the garden. Taking his directions from the low sun, he headed west across the south face of the Castle. He saw a terrace he thought he recognized; he walked across it, looking through a series of open French doors until he discovered the Family Dining Room. From there it was no problem; he headed like a homing pigeon for the entrance hall, figuring he was bound to run into somebody; sure enough, he had turned no more than four corners before he encountered Mary, who was happy to direct him to the muniment room.

There was a bobby at the foot of the steps who gave him a nod and an interested look. "Evening, sir."

Tom returned the nod and the greeting

and asked if his friend Miss Koerney was in the room.

"She was here, but she might have left, I don't know; I was away myself for a bit. Shall I have a look for you?"

Tom thanked him, and the man turned to the steps but then turned back. "I say, sir, is it true you're on the job?" O'Rourke was a fan of American TV cop shows and had picked up the slang.

Tom admitted that it was true.

"Well, then, why don't you come up yourself?" suggested O'Rourke, who was friendly to a fault. He led Tom up the steps and opened the door.

George Griffin was feeling unusually friendly as well, as he scented an imminent and successful solution to the case, possibly even a sensational solution. Kathryn had told him enough about the manuscript to make it clear that its discovery was likely to make the BBC evening news and the front page of the *Times*. He himself was about to crack what might be a conspiracy murder involving titled families in stately homes, and if that alone wasn't enough to get his picture in the papers, the connection with the manuscript would guarantee it. So when Tom was ushered in by O'Rourke, Griffin invited him to stay.

"We're about to nail Derek Banner as an accomplice after the fact," he told Tom as if he were speaking to a colleague, "and then he is going to give us the killer." Excitement and satisfaction emanated from him in equal quantities.

Tom had seen immediately that Kathryn wasn't in the room, but the policeman in him was hooked by Griffin's disclosure. He decided to stay, at least for a few minutes. *Besides,* he thought, *if I can tell her they've found out who killed Rob, she might be in a slightly better mood. And I'm going to need all the help I can get.*

Sergeant Duncan appeared at the door with Derek; Derek cried angrily at Griffin, "What is this inquisition? I've told you everything —"

Griffin interrupted with a snarl, "Sit down, Derek!" and pointed to a chair.

It wasn't just the tone of voice; it was the familiarity of "Derek" without the "Sir." Even "Banner" might have passed as civil, but as Griffin was using it, the Christian name on its own was a mark of contempt.

Derek stood still. A guarded look came over his face.

"We've been having a talk with your delightful friend, Miss Crumper," Griffin continued. "She corroborated your story.

Every bit of it. But it's the part at the end that interested us most. Tell us, Derek: what did you see on the parapet? What surprised you so much, you hung up on the lovely Crumpet?"

Derek, still without speaking, moved slowly to the chair Griffin had indicated and sank into it. Crumpet, of course, had asked the same question the day after it had happened. Derek had told her that a bloody great spider had dropped from the tree above him onto his head; he had dropped his mobile, it had hit a rock and disconnected, and when he had tried to ring her back he couldn't get the phone to work. He was sure at the time that she had believed him, and even now he was reasonably certain that she had given the incident no further thought. It was this policeman who had seen through the story. *But he's guessing,* thought Derek. *There's absolutely no way he can prove I saw anything on that parapet other than Rob Hillman with a cup of tea in his hand.* He decided to call Griffin's bluff: he repeated the tale about the spider.

Griffin, predictably, poured scorn on it, but Derek stuck to it and they came to an impasse. They were glaring at each other mulishly when O'Rourke said, "Inspector? It's Mr. Carlyle."

Griffin, partially annoyed and partially relieved at the interruption, turned and gave his attention to the estate manager, who had just entered the room.

"I don't know if this will be any use to you," Carlyle was saying, "but it puzzled me. As I've told you before, I've only been here about eight months, so this invoice is a bit before my time. It's from a firm of building contractors in Oxford who were apparently doing some alterations in the south wing. It's this item here," he said, showing Griffin the sheet of yellow paper and pointing to one line. "The thing is, I've always been informed that the only access to the parapet is from the staircase in this room."

The Inspector said grimly, "So have I."

He took the invoice from Carlyle, crossed the room back to Derek, and held the paper in front of Derek's nose.

"All right, then, *Sir Derek*," he said witheringly, "tell me who, on Wednesday last, used the 'roof access from south wing' to get to Rob Hillman?"

A look of horror came over Derek's face. "Oh, no!" he cried, shaking his head. "Oh, no, no, no! It can't be! It couldn't be! We were so careful! Uncle Gregory took care of everything! She can't have got out!"

Griffin threw the paper aside, put his hands on the arms of Derek's chair, and fairly shouted into his face, "*Who* can't have got out? Who went from the south wing up onto the parapet? Who did you see?"

Derek, shaking all over, covered his face with his hands and began to sob. "It looked like her, you see, but I knew it couldn't be her, because she couldn't have got up there, there was no way —"

"Out with it, man! *Who did you see?*"

Tom was almost fifteen feet from Derek but his hearing was acute. There was no doubt; the half whisper, half whimper that came from behind Derek's hands was, "My mother."

Kathryn thought, *So much for a secure facility in Hampshire.*

The Family hadn't sent their black sheep off to be locked up with strangers. They had kept her at home. It was *Jane Eyre*, after all. It was positively Gothic. It was ridiculous. What century did they think they were living in?

"Lady Bebberidge-Thorpe," said Kathryn, rising from her chair, "I apologize for intruding on your privacy. I only came because I, ah, got the impression from

Crumper that you wished to speak to somebody about Sir Gregory's death. I see I was mistaken. I'll go now."

"Sit down, Miss Koerney," said the icy voice. "I said I didn't need your sympathy. I didn't say that I was not interested in information."

Kathryn hesitated. She found the fabled Clarissa/Cruella well and truly creepy, but she also found it hard to believe that the woman could represent a real threat. Kathryn admitted to herself she was nervous, but she was determined to behave sensibly. *After all,* she told herself, *I can run a lot faster in these sneakers than she can in those heels.*

She sat down again. "What can I tell you, Lady Bebberidge-Thorpe?"

Clarissa, it transpired, wanted to hear all there was to know about her brother's death. Kathryn thought this a reasonable request and fulfilled it to the best of her ability. Trying for a courteous conclusion, she said, "So now your son is Sir Derek. I'm sure he will take good care of Datchworth."

"I have no doubt he will," Clarissa replied indifferently, "but Derek is not my son."

"I beg your pardon? Derek is — ?"

"Not my son."

"I'm terribly sorry, but I don't understand."

"Then you must not be very clever. It is a simple matter. The young man who thinks he now owns Datchworth is not my son. I bought him from a stupid girl in Italy who had got herself pregnant by some German tourist."

Kathryn struggled for speech. After several seconds she settled for one word: "Why?"

Clarissa looked at her disdainfully. "You are not, in fact, clever at all, are you? We needed an heir, my husband and I. Then, as it happened, my nephew died in a car crash and my brother needed an heir as well. Derek served admirably for both purposes. At least, so I thought at the time. I know better, now. He is an ungrateful wretch who does not deserve what I have given him. Will you have some sherry? You look as though you may not be warm enough."

Kathryn was, in fact, chilled to the bone. It hardly mattered whether or not the fantastic story was true. The matter-of-fact manner in which it was being related proved to her beyond a shadow of a doubt that she was in the presence of real madness. "That's kind of you, but I must go back to my room and change now, so I shan't be able to stay for sherry."

"No, Miss Koerney," Clarissa said, and it was unmistakably an order. "I must talk to you about your cousin."

Kathryn hesitated. Was it possible Clarissa knew who had killed Rob? *If I run away now,* she wondered, *will I ever find out?* "What about my cousin?"

"A pleasant young man," Clarissa allowed judiciously. "Good manners, for an American. He told me about a great treasure he had found in the muniment room."

"That's right. It is indeed a great treasure. I've seen it."

Clarissa regarded Kathryn thoughtfully for a moment. "He called it a fragment, as though it were a piece of a broken dish, yet he talked of Chaucer and a manuscript."

"That's right, Lady Bebberidge-Thorpe. Chaucer never finished the *Canterbury Tales,* and what tales he did finish he never finally assembled into one whole. There is one tale of which we have only the beginning, about fifty lines. It is told by the Cook, one of the less respectable pilgrims, and it's clear from those fifty lines that the story is going to be very vulgar. It is Chaucer, nevertheless, so the remainder of that story has been for some centuries rather like the lost mines of Solomon. That's what Rob found in the muniment room: the "Cook's Tale," a fragment of the *Canterbury Tales*."

Clarissa actually looked pleased. She almost smiled. "It would be very valuable, then?"

"Beyond valuable. Literally priceless."

Clarissa was nodding to herself as if immensely satisfied. "Excellent. That's what he told me. It's good to hear a second opinion that concurs."

"Lady Bebberidge-Thorpe, how did you come to have this conversation with Rob? Did he visit you here?"

"Oh, no. No one visits me here. It gets intensely dull. That's why I had Crumper arrange my escape hatch."

"Escape hatch?"

"Yes. If I try to go out into the rest of the house, they threaten to send me away to a dreadful place where people are locked up in padded cells. But what they don't realize is that I know this part of the Castle quite well. I memorized it as a girl. I always wanted this room, you see."

"It's a lovely room," Kathryn agreed, humoring her.

"They gave it to my stupid older brother.

He didn't deserve it, couldn't possibly appreciate it. But when he fell out the window and drowned in the moat, I assumed they would give it to me. I asked them to. But they boarded it up. They filled in the moat. I had to wait a long time to get this room." Clarissa's gaze went on a stately progress around the walls and windows.

"Lady Bebberidge-Thorpe. You were going to tell me how you came to meet my cousin. Something about an escape hatch?"

"Ah, yes. Crumper helped me with that; he's very loyal. He managed to get Cunningham, the old estate manager, to authorize some alternations to my quarters. Cunningham didn't know, of course, that I lived here, he had only been told that Crumper was in charge of this part of the Castle. But I knew every stone, as I told you, so with a little ingenuity . . . come, let me show you where I spoke with your cousin."

She rose gracefully and walked across the room to a dark wooden door. Kathryn, now afire with curiosity, followed her into a small vestibule containing two other doors.

Clarissa gestured at the wider of the two.

"I was given that room for a bedroom, and this —" here she opened the other door, "this was just a little space between the rooms. Gregory told me I could use it for storage. As if I had anything to store! But I knew something Gregory didn't. Only a wooden wall stood between this space — it was here, you see — and *this*."

"This" was a windowless area from which arose a narrow wooden staircase.

"It goes up to the old servants' quarters on the top floor. I know what you're thinking. It's not really suitable for a person of my station, is it? But it serves the purpose."

Kathryn walked over to the foot of the steps and looked up. She was in the bottom of a tall stairwell. In the dim light, it was hard to tell, but she thought it went up five flights, possibly more.

"At the top," said Clarissa, "I had the workmen alter a window. From the out-side, it looks like all the other windows, so anyone walking along the parapet would never know. But from the inside it opens like a door."

Kathryn said softly, "You met my cousin on the roof."

"Yes, it was most fortunate. Shall we go up?"

Kathryn shivered. "I — I'm afraid I can't. I — I'm afraid of heights, you see. And I'm getting quite cold now. I really must go back to my —"

No! Kathryn thought. *This cannot really be happening.*

Clarissa had lifted her right hand, and in it was a small pistol.

Tom was looking for Kathryn again, and cursing Datchworth for its size. "How the hell could you live in a place liked this?" he muttered to himself as he left the wing where the double-viewed parlor and their bedrooms were. She hadn't been there. "You'd need walkie-talkies to find anybody. Or something higher tech. Computer, tell me the location of Kathryn Koerney. *Kathryn Koerney has eloped with a rich red-headed Englishman.* Computer, tell me the penalty for doing away with a rich red-headed —"

Since he had reached the foot of the entrance hall staircase only to come face-to-face with the redhead in question, he was grateful that he hadn't been muttering too loudly.

"Tom!" Kit cried thankfully. "I've been looking all over for Kathryn. Where is she?"

"You tell me and we'll both know. She was in the muniment room a while — oh, Crump!"

Crumper had entered the hall from a corridor Tom had not yet set foot in. He looked worried. "Tom! I've been looking for you. My lord," he added with a small bow to Kit, "forgive me. I did not immediately see you." He turned back to Tom. "Did Kathryn ever find you?"

"She was looking for me?"

"Yes. I see she was unsuccessful."

"Crumper," said Kit, "what are you so worried about? Where *is* Kathryn?"

"I'm afraid, my lord, based on what Mary has just told me about something my father said, that Kathryn is with Mrs. Banner."

Kit, incredulous, exclaimed, "In Hampshire?"

But Crumper didn't hear him because Tom had grabbed his arm and was shouting, "For God's sake, where are they? Clarissa Banner is the one who murdered Rob Hillman!"

Crumper absorbed this information in a millisecond. Then he turned and ran back toward the hallway he'd come from, shouting something Tom couldn't make out. Tom, in hot pursuit, became aware that he had company. Kit's wheelchair, propelled by arms moving almost too fast for the eye to see, was flying down the corridor trying to pass him on the right.

One percent of Tom's brain was thinking, *Shit, I can't even outrun the bastard,* while the other ninety-nine percent was fighting over whether to be very afraid or to protest reasonably, *What possible reason could Clarissa have to harm Kathryn?*

Kathryn, carefully climbing the creaky stairs with Clarissa in her wake, had arrived at the same question.

Given the choice of being shot in the dim privacy of Clarissa's secret staircase or obeying her order to ascend to the roof, Kathryn had opted for the roof. *With any luck,* she thought, *there'll be a cop up there.* Failing that, she had reasoned, the time it would take to get to the parapet would at least provide opportunity to think. She was thinking with all her might.

Her thought processes were either hampered or heightened, she wasn't sure which, by the deafening thumps of her heart and the quivering weakness in her legs that made the stairs seem like Everest. She had instinctively put her hand on the banister, but it had moved under her touch and she had decided not to trust it.

"Lady Bebberidge-Thorpe," she said in what she hoped was a calm and courteous voice. "I do not understand why you are threatening me in this way. I am not at all a threat to you."

"Heavens, girl, you really are slow, aren't you? I need that manuscript, that fragment, for myself. Your cousin told me there was some plan to give it to Gregory's college at Oxford. That sounds like Gregory. Foolish beyond permission. But your cousin also told me that Gregory didn't know about the fragment yet, no one did. Are all Americans stupid?"

"I admit that many of us are," Kathryn replied, cravenly flattering the woman's egomania. "But there's no reason to, um, silence me. Everybody knows about the fragment now. It's no longer a secret. I told the police all about it."

"You would, of course, say that. Keep moving."

Kathryn had halted for a moment, stunned by Clarissa's easy dismissal of the truth. It was at that instant that fear turned to dread. This crazy woman was dead serious. And she, Kathryn, was about to be dead, period, like Rob, if she didn't try something more drastic than persuasion. A favorite phrase of her father's floated through her mind: *Never waste your time trying to reason with unreasonable people.* Time. She was wasting time.

What were her advantages and how could she use them? She realized at once that she had, at that moment, a classic advantage for combat. She was higher than her enemy. Also heavier and stronger. She would knock Clarissa down the stairs. She would turn suddenly and — No. Turning would take too much time, and she might lose her balance. She would remain facing forward and kick back with one leg. She thought she was close enough. She needed something to help maintain her balance. The banister was no good. The stairs. The stairs themselves. She would start a sentence to make the attack more unexpected; she would pitch forward and grasp the step three — no, four — steps higher than the one she was on at the time, and kick back with her right leg as strongly as she could. That would at least throw Clarissa off balance, and leave her vulnerable to a full frontal attack.

Do it now, Koerney, she told herself, *before you get paralyzed by the absurdity of the situation, before you start thinking it can't really be this bad, just behave reasonably and it will all go —*

Forgetting to start a sentence, she threw her hands down to the fourth step above her feet and simultaneously lashed back with her right leg. Her foot met only thin air, however, and the force of the movement rolled her over so that her left leg folded under her and she sat down with a thump facing Clarissa. Clarissa had thrown herself toward the wall to avoid the blow, and instantly backed down three steps. She held the gun up and regarded Kathryn with a narrow eye.

"I wonder if I have underestimated you," she mused.

Kathryn was thinking it was she who had underestimated Clarissa. She was sure of it when Clarissa continued.

"Perhaps I had better warn you, Miss Koerney, in case you decide that this gun is too small to do you any serious damage. My intention is to aim for your face and fire repeatedly. I believe I can hit you at least three times. Even if the bullets don't kill you, they should cause sufficient brain damage to render you incapable of remembering who Chaucer was, much less of reading his work." There was a brief pause. Then she spoke again: "Move."

Kathryn moved. She got to her feet,

turned, and once again began to climb the stairs. She began to wonder if she shouldn't devote some part of her brain to the business of confessing her sins.

Fortunately for Kit, the route from the entrance hall to the Round Room was all on the same level; with no steps to impede him, he arrived neck and neck with Tom. Crumper was banging on a heavy old door and simultaneously rattling the doorknob. "Mrs. Banner! Dad!" he shouted, to no effect. He was explaining breathlessly to Tom and Kit at the same time that he had tried before and gotten no answer. "I don't have a key to this door, only my father does — *Mrs. Banner! Dad!*"

Tom was looking at the door, thinking in despair that they would need a battering ram to break it down.

"*Jimmy!*" cried a reproachful voice behind them. "What are you — ?"

"Dad, thank God! Quick, open the door!"

Before Old Crumper said a word, it was clear he did not plan to comply. He was putting on his dignity as if it were a cloak, and he was starting to fold his arms. Before he could do so, however, his lapels were grasped and pulled forward and down so suddenly he could hear them tear. He was face-to-face with Aristocracy, and it said, in the voice of seven marquises put together, "You — will — open — that — door."

"Yes, my lord! At once, my lord! Here is the key —"

The key was wrested from the old man's grasp by his own son, who opened the door in less than a second; Crumper and Tom tumbled into the room, Kit almost rolling over them; Kit and Tom were shouting Kathryn's name. The Round Room was empty. Tom turned to Crumper, crying, "Go, Crump, get Griffin or any cop you can find!" Crumper was back out the door almost before Tom had finished his sentence. Kit had sped across the Round Room to the only other door, which was standing open, and swore furiously when the arms of his chair clanged against the stone doorposts. He couldn't get through it. Instantly he spun his wheels back to get out of Tom's way. Tom pelted through the opening, looked right toward a small doorway that opened onto a closet, and wrenched open the door to the left. He swept the bedroom with a glance, found the smaller door that logic said should be there, and ran to it. There was no one in the bathroom, either. Even as he ducked to look under the bed he called to Kit, "She's not here!"

"Over here, Tom!" Kit was pointing toward the place that looked like a closet. "There's light through there!"

Tom came, gasping for breath now and cursing himself for being overweight and unfit. Kit was right; the back of the closet gave way to a stairwell. Tom looked up, saw no movement, started to shout Kathryn's name again but decided to save his breath, and launched himself at the stairs.

He grabbed at the banister to assist his legs and lungs; with a loud crack it broke; he fell backward down the few steps he had already climbed and hit the back of his head against the stone floor.

Kit heard the cry, the fall, and the silence. "Tom!" he shouted. "*TOM!*"

Nothing.

Kit put his hands on the arms of his chair, put his weight on his hands, and with a mighty push flung himself forward onto the floor. He began to walk on his hands, balancing his torso and dragging his useless legs behind him. He got to the stairwell, saw Tom stretched out motionless, and said, "Oh, Jesus." Praying that

Tom was merely unconscious, he struggled past him and reached the stairs.

If the banister had been solid, he could have swarmed up it like a monkey, but having witnessed Tom's fate, he dared not try it. He put his hands on the steps and straightened his arms. Step by step he pulled himself up the stairway, walking on his hands. The muscles in his arms were screaming by the time he reached the second landing, but he stopped only to take off his belt and cast it aside; the buckle was catching on some of the steps and slowing him down. His progress was excruciatingly slow anyway; it was taking him forever; if Kathryn was in danger, he would never get there in time. But he labored on, sweating, straining, weeping, cursing, and praying harder than he had ever prayed in his life.

On the top floor both Clarissa and Kathryn had heard the shouting. But then it had stopped.

Clarissa said mildly, "I suppose that was intended to be a rescue party, but apparently it has gone off in another direction."

Kathryn had come to the same conclusion, and was now suffering the ghastly feeling that comes to a frightened person whose hopes have been raised only to be dashed.

They were in the old servants' quarters now, moving down a dark hallway punctuated by dim rectangles of light, open doorways into now abandoned rooms. Kathryn moved her eyes right and left without moving her head, desperately hoping to spot an escape route, but as far as she could see all the rooms were just that: rooms. Dead ends. There would be no point in ducking into one of them; Clarissa would have her cornered.

Kathryn had commended her soul, her mother, and several friends into the keeping of God. She had bundled all her sins into one three-word confession that said it all: "Lord, thou knowest." She had used it before when she felt overwhelmed; it was the only time she used sixteenth-century language in private prayer.

Having prepared for the worst-case scenario, she now, quite sensibly, had turned both her mind and her prayers back to an attempt at a happier ending.

I am dressed both for fight and for flight and she is dressed for neither. The gun is small. It will hold either six or eight bullets, but it may not be full. Assume it's full. Assume there are eight. That would be enough to kill me, cer-

*tainly, but only if they were well aimed. She's
right about three bullets to my face. So I won't
show her my face. And I shall get the back of
my head as far away from her as possible, the
minute I see a place where I can dodge around
a corner and make her waste a few shots. And
possibly pick up something to waylay her with
when she comes around the corner after me.
Damn this efficient household, these rooms are
completely bare. Not so much as a curtain
rod. I'd settle for a doorstop. Maybe I should
make a run for it now. Down this hall and
into the last room. There won't be anything
there I can use for a weapon, but then, there's
not likely to be anything on the roof either.
Maybe I should go for it before I get to the
roof.*

But suddenly the choice was no longer
open to her. "The door on your left,
please," said Clarissa. Kathryn obediently
went through the door. As in the other
rooms they had passed, the windows were
narrow rectangles set under low eaves. As
Kathryn entered, however, she saw that
below one window a short flight of wooden
steps had been built. Clarissa's escape
hatch. Kathryn walked over to the steps,
stopped, turned, and with a polite gesture
said, "Ladies first."

Clarissa, like Victoria, was not amused.

Neither was she offended, however; she simply said, "No," and indicated with an economical movement of the gun that Kathryn was to proceed. Kathryn ascended the steps and opened the window door. Ducking a bit to avoid hitting her head, she stepped out onto the parapet, turned to her right, and immediately broke into a run.

At any other time, she would have been impressed by her surroundings. Towering above the surrounding countryside, Sir Horace's Victorian walkway had been designed to provide a view to take the breath away. Even in the fading light of the English summer evening — it was nearing ten p.m — the grounds of Datchworth and the lands surrounding it would have been a sight to gladden the heart of anyone under any circumstances remotely resembling normal.

At least, Kathryn reflected, she was in no danger of falling off, even though she was running as fast as she could in the narrow space between the guard wall on her left and the steep, almost vertical, roof on her right; the edge of the guard wall came up to her waist. She might sideswipe it, but she wasn't going to fall off of it. Even as the expected shots rang out behind her, some small portion of her mind was wondering how Clarissa had managed to push Rob over it.

The answer to this question came, sudden and unwelcome. Rounding the corner she had hoped and prayed for, she fell to her knees, her heart in her throat, to avoid going over the edge. The parapet's wall on the west side of the Castle was only two feet tall. She scrambled to her feet, oblivious to the blood on her legs, and jogged as fast as she dared.

Behind her the shots had stopped. Clarissa had to get around the corner before she could fire again. How many shots had there been? Kathryn cursed herself for not having counted them. She'd been too frightened.

Suddenly she realized that the sloping roof at her right was not very steep, and it was punctuated with large dormer windows. Kathryn skidded to a halt, threw a quick look behind her to make sure Clarissa was not yet in sight, and climbed up onto the roof, blessing the rubber soles of her shoes. She crouched behind one of the dormers and applied herself to the difficult task of breathing quietly. Chanting silently in her mind a prayer to her favorite mystic, *Mother Julian, show me your peace,* she matched her breathing to the rhythm of the chant. She thought she could hear footsteps.

When Clarissa spoke she was so close, Kathryn's heart stopped. "Come, Miss Koerney, this is foolish. You can at least attempt to behave with dignity. What would your mother think?"

Some day, if I live so long, Kathryn thought, *I'm going to find that hilarious.*

There was silence. Clarissa was not moving forward.

Does she know I'm here? Kathryn wondered. *Behind this particular dormer, or is she just guessing that I'm behind one of them?*

Again Clarissa spoke. "Miss Koerney. You are wasting my time. You cannot possibly —"

She was interrupted, incredibly, by somebody calling her name. "Mrs. Banner!"

Kathryn's heart stopped again. Kit's voice. How the hell had he got up here? And did he know Clarissa had a gun? The second question was answered immediately.

"Don't threaten me with that toy, Mrs. Banner. I'm not that easily frightened."

Clarissa replied, icicles hanging from every word, "My name is Bebberidge-Thorpe."

"No it's not, you silly cow."

Kathryn was horrified. Didn't Kit realize she was dangerous?

"Your name is Banner, don't you remember? You married a nouveau-riche gutless wonder to get out of a house where everybody saw through you, where everybody knew you were nothing but a heartless bitch with a pretty face who would stoop to —"

Kathryn understood what he was doing in the split instant before she heard the first shot. She slid rapidly, noisily, down the roof to the parapet. Clarissa couldn't hear the noise for the gunfire, and of course she had her back to Kathryn.

Kit was actually crawling *toward* Clarissa, shouting more abuse at her in a louder voice, as if he assumed the bullets were blanks and he was invulnerable.

Kathryn grabbed Clarissa from behind and immediately fell to the left, onto the sloping roof and away from the perilous drop. Her left arm was around Clarissa's neck; her right hand was holding Clarissa's right wrist, trying to point the gun skyward. To her horrified dismay, she found she had underestimated Clarissa's strength. The woman twisted in her grasp and managed to free the hand that held the gun.

Before Clarissa could do anything with it, however, she was yanked off her feet by Kit, who had reached up and caught hold of the sash of her dress. Clarissa fell on top of him. Without a second's hesitation he grabbed a handful of her hair and slammed her head against the roof tiles. The gun fell from her slack hand and she lay still.

Kathryn pushed herself up off of the sloping roof, leaned over Clarissa, and picked up the gun. She was shaking so hard she couldn't stand, so she sat down on the narrow floor of the parapet. It felt good to have the two-foot wall at breast level.

She looked at Kit, trying to collect herself enough to speak. He was looking at her, doing the same. She got there first.

"Did you kill her?"

Kit took another breath. "God, I hope not."

"Are you hit?"

"I don't think so."

"Good."

It was all she could think of to say.

They sat without further attempt at conversation, too exhausted even to hold hands, until the police found them.

CHAPTER 28

Two Days Later

The first thing he was aware of was that his head hurt. God, did it hurt. Other things, less painful, began to introduce themselves to his notice. He was in bed. It wasn't night-time, though; warm light penetrated his closed eyelids, coloring them orange. He thought about opening them but he was afraid that it might make his headache worse.

He never had headaches. Where on earth had he gotten this one? Suddenly it came flooding back: Datchworth, Clarissa Banner, Kathryn. Kathryn! He opened his eyes. He appeared to be in a hospital bed, but the room looked too good for a hospital. There was real wallpaper and a decent-looking painting and a huge television on a tall stand that made it easily visible from the bed. Best of all, however, was the armchair, because sitting in it, reading a book and looking entirely healthy, was Kathryn Koerney.

"Kathryn!" he said. Or at least, tried to say. All that came out was a harsh rasp that sounded like an unsuccessful cough.

She looked up in delight, however, as if summoned by the voices of angels. "You're awake! Oh, thank God! Here," she said, jumping up and coming to the bed. "What you need is water." She had picked up a pitcher and was filling a glass. "Your mouth probably feels like Death Valley. Unfortunately they don't have those cute hospital straws over here that let you drink lying down. . . ."

She had pressed a button at the side of the bed, and with a loud hum it was raising him to a more or less upright position. He tried to speak but it was hopeless; she shushed him and told him to wait until he'd had a drink. He decided this was good advice and followed it. He drank the entire glass of water, although toward the end his hand shook from the effort of holding the glass. She saw it, steadied his hand as he finished the last sip, and then took the glass and put it on the bedside table.

"Better?" she asked.

"Kathryn." At least this time it sounded more like her name and less like the rattle of a dying man. "I'm so sorry."

"Don't be silly. You have nothing to apologize for. It wasn't your fault. How could you have known the banister would break?"

" 'S not what I meant," he whispered. "I mean, I'm sorry I yelled at you, said those awful things."

"Oh, *that!* Forget it. We were both stressed-out; the whole house was awash with negative emotions, so it's no wonder it got to us, too."

"But still. The things I said . . ."

"The things you said, my friend, were mostly true."

"No, they weren't. I was just —"

She laid her forefinger on his lips to hush him. It was the most intimate gesture she had ever made to him; he closed his eyes the better to savor the sensation. He would have given half the planet earth to be able to extend his tongue and lick her finger.

"You were absolutely correct, Tom, I was enjoying hobnobbing with the wealthy and the titled. And although I honestly don't fancy a life as lady of the manor, my ego was tickled pink that a marquis, no less, had fallen in love with me."

Tom swallowed hard. "Was it mutual?"

"It was and is." She sighed, sat down on the edge of the bed, and gazed out the window. "I just wish he were — oh, an English teacher."

Misery held Tom's tongue. He needed desperately to change the subject. "Speaking of English teachers, did you find something in the manuscripts that, ah, explained . . ."

"Yes. Yes, I did. I forgot you've slept through all of it. Headlines from here to Timbuktu. 'Sensational Literary Find Solves Murder.'" She explained about the Chaucer fragment, but her tone was so obviously bitter that he was puzzled until she got to the end. "One's desires," she concluded, "can render one's brains useless. Rob should have noticed the parchment was unused on one side. I should have noticed that the wife was supposed to be carrying on while her husband slept, but Chaucer makes clear that the husband himself is a late-night reveler."

"It's a *fake?*"

"The Lord High Muckety-Muck Manuscript Expert at Oxford is flying back from somewhere to look at it, but yes, he's going to say it's a fake. A sixteenth-century joke. A novelty." She spat out the last word as though it were an obscenity, rose abruptly from her chair, crossed to the window, and glared out of it.

"Oh, shit, Kathryn," Tom said with feeling. Her cousin had died for a joke. He could think of nothing else to say, so after a short silence he repeated it. "Oh, shit." It sounded appallingly inadequate to the occasion.

After a while, however, she turned and went back to the armchair, saying as she sank into it, "Do you know, I think that is the most intelligent remark anybody has yet made to me on the subject?" Then, before he had time to feel gratified, she added, "Would you like to hear about my adventures with Clarissa?"

Tom recognized the deliberate change of topic; he assured her he wanted to hear every little detail.

"Well, then." Kathryn settled herself in the chair. "Do you remember that you added a couple of relatives to the family tree, people Crumper had told you about? We didn't give much thought to them, did we? But one of them was Clarissa's first victim."

She told Tom what Derek had finally told the police: that twelve-year-old Richard Bebberidge-Thorpe, Sir Gregory's older brother, had "fallen" out of his bedroom window into the moat and drowned. That months later, his room had been cleared out and various and sundry of his belongings stored in one of the attics. That decades later, Sir Gregory's son Gerald had asked if he could have the old set of golf clubs he'd seen in the attic, and his father had said yes. That a friend of Gerald's had been the first to try the wood, and had asked him rudely, after the manner of schoolboys, what Jerry'd been using the club for, bashing rabbits? Because there was pale brown hair stuck to the wood. That Sir Gregory had taken the club, bought his son a new one, and sent the old one to a laboratory in London to be tested.

"It was human hair," said Kathryn, "stuck to the wood with human blood. Sir Gregory knew then what had happened, because Clarissa had always simply taken whatever she wanted, and she wanted her brother Richard's room. Which is understandable, actually, it's a wonderful architectural eccentricity, huge and perfectly round —"

"Kathryn," Tom murmured.

"Yes?"

"I've seen it."

"Oh, of course you have, what an idiot I am. Where was I? Oh, blood on the golf club. Later, when DNA fingerprinting had been developed, Sir Gregory had the golf club tested again and then he had irrefutable proof. But he kept it to himself. He had not believed his sister then presented a danger to anyone, because by that time she was married to John Banner, a man who could buy her literally anything she wanted. Desperate measures would not be necessary.

"But in 1995 Dotty Mallowan decided to marry Harry Tandulkar, and Clarissa went 'round the twist. She'd always hated the very thought of having Will and Harry as relatives; they claim she refers to them as 'filthy niggers,' which seems rather hard to believe in this day and age, but having spoken to her I can believe anything about her as long as it's unpleasant. At any rate, if Harry married Dotty, as you pointed out yourself, and Kit died without male issue, any son of Harry's would be the next Marquis. So, Clarissa — my God, Tom, it's so bizarre. Clarissa actually told Derek he had to kill Harry. So Derek and Sir Gregory decided to lock her up where she couldn't do any harm. But they couldn't have her properly medically committed without letting strangers in on the dire family secret, so they put her under house arrest at Datchworth, imprisoned in the room she'd originally killed for, and set as her servant and reluctant jailor Crumper's father, 'Old Crumper.' Crumper tells me you met his father briefly in the mad chase."

Tom nodded. "Yes. Suddenly there was this old man, and Crump was calling him 'Dad,' and it just seemed like part of the craziness, you know? The idea of Crumper having a father, when anybody can plainly see he wasn't born, he was, I don't know, ordered out of an old Hollywood film, know what I mean?"

Kathryn chuckled. "I know exactly what you mean. Let me fill you in. The old Hollywood film in question is the Datchworth Castle estate. The Crumper family has worked on it for generations. *Our* Crumper's father, *Old* Crumper, is named Albert. As a child, Bertie Crumper, like all the other Datchworth children, watched the Family from afar, and from afar I imagine that Clarissa Bebberidge-Thorpe, who is still beautiful at seventy-five, must have looked like an angel from heaven. From my short conversation with Old Crumper, I gather that he is blindly devoted to her despite the fact that she is a heartless viper and mad to boot, so I'm guessing that what we're dealing with is idol worship conceived at a very early age. Crumper, *our* Crumper, says his dad worked like stink to 'better' himself to get off the farm and into 'house service,' and maybe he did it to get closer to Clarissa. But I wander far from my tale."

"Yeah, you never could stay on the subject."

"You are taking shameless advantage of the fact that I dare not throw anything at you for fear of making your head hurt worse."

"Yes."

"Fair enough. Where were we? Ah, yes. Derek and Sir Greg put Clarissa under house arrest in the Round Room with Old Crumper as her butler and jailer. They thought she couldn't harm anybody there. They underestimated her. As did my cousin Rob, apparently. As indeed did I."

Kathryn told Tom how Clarissa, serenely claiming the Bebberidge-Thorpe name and title on the basis that she was the next eldest, had explained just as serenely how she had pushed an unwary Rob Hillman over the parapet so that the newly discovered treasure would remain at the Castle rather than go to Brasenose College.

"She thought she could take Datchworth

and the Chaucer fragment with it. With Sir Gregory dead" — here Kathryn took a breath — "she was going to disown Derek on the grounds that he was not actually her son but an illegitimate Italian peasant."

"*What?*"

"Gets better all the time, doesn't it? She told me about it but I didn't know whether to believe her or not. When the police and the guys in the white coats took her away, she was screeching it at the top of her lungs. The story got to Morgan Mallowan by the next morning, of course, and Harry came storming over to demand that Derek take a DNA test and if he couldn't prove kinship, Harry was going to claim Datchworth for himself. Derek told Harry where to go and to take his DNA tests with him. I found it all very unattractive, so I told Derek to check Sir Gregory's will to see who inherits if he doesn't. Lo and behold, Sir Gregory left the entire Datchworth estate, every stone and every penny, to Derek Several-middle-names Banner of such-and-such an address, Oxford, further to be identified as 'the infant baptized at Saint Something's parish church, Little Nowhere, Surrey, on such-and-such a date, and subsequently reared as the child of Mr. and Mrs. John Banner of Banner

House, Little Nowhere, Surrey.' The word 'nephew' does not appear."

Tom whistled.

"I couldn't agree more. Anyway, that at least got Harry out of the house. He may get the 'Sirdom' but he won't get the Castle."

"He can buy himself a dozen castles," Tom remarked, "with the Banner millions."

"You know, for somebody who's been unconscious for two days, you're picking up the pieces mighty fast."

Was it his imagination, Tom wondered, or was she sounding more American again? And she was certainly saying nice things to him. Things were looking up.

Then he made a fatal mistake. He asked how she had gotten safely out of Clarissa's clutches.

She told him.

"And then Inspector Griffin was there, and other cops, and they more or less picked us up and took us downstairs." She was silent for a while, looking out the window. Then she said quietly, "He just kept coming, walking on his hands, shouting insults at her while she shot at him."

Tom became aware that his head hurt

like a son of a bitch and all he wanted to do was go back to sleep again. And possibly never wake up.

He did fall asleep again, and he did wake up, but not of his own volition. An irritatingly bright voice was calling his name. "Come, Mr. Holder! Wakey-wakey! We know you can do it, your friend told us so."

It was a nurse. She was taking his pulse and temperature and chattering about how Dr. Somebody would toddle along in a minute to see how he was getting on. Kathryn was no longer in the room. He couldn't remember her leaving.

He tried to stay awake this time in case she came back, but the painkillers defeated his efforts. Fortunately, they also defeated about half of the pain, so he was a bit more comfortable as he drifted off.

The next time he woke up, the armchair was occupied by Crumper.

"Shouldn't you be serving tea to somebody?" Tom's voice was getting stronger, that was one comfort.

Crumper dropped his newspaper and grinned. "Why do you think I'm here?" He rose, turned his back for a moment, then smoothly revolved toward the bed and posed, teapot in one hand, cup in the other, face politely blank, a perfect self-parody. "Will you have Earl Grey, sir?"

"I'd laugh but it would hurt. Yeah, sir will have Earl Grey."

"Very good, sir."

Tom received the steaming cup and studied his new friend with satisfaction. "Y'know, Crump, when I first met you I thought you were a cartoon character."

Crumper poured himself a cup and went back to his chair. "Sometimes I overplay the part," he acknowledged.

"What I can't get is how a guy with your intelligence doesn't get bored doing that stuff."

"There are different types of intelligence as well as different degrees of it. I have the kind that directs itself to order and organization, but is lacking in imagination, not to mention academic discipline. I'd have been a disaster at university, but I'm brilliant, if you'll pardon my complete lack of modesty, as a butler."

"I'll pardon it because you're dead right. You are brilliant."

"As a butler," Crumper repeated. "You, on the other hand, have the kind of intelligence that takes imaginative leaps. You would do well at university."

"Thanks. I'd like to think so. My scores were good enough, but my folks didn't have enough money to send me."

"I suspected that was the case. The question is, how are you going to manage it now?"

"Manage what?"

"Going to university. Or, as you Americans say, going to college. I understand that one of the best in America is in your town."

"Crump, what are you going on about? Where do you come up with sending me off to college at the ripe old age of fifty-five? Who was talking about college anyway?"

"No one. But you should be."

"Why, for God's sake?"

"Because it's the only way you'll ever have a chance with her."

It took Tom a good minute to recover from this remark sufficiently to reply to it.

"It would take more than college," he said glumly.

"I'm not convinced it would. You have met my daughter?"

This nonsequitur was so abrupt, Tom hardly knew what to say, and settled for, "Uh, yes?"

"I also have a son you have not met. Julie opted for the local comprehensive, that's public high school to you Americans, because she has no ambition. But David was always precocious, and Sir Gregory was kind enough to send him to Winchester, as he sent me. Winchester, I should explain, is what you would call a prep school, a very good one. David went to Cambridge and he now teaches chemistry at a girl's school in Abingdon. He is engaged to be married to a lovely girl he met there who teaches French." At this point Crumper lifted his cup to his lips and deliberately threw away his punch line. "Her grandfather's a duke."

Tom laughed until his head hurt, which was about a second and a half. "O.K., Crump, you've made your point. So give me a small fortune and I'll quit the force and go to college. I'll lose forty pounds and fifteen years and grow my hair back, and then I'll divorce that woman who never loved me anyway" — Crumper's eyebrows rose, not in disapproval but in recognition of the information Tom had not previously shared — "*but* Crump, old buddy, she would still be in love with the skinny carrot-top!"

Crumper could not stop himself from saying in a perplexed tone, "There's no accounting for taste, is there?"

"Will you be serious, or should I go back to sleep?"

"I shall be serious. And seriously I shall admit that Kit Mallowan is no mean rival. He is a very fine human being. Tremendous courage. Wonderful wit. Kind, generous, easy to know."

"Gee, thanks, Crump. This is really helping."

"But he has a massive disadvantage when it comes to your lady friend."

"Yeah, I know, the house and the title. But so far that hasn't put her off."

"That's because she hasn't known him long enough."

"You're saying there's something unattractive hidden behind that almighty impressive exterior?"

"No. I'm saying the almighty impressive exterior goes clear to the bone."

"You're going to tell me what that means, right?"

Crumper hesitated a moment. "I might be mistaken, Tom. I wonder if I might be wrong in getting your hopes up."

"Not to worry. My hopes have never been within twenty miles of up."

"All right, then. I believe that Kathryn sees Kit Mallowan as an ordinary human being who has the ill fortune to be lumbered with being the Seventh Marquis of Wallwood. She is probably misled by his references to the house and the title as the 'Greater Beast,' as if they were as much of a curse as the 'Lesser Beast,' the wheelchair."

Crumper studied his teacup, then said, "But I was present, I believe, when he first used those terms. He was playing backgammon with Sir Gregory and I was serving sherry. He said to Sir Gregory, 'When it comes to marriage, there are two things standing between me and a bride. Two beasts, so to speak.' Then he tapped the arms of his chair and said, 'This is the lesser one.'"

Tom promptly validated Crumper's opinion of his intelligence. "So the beasts are dragons in front of the tower that holds the Princess Bride. It's about how women see him. He doesn't want to be pitied and he doesn't want to be —"

"Coveted," Crumper supplied.

"Yes. So the house and the title are not beastly except for the fact that they attract gold diggers and social climbers."

"Precisely. They are not beastly *in themselves*."

"So Kathryn thinks Kit Mallowan is stuck, poor man, with being the Marquis —"

"Whereas in fact Kit Mallowan quite *en-*

joys being the Marquis."

Tom let out a thoughtful "Mmmmmmm" and sank back onto his pillows.

Crumper stood up. "I must go. The nurses in these places are more polite but they're just as tyrannical, and they said I could only stay half an hour."

Tom dragged his thoughts away from Kathryn. "Huh? What places? More polite than what?"

"More polite than the ones in National Health hospitals. You don't think every ill person in Britain enjoys this sort of luxury, do you? This is a private hospital. Very posh. Very pricey. You are a fortunate man."

"But Crump!" Tom cried in alarm. "Who put me here? Who's going to pay for it? My travel insurance won't cover this!"

"No, but your traveling companion will. And Tom, one more thing." Crumper stopped by the door, enjoying the surprise on Tom's face. "I seriously doubt that any man who doesn't have the balls to get out of a loveless marriage deserves Kathryn Koerney."

Crumper was gone, the door closed behind him.

Tom closed his eyes. "Don'tcha hate it," he muttered, "when people are right?"

He drifted off to sleep again, and in spite of the headache, some of his dreams were surprisingly pleasant.

ABOUT THE AUTHOR

Cristina Sumners holds a B.A. in English from Vassar, an M.Div. from the General Theological Seminary of the Episcopal Church, and an M.Phil. in medieval English studies from Oxford University. She has taught English and religious studies, and has served churches in Texas and England. Married to a scientist, she lives in Taos, New Mexico, where she is at work on her third suspense novel, *Familiar Friend.*

The employees of Thorndike Press hope you have enjoyed this Large Print book. All our Thorndike and Wheeler Large Print titles are designed for easy reading, and all our books are made to last. Other Thorndike Press Large Print books are available at your library, through selected bookstores, or directly from us.

For information about titles, please call:

(800) 223-1244

or visit our Web site at:

www.gale.com/thorndike
www.gale.com/wheeler

To share your comments, please write:

Publisher
Thorndike Press
295 Kennedy Memorial Drive
Waterville, ME   04901